Suspense, Drama, with a Touch of Humor

DIVAS 'til DEATH

A Callie Kinsey Mystery

MARY CURRAN

DIVAS 'TIL DEATH
A Callie Kinsey Mystery
By Mary Curran
Copyright ©2023 by Mary Curran
All rights reserved.

SECOND EDITION

This publication may not be reproduced, stored in any retrieval system, or transmitted, in any form, or by any means, electronic, mechanical, photocopying, recording, or otherwise, without the prior written permission of the publishers.

This is a work of fiction. Names, characters, businesses, organizations, places and events, other than those clearly in the public domain, are either the product of the author's imagination, or are used fictitiously. All resemblances to actual persons, living or dead, events or locales are purely coincidental.

NO AI TRAINING: Without in any way limiting the author's [and publisher's] exclusive rights under copyright, any use of this publication to "train" generative artificial intelligence (AI) technologies to generate text is expressly prohibited. The author reserves all rights to license uses of this work for generative AI training and development of machine learning language models.

ISBN-13: 979-8387820281
Also available in eBook
O'Neill Books

Cover design: Angelee Van Allman
Cover Art: Kristi Rauckis
Interior Design: Ellen Sallas

PUBLISHED IN THE UNITED STATES OF AMERICA

To Mom and Dad who always believed in me.

1

SUPERMAN CHANGES IN A PHONE BOOTH, I USE MY CAR. I'm no hero, just super late for a riding lesson. I kick up the music and set the cruise control to begin a non-sexy striptease when an incoming call interrupts the moment.

Mom, flashes on the display screen. The ringtone might as well be an air raid siren. My usually carefree mother is categorically against changing while driving.

"Hi, Mom," I say as cheery as possible.

"What's wrong?"

If she was an average mom, explaining the intuition would be simple. All moms have eyes in the back of their heads and the uncanny ability to detect when a child is up to no good, right? That's not how I was raised. I am the byproduct of a former hippie. The full-fledged, free-love kind. For bedtime stories, she used to recount exotic tales about the various men that *might* be my dad. Despite her colossal shortcomings in parenting, my mom somehow manages to sense when I'm up to no good.

"Nothing's wrong," I say, realizing immediately that she can hear exasperation as I wiggle free of my skirt. "This back road is so bumpy after the rain, I can hardly hear you." Normally the out-of-control tension in my life melts as the cement structures of the city fade into the rearview, and the road ahead transitions to horse country. Not today.

"You said it was urgent," my mom sounds confused. Completely not her fault. I had placed a panic call. I am still a wreck.

"You know me. That was an hour ago. I'm running late to see

Cassidy." My voice goes all squeaky, like a little girl talking about a puppy. My left leg slides easily into the breeches as I talk, but as I go to stuff the other in, my foot catches, leading to an involuntary grunt.

"What kind of predicament are you in now?" she asks.

"Nothing," I wince, as I try to break free. The tight khaki material some clothing manufacturer labeled 'stretch comfort' begins winding around my ankle like a boa constrictor. "They finally announced that the station was sold. I wanted to talk it over with you, but I'm pulling into the stables and I'm really late. Can I call you when I'm heading home?"

"You're changing your clothes!" This is not a revelation, it's a declaration of war. With the onset of smart phones and texting, my usually liberal mother considers any type of distracted driving intolerable. No one has supported a cause this vehemently since anti-war protests in the '70s. On more than one occasion she's even called the police on me.

"Last I heard she was traveling on I-75 South," she told a state police dispatcher last week. "I don't know her license plate number, but you'll recognize her. Callie Kinsey from Channel 5 News. Drives a ridiculous little, blue BMW convertible. Curly brown hair, greenish-blue eyes. Exceptionally pretty, if you're single."

How do I know exactly what she said? Let's say the recording has been making the rounds. My mom does not feel one ounce of remorse that her call is practically viral on the internet.

"Do you think after reporting me last week I would seriously risk changing clothes in the car?" The car rambles onward with reckless abandon while I steer with my knee using all my strength to hike up breeches. Tugging makes the tangle worse. If I lose control of the car, I'll never hear the end of it.

"I can't miss my lesson. I'll call you the minute I'm done." With a quick "love you," I basically hang up on my poor mom. A crater sized spring pothole appears out of nowhere. Karma strikes like a lightning bolt as the jolt sends my hip bone crashing painfully down onto the driver's door armrest.

Knowing that my mom is probably already dialing the county sheriff's department, I ease to the side of the deserted road, and throw the car in park a block shy of the stables. I need a minute to mentally regroup anyway. Nonstop negative thoughts have been churning in my brain all day. I work as a television news reporter. A competitive business to start with. Now, with the station sold to a former NFL star so hell-bent on winning, we all fear losing our jobs. The general manager gathered us in the studio today to help calm rumors of mass layoffs. Unfortunately, his pep talk backfired, and the delay has me running even more late than usual.

I open the car door, revealing scenery straight out of a fox hunt oil painting. Forested trails and private stables pepper the surrounding landscape. I easily pull the pants off in one swoop. The scent of fresh pine swirls through the crisp breeze. Locals call this area horse country; I call it heaven. I don't know how I would cope if I lose my job and have to give this up.

It's also pretty desolate this far out. So, sporting only a purple thong on my lower half, I stand up, stretch and inhale the fresh air. After a brutal winter, the heat of the sun feels great on my bare legs. As I sit back down on the edge of the seat to finish changing, a beam of light directs my attention to a black blob at the bottom of the ditch. Something about it strikes me all wrong. I bounce back up to get a better look.

Subconsciously, I ball up the breeches I'm holding. Clutching them like a Teddy bear, I creep on tippy toes closer to the edge of the gravel shoulder. Fearing it may be a sleeping animal, I keep every movement soft and quiet, careful not to startle whatever lies so still. A carcass is the most likely explanation. With below average temps and above average snowfalls, we lost a lot of deer this winter. There is also a distinct possibility it is nothing at all. When friends at work forced me to fill out an online dating application recently, I listed 'jumping to conclusions' as a hobby. But the long, cold season also caused a dry spell of decent stories, and the new station owner made it clear he's only keeping the A-team. It's at least worth investigating.

My eyes fixate on the mass. The object becomes more and more surreal. One thing is certain, it is impossible to identify from this vantage point. As usual, curiosity overrides common sense, leading me to ease my way down the embankment, bare feet, bare fanny and all. A putrid odor catches my nose. I cover the lower half of my face with the breeches. Thankfully they also shield my eyes from the grizzly sight. A corpse clearly lies in the ditch, and it is not an animal.

As a reporter, I stick to covering the news, not finding it. Body bags and police tape usually keep me at a safe distance from gruesome encounters.

My pulse steadily increases to near pounding. It's not every day you find a dead body dumped in an haute couture zip code. With the mud, it's impossible to make anything out clearly from the side of the embankment. The only discernible markings are fragments of royal blue material, but there's no way I am going any closer. I look around for signs of a struggle or personal belongings. Nothing. On the opposite side of the ditch lies a trampled area. A path exactly the width it would take to roll a body down the embankment. My knees buckle. This is most likely a murder, and right in the midst of pristine horse country. The whole crime could have taken place within a few feet of where I am standing. A good-sized pond butts up to the area, not more than ten feet over. It seems strange the perpetrator didn't roll the body into the water where it would be far less likely to be discovered.

I am so engrossed, I don't hear the rumble of an old beater truck roar up behind me. By the time I do, it is too late. The driver pulls beside my car and catches me striking quite the pose. To hold my balance as I leaned forward to peer down into the weeds, I had placed my hand on my thigh and stuck my bare rear end out toward the road. We're talking a shot directly out of some cheesy hot rod magazine. All I need are some high heel hooker shoes to complete the picture.

"Can I help you?" the burly guy calls out. I stay hunched over so I can't see his face and he can't see mine. I don't consider myself a celebrity or anything, but I already have my mom's 9-1-1 call circulating. I don't need a photo of me half naked on the internet.

"No, I thought I might be sick," I say holding my stomach.

"I work for the..." he tries to interject.

"No, no. I'm all right now." I keep my head down, allowing my curly mop of hair to fall toward my face and make my way back to the car, hoping the car door will shield his view.

"Well, all right," he says as he puts the old truck back into gear. "You're going to find yourself with a cold next if you don't get some clothes on. Not quite warm enough for a French bikini just yet." With a nod and a salute, he ambles off.

I leap into the driver's seat to catch my breath and cover my lower half with the blouse I tossed aside earlier. In the safe confines of the convertible, I begin to doubt what I saw, but I'm not going any closer for further analysis. That's a job for the police. I try to dial 9-1-1. Intense shakes render my muscles uncooperative. Desperate to make it to the safety of the equestrian center, I try to put the car in drive. The gear shift feels like a pound of lead. Physical struggles create more mental doubts. I can't understand why no one else discovered the body. It has obviously been there for some time. I keep willing the situation to be a trick of my imagination, but the images of the body and patches of royal blue flit through my mind over and over. It dawns on me that I've seen that material somewhere before.

Nausea seeps in. My body involuntarily confirms the worst. I know exactly who this is. This scene is real, and I have to pull myself together. It's an even bigger discovery than I first imagined. For starters, I better get dressed. Then I'll figure out the best way to handle this whopper of a story.

2

GASPING, I HIT THE ACCELERATOR AND SPEED DIAL simultaneously.

"I can't hear you!" the assignment editor screams. I am so shook up, I accidentally called the station instead of 9-1-1. AC/DC's *Highway to Hell* blares while I try to speak. My dad must have been a rock and roller. How else can you explain a Gen Y playlist that mainly features old-school rock songs?

"I think I just saw a body!" I blurt as I turn down the volume. So much for poise.

"It, ah—" I regroup. "Something suspicious was wedged at the bottom of a ditch, covered in mud and weeds."

"Where are you?" As air traffic controller of the newsroom, we call Al Hagen *Obstinate Al* because he's chronically crabby. "And what are you talking about?"

"I need to call the police. I was driving out to ride my horse. There may be a body in a ditch. And not just anybody. Al, I think I found Talia Lang, the missing socialite."

"What?!" Al exclaims in disbelief.

"I know. Most of the body was covered in mud, but I clearly saw royal blue fabric. Her husband said she was last seen wearing a royal blue evening dress. We aired a photo he gave police from the night—"

"That's a negative," Al interrupts me. "Her husband retracted the report."

Confusion whirls through my mind like smoke swirling from a

Genie bottle. "I'm telling you, I saw a petite body lying there in some type of royal blue dress." Goose bumps stand straight up on my arms.

"Listen Callie, we'll investigate, but take a breath. We're all under a lot of strain," I can tell by the change in tone that Al twirled his chair away from the desk to whisper privately. 'Under a lot of strain' conveys you sound cray-cray.

"Talia Lang rides at the same equestrian center as me. I don't know why she'd come to see her horse in an evening gown, but it's not impossible that she'd be out this way."

"Okay, but we know her husband pulled the report, so let's withhold mentioning any names and stick to routine response. You found a body in a rural area, and that warrants coverage, debutante or not," Al says. "You are a solid hour from downtown, and we're only two hours from airtime." Al starts barking orders in the background. Like triage in a hospital emergency room, he begins mobilizing the most important trauma specialists first. In the world of television news, that's a camera crew and a live truck.

"Hey," I butt in. "One of us needs to call the police."

"I'm on it." He turns his attention back to me. "Send a pin." It only takes a second to stop the car and send the location. Not wanting to be alone, I'm content to stay on the phone listening to Al work his magic. After completing standard procedure of alerting local police and getting a crew in route, Al discloses to the news team that the body of the socialite may have been discovered. The revelation sounds a five-alarm scramble. All staff producers, writers and station management hustle into a conference room. Our new owner, Nigel Mitchell, Super Bowl champ turned media mogul, threatens to only keeping the A-team. This may be the touchdown I need to save my job.

A small boulder with Chanticleer etched in curly French font marks the stable entrance. I happen to ride at the most elite equestrian center in the area completely by accident. A Google search led to Maggie who gives lessons at the upscale hunter/jumper facility. It only took one or two lessons to become absurdly obsessed with horses and the desire to live an upscale country life.

At the top of the gravel drive sits a refurbished French rustic main house. Based on a home in Bordeaux, the inside features stone walls and a series of magnificent fireplaces, all imported from European chateaus. Off to the side, the guest house, with a built-in pool framed by a rock garden, the stables and pole barn, are all painted light taupe with black trim as if they too could blend in with the French countryside. Matching black fencing stretches across acres and acres of rolling paddocks.

In the winter months the beautiful property turns as dormant as the surrounding landscape. Half the boarders winter with their horses in Florida, the others typically choose not to ride when it's cold. Unfortunately, on a day I need to fly below the radar, the entire flock of fair-weather riders seem to be returning like swallows to Capistrano. A small crowd of people and horses mill around gabbing happily with each other on the front lawn. I dodge the group by heading to a side door, phone still glued to my ear.

The polished mahogany walls, rubber mat carpeting and hanging light fixtures in the main aisle way adorned the cover of Architectural Digest a few years ago. A framed copy of the magazine cover hangs in the main hall. The stalls spread out in an X-shape into four wings. Every stall has a door that faces the inside and a picture window facing outside, the equivalent of an ocean view room at a swank hotel. No one has ever said it, but my area of the stables appears to be the low rent district.

Most people aren't aware of the huge amount of affluence in Detroit suburbs. Henry Ford wasn't the only captain of industry. Many Michigan businesses flourished during the industrial revolution, most produced third and fourth generation trust fund babies. Those that own horses, ride at Chanticleer.

I peek down to the area where Talia Lang rides with a group called the Divas. That area of the stable has been abandoned while the women traveled to Palm Beach for the winter horse show season. Even their area suddenly bursts with activity. The horses, back from competing on the fancy horse show circuit, look absolutely polished. I recognize Talbot Bates Chandler immediately. Tab, as her friends call her, comes from old school money. She regularly makes the social pages handing out giant cardboard checks to non-profit organizations. I pause, wondering how they will take the news if I found their friend. The gaze lasts a pinch too long. They totally bust me for gawking.

"Callie, you're positive it's her?" Rick, the news director, jolts me back to the call at hand.

"I, yes, well..." I spin away from the Divas and power walk toward the south wing where my horse awaits. "My gut tells me it's her, but don't go running any breaking news reports." Once I make it safely around a corner, I slow down to pull my thoughts together.

"We have to be cautious," I say. "If her husband retracted the missing person's report, I get there's no logical way it could be her. But on the other hand, every gut instinct tells me it is."

"A classic case of covering the scent of foul play, right?" Cynicism runs through Rick's veins like caffeine runs through mine.

"Maybe, but let's let the cops make the ID, not us," I caution.

"Absolutely. There's a lot of liability here, Run me through the entire scenario once more." Rick operates like an old school newspaper editor during any breaking news, always calmly collecting facts.

Cassidy, my big bay with a wide white blaze running down his nose, gives a whinny as I walk up. On my budget I don't participate in the myriad of optional extras, but full groom service is mandatory. My horse stands peacefully in the cross ties of a grooming stall, fully tacked and ready for action. A great old master of the show ring, he's the perfect first horse as I muddle through beginner jumping lessons. I gently stroke Cassidy's neck as I launch into a recap.

"Callie, stay on the line," Rick orders as I finish explaining what I saw. "Courtney needs to work out some logistics, and I'm going to run down to Tom's office to let him know what we've got here."

"No worries." I press mute on the phone. "Hey big guy," I say. "Looks like your momma can't ride today. I have to work."

I pace a small circle in front of Cassidy, waiting for Rick to return from the general manager's office, and catch sight of a bronzed face. A bleach blonde spies from behind a wooden beam at the corner of the aisle way. Our eyes meet and she pulls back quickly. The Divas must have heard part of my phone conversation. I have interviewed mayors, governors and heads of state – but the thought of encountering the über elite of Chanticleer, especially on the day I may have found their friend, reduces me to a puddle of nerves. Instead of relying on normal instincts to introduce myself, I'd rather hide.

I step into Cassidy's stall and stick my head out the window. No sirens wail in the distance. Even if the police arrive, I still have to wait for the camera crew. The best way to avoid contact with Talia Lang's circle is to hop on my horse. Cell phone still attached to my ear, I grab my helmet and Cassidy's reins and head toward the barn doors.

"Who's locating the original missing person's report?" I ask as we start to wrap the call. The rubber flooring absorbs any tell-tale clip clops of my horse. "The cops will never release identification of the body before notifying family members, so it's doubtful we'll be able to contact next of kin before we hit the air." I sound distinctly winded from walking briskly. Even though *chasing a story* is only a figure of speech, we're always in some type of rush. The exertion goes unnoticed by my colleagues back in the newsroom. "The only angle for a decent piece will be relaying similarities between the missing person's report and what we're seeing live at the scene."

"I like it," Rick chimes in. He's back from the GM's office.

"We'll email the report as soon as possible," Obstinate Al directs.

"You're sure the police are on the way, right?" I'm already writing the lead in my head as I disconnect the call and climb the steps of the mounting block. I formulate a million questions too. Mostly, why hadn't there been a full court press by family and friends to find this woman? I pull Cassidy up before we walk into the ring and hit redial.

"She's been missing a week, right? The husband may have cancelled the report, but obviously she really was missing. Why wasn't anyone else looking for her?"

"Just hung up with headquarters. Desk sergeant made it sound like a big misunderstanding." Al explains. "The husband claimed she went back down to Florida without telling him."

Maybe Rick is right. The husband rescinded his statement as part of a sinister cover up, but given her social stature, the lack of effort by family or friends to find her strikes me as extremely odd.

3

"NO SIGNATURE ENTRY TODAY?" MAGGIE, MY EVER-PATIENT trainer asks in her soft Irish brogue. Normally she chastises me for recklessly blasting in like I'm in the photo-finish of the Kentucky Derby when I'm running late. Today she gives me a well-done smirk as I saunter into our outdoor sand ring.

"I'm a little preoccupied," I admit, pulling Cassidy to a stop beside her. I'm not ready to divulge that a big story may be brewing. Maggie, who came to the states about ten years ago working for Irish Olympic show jumper, Declan Fitzgerald, possesses a strong sense of what we will politely call "curiosity". I don't want to get her on the scent of potential gossip. Maggie and Declan met the Divas while showing at the Palm Beach International Equestrian Center. A great rider in her own right, Maggie came up to give a few summer clinics and never left. She and Declan concocted a unique arrangement. She lives in the gorgeous, refurbished farmhouse on the property and runs the entire program up north. Declan handles the women when they head south in the winter months.

Maggie sits on her favorite perch, a fence post by the in-gate to the arena. She's still wearing khaki breeches and her well-worn black tall boots from working horses earlier in the day. Her thick brown hair is pulled in a ponytail and hidden under a red CWD Sellier baseball cap.

"You wouldn't have gotten the attention of these women if you shot into the ring through a cannon today. They're riled about something. Do you have any idea what it could be?"

Judging by the gleam of the horses and glow of their skin, the Divas ride five-astride. The Divas insist on private lessons and ring time. I haven't seen them in the two full years I've ridden here, and now I can't seem to shake them. This time I recognize Lydia Mulholland. Her husband, Cameron Mullholland, was the lead county prosecutor for over a decade. Their affair ended his marriage. Cameron resigned as prosecutor, married Lydia, and went on to make a fortune in commercial real estate.

"Is that Sperry Davis?" I gush at Maggie, turning my horse so the women can't see me questioning our trainer.

"The one and only," Maggie says, tucking her blue-checked blouse neatly into her trim waistline. She often quotes her Irish grandmother about the need to look proper.

"I've been trying to interview her forever."

"I know," Maggie says. "You badgered me for an introduction the entire first year you were here."

"How could any man cheat on her?" I ask. Even under an awkward black riding helmet, Sperry's distinct cheekbones and almond eyes put her on par with any super model. Like Christie Brinkley, Sperry caught her husband having an affair. Unlike anyone, she hired a private lab and used high-tech CSI-style tactics to prove he had the woman in their bed, then took him to the cleaners.

"Someday I'm going to convince her to let me do a profile on her," I say, as I shorten up my reins. "I'm going to call it: 'the new C.S.I., Catching your Spouse at Infidelity'."

"Good luck. You know how elusive she is."

"No kidding. What are they doing here? Did I get our time screwed up?"

"They actually asked permission to ride during your lesson time," Maggie whispers under her breath. "So the question is do *you* mind? They said the horses need a stretch after trailering in, but I don't buy it. I think they're up to something." So do I, but I can't feed Maggie's interest.

"I just hung up with the station," I try to sound light, while feverishly formulating a strategy to avoid these gals. "Of all days, I got called back in to work a night shift. I'm going to have to hop off."

"Cassidy's been standing tacked up a while," Maggie says. "Give him a quick hack and let him stretch those limbs in this gorgeous sunshine."

We have a massive ring. Avoiding the women won't be comfortable, but it is doable. "Okay, a couple quick laps, but then I have to get going." I give Cassidy a little squeeze to ease him into work mode. The other women continue to walk in clump formation.

At a walk it's easy to keep a good distance, but when I eventually pick up a trot, I make it halfway around the ring before having to zigzag around the women.

"Oh, come on," Lydia Mullholland, the prosecutor's wife says, her reins drape lazily in a big loop on her horse's neck. With their perfect figures and expensive riding apparel, they could be models for a classy equestrian catalog. Quite the contrast to the racy pose I struck for that old guy earlier.

"I heard it," the blonde says indignantly.

I can't quite pick up what they're talking about. Tracking a nice unassuming circle, I pretend to stay absorbed in my ride, but conveniently move myself within earshot. With my curly hair tucked in the helmet, I don't know if they realize it's me yet.

"Hech," Lydia coughs and dramatically tilts her head in my direction. The women fall silent. Cassidy trots steadily on.

"Ask her," the blonde who came snooping over earlier says as I tread across the opposite side of the ring. I steer Cassidy wide to loop past them again.

All five sets of eyes glare at me. Mark unfounded paranoia as another of my signature traits. Although, in this case, I'm sure I'm right.

"He looks terrific," Maggie yells to me. "You've got him nice and forward. Let's trot a little the other direction."

Cassidy and I make a half circle and change direction passing them again.

"Nice day," Tab Chandler, sitting on a light bay horse with a dark mane and tail, says as I pass.

"It is," I muster as I squeeze Cassidy even more forward.

"Ask her," the blonde pushes.

"Stop," Tab scolds, "we have to handle this right." She looks over to see if I'm listening. I continue to act absorbed in riding Cassidy.

Any other day I would love to meet them, but the fact that I may have found their friend's body makes any type of introduction inconceivable.

At the far end of the ring I bring Cassidy to a halt. I want to create a little space between us and the women before easing into a canter. The blonde turns and sees that I am behind them.

"Stop being in denial," she all but shouts. "I distinctly heard missing woman, ditch, blue taffeta." The well-bred faces sink into gloom. Crime of any type doesn't touch this community, let alone murder. And definitely not the loss of a dear friend.

No doubt the Divas heard me earlier, jeopardizing the story. I pick up a canter and head back to the in-gate. I may have entered the ring slowly, now in pure panic, I practically gallop back out.

4

A LOCAL SQUAD CAR SITS PARKED ON THE SHOULDER. Not eager to venture out by myself, I fumble, straightening a few things in my purse waiting for the crew to arrive. Within minutes, the commanding live truck displaying call letters *WMIV Channel 5 News* in bright orange rolls down the dirt road kicking up a giant cloud of dust.

A quick glance in the rearview mirror ensures no sign of helmet head before popping out of the car. I freshened up as much as possible and changed back into my street clothes before returning to the scene. After years of cursing my curly hair, I will admit, whether I spend one hour or one minute styling, it looks the same. I may never have a good hair day, but I rarely have a hideously bad one either. No one would guess I just hopped off a horse.

"It's beautiful out here," Ben says as he greets me while simultaneously opening the back door of the van to haul his gear out. Another squad car and an unmarked sedan pull up, as well. Ben never waits for instruction. It's what makes him one of the best photographers in the business.

"Yea, it's beautiful," Wally chimes in. He's everyone's favorite, quirky station tech. Having an extra person on the shoot catches me off guard. Wally, a slim, green bean of a guy with hair that flops in front of his eyes, sounds and acts like a rad surfer dude. He knows his stuff and is excellent at crunch time. Given the remote location and size of the story, management made the decision to fully staff. If technical difficulty occurs with the live truck or equipment, they'll have two sets of hands to correct the problem and less risk of missing airtime.

"How many times have I told you how incredible it is out here?" I punch Ben in the arm and wince. His muscles resemble cement.

"Are you the one that called in the discovery?" the guy who arrived in the unmarked car yells over. I recognize the state detective.

"Yes," I shout back and make my way toward the edge of the ditch. Ben and Wally follow, as the detective eases down the embankment.

"Got a body all right," he confirms before making it to the lump, relaying his findings to a burly uniformed officer standing at the squad car. A younger officer tucks a roll of yellow crime-scene tape under his armpit and gingerly makes his way down the small hill to the site.

Ben pops the camera on a tripod and immediately begins to capture footage. The detective makes a call setting a flurry of activity in motion. The detective assures Ben it will be almost an hour before the medical examiner and crime scene investigators will arrive.

"We got all we're going to get for now," Ben says. "Which direction will we find those big, gated estates? We need some establishing shots to show how fancy this area is before the sun sets."

I start to object, but back off. The truth is, I have to be in on the plan because Ben will take off on his own regardless of whether I'm on board or not. Good photographers always think of stories in terms of pictures. It's their job and it often puts them at odds with reporters. In this case, I have to admit Ben is right. Most lifelong Detroiters don't know this gorgeous area exists. Capturing the landscape will go a long way in describing the privileged rural setting. And I'm already thinking maybe we can snag a couple of interviews back at Chanticleer.

"Go ahead. Double check with the local guy," Ben urges. "You'll be a wreck if you don't."

I introduce myself to the husky guy, who turns out to be the local police chief. He promises nothing major will happen at the scene for at least thirty minutes and agrees to do an interview when we get back after he's been briefed on initial findings. Knowing we have a ton of footage in the can, I agree to make our way down the road, but only as far as Chanticleer.

"From this vantage point we can capture the stables, the horses and the rolling pastures behind Chanticleer all in one swoop," Ben says with excitement as he exits the truck at the equestrian center.

"Wow, man, this sure beats dingy alleys," Wally adds as he pops the legs of the tripod open.

"And it's the perfect backdrop for grabbing a couple interviews. Talia's friends suspect something is going on." I survey the parking lot. Three Range Rovers and a Mercedes sit parked on the side closest to the drive. "They're still here."

I make my way to the door, then hesitate. I have no business heading to the west wing, especially when all I have is speculation. To my relief, the women are not in sight. Busy grooms put horses and tack away. Maggie leads a gray horse up the aisle way.

"Please don't need me for anything," Maggie says, swiping a sweaty chunk of hair back under her ball cap. "I can't keep up with George gone. Crazy buzzard has left me with an unbearable workload." Maggie shrugs toward the barn office where George McNabb, our barn manager, usually camps out. A Desert Storm veteran, George is on probation for letting pain meds and alcohol get in the way of his work.

"I found what I'm looking for," I say, as my gaze shifts to the window. Inside, to my dismay, all five women huddle around the desk. The barn manager's office sits at the foot of the clubroom stairs at the center of everything. Back in work mode, I should have a tinge more confidence, but these women are fierce, and I don't have any solid facts. I start to make my way back to the news truck. It's prudent to wait for official word before approaching anyone for an interview.

I strut toward the front door, then do an abrupt U-turn. It may be wise to wait, but definitely not smart. Mustering every ounce of courage in my body, I make my way back to the office and reach for the door handle. Locked. It's already difficult enough to confront any loved ones during a crisis, it's less than ideal to have to bang on a door to share devastating news.

"Good luck," Maggie says pushing on to put the horse away. I need more than luck. Gossip shoots through this community with impressive speed. The women likely have every heavy hitter in town in their contacts. They are either trying to confirm what they heard earlier or are spreading word that a body has been found. I have to intercede.

I knock tentatively on the door. The women pull a little tighter, keeping their backs toward me. It looks like campaign headquarters for a political candidate. Tab Chandler and the super skinny woman feverishly type text messages while Sperry Davis, Lydia Mullholland and the blonde talk on their phones.

I can't let them leak my prize story all over town. Actually, it's more like a floodgate. I put pride aside and scribble 'can I please talk to you?' across a page in my reporter's notebook. I knock and hold the note up to the window while mouthing the words. They continue to disregard me. My stomach churns and grumbles louder than the nearby horses nickering for their dinner. I head toward the news truck wondering how to admit that I got snubbed by the snobs.

"Pack it in," I say as I approach Ben. He leans with one arm on the camera, lazily waiting for me to return.

"Thought you wanted a couple of interviews?"

"No one's available," I mutter. I convince Ben and Wally that the more urgent task at hand involves venturing back up the street to prepare for our live shot.

"It's like a country club. They're big into maintaining privacy." Guilt leads to a confession once we all pile into the live truck. "You should have seen them. They were completely holed up in the office with the door locked."

"I'm sure they're in shock," Ben says.

"Yea," I concede. "This is definitely a little too close to home. After we're off the air, we'll track down a few neighbors. They'll be more likely to talk."

"If you can find any," Wally says, referencing that we are in the middle of nowhere.

"No kidding, this area gives meaning to a country mile," Ben laughs. His joke falls flat on me. I'm preoccupied. Our jobs are on the line. I need a good story and I'm off to a bad start. The Divas live in a closed-door community and slammed the entrance in my face. I'm actually relieved to return to the crime scene where flashing police lights make me feel back on top of my game.

Although he can't yet release much information publicly, local Police Chief Joseph Zurn proves a hundred times more cooperative during our live report. With yellow tape flapping behind us, he confirms that a woman's body has been discovered.

"It will be up to the medical examiner's office to officially make identification of the body and determine whether she is a victim of foul play." The chief's rather large belly presses the buttons of his tan uniform shirt to the point of bursting.

"According to a description given in this missing person's report," I reference the pages for the camera, "there are a number of indications that this could be missing socialite, Talia Lang."

"That would be speculation," the chief says. "Identification could take days."

Off the air, the old-school chief confirms that the corpse is likely Talia Lang.

"What do you think she was doing all the way out here in a formal dress?" I ask. The chief and I stand at the top of the ditch. He peers over at investigators busy at their jobs. "This missing person's report lists her address in Birmingham."

"They keep a place in town, but the Langs primarily reside out here. An estate a mile or two up the road. We sent an officer up there." The chief kicks at the dirt.

"Are you considering the husband a suspect?"

"Routine. Spouses are always questioned."

"Here's what I don't get. Even if he said she wasn't missing, why weren't friends and family members pushing to find her?" I ask him.

"This is definitely off the record young lady. Supposedly, those closest to her are the ones that talked him into backing off. They were positive she wasn't missing. They thought she was," he pauses for effect, "*mis*behaving."

"An affair?" I look over where a black body bag is being hoisted onto a gurney. Our producers have been collecting photos of Talia Lang all afternoon. We have a photo of Talia in a tasteful, gold ball gown looking happy and cozy with her husband while making a huge donation at the Talbot Cancer Center fundraiser last fall. There's one of her in jeans and a t-shirt holding a rescue dog at a local animal shelter, and another in a rather frumpy, floral dress, tucked in the back row of a group at a Birmingham Women's Guild luncheon. Her wavy chestnut hair always hanging free, an effervescent smile on her face, Talia Lang looks like a standard privileged housewife, nothing remotely close to a vixen.

"We don't see random murders in these parts. Homicides generally result from crimes of passion. Jilted lovers. Once in a while enemies with an axe to grind." The chief speaks slow and steady, conveying a knowing that *justice will prevail.* A totally different demeanor from the big-city guys, where homicide cases are rarely solved.

By eight p.m., every news agency in town swarms the scene. Giant live trucks park nose to tail along the normally deserted piece of road. Lights shine bright making the ditch look like a shopping mall parking lot.

While the others scramble to play catch-up and collect basic facts, we have the rare chance to eat dinner. I recently pledged to quit eating junk food. We find a pizza place that serves salads and agrees to send the order directly to the news truck on the side of the road.

"We deliver to bonfires, fishing sites, even deer hunting blinds." The teenager boasts while holding his hand out for the cash. We devour the food in quick fashion and leave the live truck parked in its primo spot next to the ditch while we use my car to sneak out and find the husband.

Without question, the toughest part of news entails calling on grieving families. I've learned it goes best in person. Believe it or not, many people find it cathartic to share their story with the media. That doesn't make knocking on the door any easier.

Out of respect, I approach the home alone. Ben stands with the camera beside a bush on the side of the drive. He attached a wireless mic so we can capture the initial interaction on tape. Wally stays cramped in the back seat of my car.

I'm not getting a good vibe as I cover the distance of the expansive concrete steps. I ring the front bell of the red brick Tudor mansion anyway. My gut instinct never fails. Lang answers the door holding a shotgun.

I stare at the distraught man, unsure of what tact to use as a greeting. His eyes are puffy, his hair stands on end like he had been tugging on it.

"I am so sorry to disturb you, Mr. Lang. I'm Callie Kinsey. Channel 5 News." He swipes the business card out of my hand before I offer it. He glances at it, then drops it in his shirt pocket. "We have been covering the discovery up the road."

Both of his hands return to the gun. One on the trigger, the other balances the long barrel. He keeps it pointed at the ceiling but tightens his fingers on the handle. He may as well squeeze my heart. "I wanted to introduce myself in case you want to make any type of a statement or plea to the public."

"You can go to hell! If you aren't off my property in twenty seconds, I'll shoot." Lang cocks the gun. "It won't be a warning shot."

The fury in his voice could blow me back to the car like a gale force wind. He raises the rifle. I don't need any further encouragement.

"Sorry to have disturbed you," I turn for a hasty departure, hustling down the ragged brick paver drive at a jog, praying a heel doesn't get stuck.

"I'm suing that damn station and I'm suing you personally!" Lang yells as Ben collapses the gear, dumps the tripod in the trunk and haphazardly tosses the camera to Wally in the back.

I reach over and start the car from the passenger side. Ben jumps in the driver's seat and we peel out.

"I got it all!" Ben says.

I can't reply. I don't even take a breath until we have sped down the narrow dirt road back toward the crime scene. That display of rage did not do Lang any favors.

5

"DON'T YOU RIDE AT CHANTICLEER?" RICK BELLOWS SO loud he might as well be on speakerphone. Anyone within a hundred yards can hear me getting chewed out. "You begged to cover this story because you *knew* everyone out there!"

Turns out I was scooped. Buried might better describe it. For the eleven, I thought we would blow the other stations out of the water. We used slow motion footage of the entire encounter at gun point and a good 'Go to hell!' sound bite from Dale Lang.

"You didn't have one interview from anyone at your fancy equestrian place. Leslie Littleton at Channel Two led with footage of Talia Lang riding at some horse show. You were probably on the sidelines watching, like you did with your coverage today. They are all on pins and needles waiting for authorities to identify the victim. Her friends are praying it is not Talia Lang saying she was such a great person. You kept reiterating that a body was found and how no one could talk or give details on the case yet, including the husband who nearly shot you."

I am devastated. Rick's tirades can last forever. Normally, my forte is talking my way into anywhere and out of anything. I don't even try. I skulk around to the front of the live truck where no one can see me or hear Rick. I lean on the grill and listen to my boss rant and rave.

"So much for making yourself a superstar."

I know better than to make excuses. I have no defense. The Divas at the barn double-crossed me. Plain and simple mean girl treatment.

The dark country sky displays an endless array of stars. Some people might wish on a lucky star to get out of this predicament, I require comfort food. I make up my mind to call Shorty's back as soon as Rick finishes his tirade.

"This story isn't over," I finally say. "We found it first and we'll stay on top of it."

I hit the end button, then immediately hit redial. Whatever is included on the famed meat lover's pizza sounds perfect.

As camera crews roll in cables and pack away gear, I walk along the side of the dirt road watching for the teen to return in his well-worn delivery car. My mind mulls over this dilemma. I need to reclaim the story. But how?

I climb into the back of the news van, tune in to the local classic rock station and blast a little Bon Jovi. Without a doubt, I am living on a prayer and I must admit, repeatedly jabbing the end of a ballpoint pen into my notepad is not generating any earth shattering ideas.

"Excuse me."

I nearly jump out of my skin at the sound of a guy's voice. I did not see this blonde headed kid approach the truck. He sticks his head in, surveying the wall of monitors and our state-of-the-art editing equipment.

"Are you from Shorty's?" I ask, expecting him to be holding a pizza in his hands.

"Curious what's going on," he says. "I work up the street."

"At Chanticleer?" I ask. The equestrian center is the only business in the area.

"Yea." A quick onceover confirms no pizza box in his grips.

"I ride there. I don't recognize you." The kid, early 20s with bleached-blonde hair, wears a preppy short-sleeved checkered shirt and jeans. He takes a step or two back after I call him out.

"We just got back from Florida," he says shyly. I should have noticed the tan. He likely works with the Divas.

"They think Talia Lang was discovered here this afternoon." For some reason I leave out the part about me being the one to find her. It doesn't seem appropriate. He stares where police still scour the ditch.

"I'm Callie Kinsey," I say, reaching out to shake his hand.

"Covey," he replies with downcast eyes. I hand him a card.

"Did you know Mrs. Lang?" Before he can answer, my cell phone blares "T.N.T" by AC/DC into the black, quiet night, startling both of us. I look at the caller ID. It's the chief.

"Can you hang on for one second?"

Covey looks tentative, like a stray dog uncertain about who to trust.

"Chief Zurn here." The friendly tone from early has disappeared. After getting chewed out by Rick, my confidence sinks.

"Yes Chief, what can I do for you?"

"Glad I caught you. Are you still at the site?"

"Yes," I respond hesitantly. In the brief second of saying hello to the chief, Covey sneaks off. I jump out of the truck and look both directions. No sign of the kid. He vanishes into thin air before I ask him about the victim.

"Listen, I've got a car on the way out," the chief instructs. "Don't go anywhere."

No chance, I launch a conversation in my head. *We'll be out of here quicker than you can say Mayberry.*

The chief, unable to read my mind, continues. "We got word from the coroner's office. The medical examiner officially identified the body as that of Talia Lang. They will conduct the official autopsy tomorrow, but they are also confirming she likely died as a result of foul play and this will be classified as a murder case. We want to make an official announcement. The sooner we make a plea for eyewitnesses to come forward the better."

I leap into action. "Don't power down!" I yell to Ben and Wally, as I trip over a rock trying to run toward the back of the truck. "Fire this back up, we're going back on the air!" I pull the phone off my ear to read the clock: 11:08, plenty of time to get the story on before the end of the newscast.

The chief yells through the receiver to get my attention.

"Now listen young lady, if anyone has any information that could help our department, they need to call immediately. I have an officer on the way or you can interview me by phone."

By the time the officer pulls up in a squad car, I am already on the air giving the update, complete with a phone-in interview. The chief gives me an exclusive. The producer chirps "good job" in my earpiece while we're still live. Less than 10 seconds off the air, Rick calls to apologize for being hard on my earlier.

Gavin Phillips, a reporter from Channel 8, hustles over.

"I saw your lights go back on. Anything new?"

"They wanted a live look at a few budding trees for weather." I hold my breath as he walks back to their truck. He's a nice guy, but there is no way I'm letting the other stations know the case is heating up.

"You guys are pretty competitive," the newly arrived officer says as he steps out of the late-night shadows. "Troy Kirkpatrick," he extends a hand. It's difficult to get much of a look at him in the moonlight. I can tell he is tall, has thick brown hair and appears quite cute.

"I have an important message from the chief."

"I think we just delivered it. Confirmation of murder and a plea for eyewitnesses."

"You were still on the air when the studio disconnected the call, so he asked me to relay a request. The chief wants you in his office first thing tomorrow morning." Troy pulls back his sleeve to check the time. He sports a Shinola, a big-name Detroit handcrafted watch.

"And that's promptly seven a.m.," he says, raising his eyebrows as if that would shock me.

"I can't be back out this way at seven," I say.

"This is not a friendly visit. It's official business. Trust me. You will never meet a friendlier man than chief, but he's serious when it comes to leading up an investigation. You do not want to cross him by being late."

"It will be past midnight when we pull out of here. I live almost an hour away." Cute cop stands looking pleasant. I am getting nowhere. "I'd have to camp out here to make it to his office that early."

"Looks like you'll be navigating your way through a pup tent in hot rollers and high heels," he cracks another smile. Now that we're in the light, I can see he stands at least six-foot-two and in rock-solid shape.

"Now that's an image." We both laugh.

"You're going to need stamina." Troy Kirkpatrick pulls a pizza box from behind his back. "Special delivery," he says with a slightly seductive edge. "They said this one's on the house."

Talk about being mortified. With all those toppings it probably weighs a ton. I refuse to look like a cow in front of this cute cop.

"Oh, yea," I say, "I ordered that for the other crew. It's kind of an inside joke. They were jealous when we had one delivered earlier."

"I don't know," Troy peeks inside the box. "Not sure I would have initially taken you for a meat lover, but this seems to have your name written all over it."

"Depends on the kind of beef." The flirty retort inappropriately flies out of my mouth. Thankfully, the dark night hides more than a hint of red rushing to my face.

I don't give Troy a chance at a comeback. I thank him, grab the box and run it down to the guys from Channel 8 to escape any further embarrassment. I return composed and ready to redeem myself, only to discover Cute Cop has peeled out.

"Where did the officer go?" I ask, looking around. Ben and Wally busy themselves wrapping cables and loading equipment at the back of the truck. I know they had been spying on my encounter.

"Textbook flirt and flee," Ben taunts. He lets me stew for a few seconds. "Or perhaps he had to get back to work. There is a murder investigation underway."

"And the public to protect," Wally adds. "Some of us are on duty."

"He wanted us to be sure and tell you dispatch sent him on another call. And he said to tell you that your mom is right," Ben says while he continues to work. "Whatever that means."

"O-M-G, you know exactly what he means." *Exceptionally pretty, if you're single,* echoes in my mind. Leave it to my mom.

Heat fills my cheeks to my chest and, if I'm being honest, maybe even a little further south. I don't know what I'm doing checking a guy out when I finally have a decent story fall in my lap. I have to focus on preparing to meet with the chief.

6

"WOULD YOU LIKE SOME COFFEE?"

"Intravenously, please." I have no idea how I manage the feat, but I am sitting before the chief at 7 a.m. sharp.

"I know this was asking a lot, but I couldn't risk having you talk to anyone else before us." The chief seems genuinely sorry for dragging me out of bed. This makes two mornings in a row I've been up and out pre crack of dawn. The fact that my car has not been in the driveway either morning will create wild speculation with the town gossip, my mother. Long story, but we live in the same condo complex, and she started taking sunrise meditation walks last year. Her morning route takes her right past my place on the way to a wooded path. Not seeing my car two mornings in a row will have her concocting exotic theories over where I've been and who I've been with. If only my mom could see just who's fetching my coffee. The chief, with thinning, light brown hair pulled neatly in a comb over, belly hanging over his belt buckle is a far cry from whatever stud muffin she's probably envisioning.

"Obviously, I called you in to talk about the Lang case." The chief strides back into his office carrying two good-sized mugs, steam rising lazily off them. The spring morning carries a definite bite of frost in the air, and the ancient heating system in the township station, practically a throwback to log cabin days, has yet to respond. I clutch the mug, happy for warmth as much as caffeine.

"We need to talk about what you saw yesterday." He takes a seat behind a giant, old wooden desk littered with piles of paper and old-fashioned pink *while you were out* slips. "In fairness to you, let me back up. Maybe we should talk about what I saw first," he says. He leans forward and looks out the window. "Where did you park?" he asks.

"Yesterday?"

"No, today. Out front I suppose?"

"Yes." The coffee has not kicked in.

"As you should. We park out back," he points out the window. "That's my truck right there." My gaze follows his outstretched arm to the light blue beater truck with streaks of rust that approached me yesterday.

"It's a 1963 F-100," the Chief boasts. I want to tear out of the room. Sheer panic keeps me bolted to the chair.

"This could only happen to me." I stare in disbelief.

"I think I've pieced together part of what you were doing out there," the chief says with a grandfather like tone. "Officer Kirkpatrick explains that you're known for changing clothes on the run. I assume you were indisposed, should we say, when the body caught your attention."

"That's pretty much exactly what happened."

"I've kept our initial encounter off the record," the chief continues, "but you do understand we don't staff a detective bureau. Now that this is a homicide, we're playing with the big boys. One of the top state investigators landed this case. He's asking a lot of questions. He plans to call you in for questioning today. I wanted to speak with you first."

That explains the early meeting.

"The investigator wants to know exactly how close you got to the body. Now, from what I saw, you weren't in much of a position to crawl about in a ditch, but I couldn't tell him that, now could I?"

"Why didn't you tell me who you were when you pulled up?"

"I tried. You convinced me you were some crazy girl with spring fever so I left you to your privacy."

"What about when we met officially at the scene last night?"

"Well," the chief says, "when your station guy called the report in, he was forthcoming in admitting that you found the body and were pretty shook up, which explains the delay in calling dispatch. Then Officer Kirkpatrick told me about the recording with your mother, so I figured no harm in saving you further embarrassment."

Cute Cop *did* hear my mom's recording. And he's talking about me.

"However, my attempt at chivalry has left me in somewhat of a predicament," the chief continues. "I need to know what happened after I pulled away. Rather than guess, I called you in this morning to find out. We have a couple of details that we can't risk being released to the public." The chief flips open a tiny leather-bound notebook, which looks like a postage stamp in his plump hands.

"I understand." I'm relieved enough to manage a sip of the coffee. "By the way, thank you for not sharing the fact that you saw me indisposed with the world."

"Sounds like you have your hands full with your mom in that department." The chief's tone indicates he's smiling on the inside. I give the signature *poor me* shrug reserved for most references to my mom.

"Now, let's get some facts straight. Did you at any time venture any closer to the body?"

"No. Finding bodies is not my thing. I really was feeling sick. I went up the drive, tried to call 9-1-1 and I was so shook up I accidentally called the station. Then I waited for a camera crew to show up before going back."

"The time lapse seems plausible. But I still need you to clarify exactly what you saw."

"Not much." I take another sip of coffee, this time as a stall tactic. I'm sitting in a police station as the sun comes up. Something tells me there is a right and wrong answer to this question. "It was hard to make out whether it was even a body."

"How much could you see from the road? For instance, did you see the victim's face?"

"No, I believe she was lying face down."

"Yes, she was. How about the manner in which she died?"

"You told me, off the record, it looked like she'd been strangled."

"The paraphernalia we believe was used to cause the death could turn out to be a key piece of evidence. Did you see exactly what was used to strangle Mrs. Lang?"

"I don't think so." I did not see anything, but if I stay vague, perhaps the chief will tip his hand.

"It's tricky to have a member of the media be the first to discover a high-profile crime scene. We need you to be incredibly sensitive. If any leaks hamper this investigation, you will be prosecuted for obstruction of justice. And that goes for any conversations you have professional or personal," the chief pauses, "even with your mother."

"I understand," I say out loud. Internally I chastise myself for being an idiot and not taking a closer look. "While I'm here, you said last night that her friends thought she was fooling around and that's why the missing person report was rescinded. Clearly the body had been there for several days. How could no one realize such a high-profile person disappeared off the radar for that long?"

"Blame the lifestyle I guess." The chief sighs, apparently troubled by the same conundrum. "Her husband claimed she flew home for a benefit dinner and then went missing that same night. He filed the missing person's report. Then he came back the next day, apologizing for the misunderstanding. According to her friends, she decided it wasn't warm enough and went south again."

"Now we know she never left town." I try to help piece the scenario together. "Wait a second," I add, "her friends returned from Florida in the last day or two. Shouldn't that have raised a red flag when she didn't show up down there?"

"That's where it gets tricky," the chief says, resting folded arms on his belly. "Will you keep this off the record?"

"Sure."

"They're the ones that supposedly convinced the husband she was in Florida, but it was a cover up. Mrs. Lang was looking for heat alright, but not in the Florida sunshine. Evidently, Mrs. Lang teamed up with a polo player this winter. She came home to make amends with her husband. When the homecoming wasn't rosy, her friends thought she galloped off to Latin America for a tryst with the polo guy. I understand you ride at Chanticleer. I'm sharing this little detail on purpose. If you hear anything on your end, let's have a two-way street with communication."

"Of course." Making the agreement is no big deal. Police agencies work with the media behind the scenes to solve crimes more often than the general public would ever imagine.

"It's imperative we keep the affair and cause of death out of the headlines."

Before parting with the chief, I pledge to keep both facts out of the news for now, but I can't get the other exciting development out of my head. Paraphernalia must mean horse equipment. If I'm known for tearing up the back roads when I'm late for a lesson, today I'd be accused of creating a super sonic boom. I can't wait to get to Chanticleer to start piecing the horse connection together.

Evidently the rest of the world isn't off to the same early start. Other than the horses mingling in the turnouts, the impressive facility appears sound asleep. I make my car creep, as if on tiptoe, up the gravel drive. The good news is, I can manage a good look around the west wing without getting caught.

I slide in through a side door and make my way straight to the off-limits portion of the barn. Frankly, it isn't that different. Stalls are stalls, and grooming areas are grooming areas. They do, however, have a private lounge, and that's what I want to investigate. To my surprise, the door is unlocked. I sneak in. Somewhere an interior designer still smiles over the masterpiece he or she created in this room. At one end, a grouping of Adirondack chairs with Ralph Lauren Aztec fabric huddle around a fieldstone fireplace. Given that the ladies winter in Florida, I doubt the warm-up area is used much, but the arrangement is gorgeous and inviting. The other end of the room favors a traditional country club locker room. Thick, rich, hunter green carpeting covers most of the floor. Tiled walkways lead to and from full-length polished mahogany lockers that stretch along the wall, each has a brass nameplate and built-in combination lock. I count them up. There are twelve nameplates total. Talia Lang's locker sits right in the middle. I'm sure the nearby glass door leads to a shower and private bathroom. The opposite wall features a full bar, also made of polished mahogany and fully stocked. Behind sits it a stainless wine refrigerator and on top, a state-of-the-art cappuccino maker, baskets full of snacks and a large fruit bowl.

Churning the chief's word *paraphernalia*, conjures images of some type of horse equipment being used in the murder. Sectioned off by the door, I find the horse tack stored in a super organized walk-in closet the size of my bedroom.

Traditional wooden saddle racks line the wall, each labeled with the owner's name on a brass plate. Another wall houses bridle hooks, labeled as well. The back wall astounds me most. Mahogany wooden bins cover the wall floor to ceiling, each labeled with a horse's name. I pull one open and find all the other pertinent items like leg wraps, protective leg boots, and so on. I peruse each item in the area as a criminal rather than a rider. What would I choose if I wanted to kill someone? Reins seem the most obvious, but a little long to use effectively without tangling. And impossible to use efficiently if grabbed in haste with the bit and headpiece still attached.

The door bursts open hitting me in the shoulder. I shriek in response to the intrusion.

"Hey!" She tries to sound gruff, but I realize immediately the voice belongs to Maggie.

"Maggie! It's me!"

"Callie? What are you doing in here? I was ready to clobber you. We have a murder on our hands. I thought you were some intruder peering around."

Maggie and I have a great relationship, but I am standing in an area I don't belong and that requires an explanation. I quickly scan the room.

"I am so sorry," I say, still trying to catch my breath. Maggie, breathing heavy herself, clutches a shovel. Her chest puffed out, ready for battle. "I looked for you when I arrived, but I was dying for coffee, and the only thing I could think of within miles of here was this Nespresso machine." I reference the bar. Judging from the screwed up look on Maggie's face as she takes in the fancy espresso machine and the color-coded disks of coffee hanging in a wire rack to the side, I'm not sure how often she ventures into this territory.

"I only had three hours of sleep and I have a long day ahead." I gently remove the shovel from Maggie's grip and place it outside the door.

"Don't even talk to me about long days. With George on suspension, that's how every day is for me lately. I do need to scoot you out of here, but I tell you what, they installed the exact same machine in the guest house. If you know how to use it, let's both go have a strong cup of coffee. We need to catch up on this Talia business. So tragic."

"For a coffee, I'll gladly try to fill you in, but I don't know much."

"If you're going to be doing a lot of running back and forth while this case is solved, you could probably stay in the guest house, if you want. The only time we use it is to house people coming to judge horse shows in the area or give clinics in the summer."

I have never seen the inside of the guest house. From the outside, the remodeled cottage looks as gorgeous as every other ounce of the property. It would give me a front row vantage point for covering the story and, hopefully, a little more time to sleep.

"Give me a moment," Maggie lifts a ginormous ring of keys out of her coat pocket. "Let me make sure I have the right key."

I stay still as a mouse to encourage her to look through the keys exactly where she stands while my eyes feverishly finish exploring the tackroom. A row of smaller hooks hold leather lead lines right inside the door for easy access. As with all the other equipment, they are labeled with the owners' names. All of us at Chanticleer have matching leather leads with our horse's name engraved on a mounted brass plate. Unlike my worn lead, these gleam, oiled to perfection. I should start taking better care of my stuff. I have to remind myself that these ladies have staff, and they aren't racing in and out while trying to manage a full-time career.

Maggie continues to fiddle with the key ring.

"Look at the amount of keys this man carries around," she says. She eases toward the door to grab a little more light from the hall. As she steps to the side, I clearly see an empty hook.

Lang it reads. My stomach drops. It's the second to the last hook away from the door. Not an easy reach. Someone knew where it hung.

"Here it is," Maggie says triumphantly as she raises the guest house key. "Of course, we'll ask Bud for permission, but I know it'll be okay."

Bud Burkhart owns Chanticleer. He bought and refurbished the property as a surprise for his wife, but the surprise was on him when she refused to move to the country.

Maggie's offer of staying in the guest house sounds tempting. There are plenty of pros to being this close to the story, but if a killer is on the loose and operating out of this barn, the con of putting myself in close proximity weighs much bigger on the no side of the equation. Luckily, I've never been one to study the odds.

"I would love to stay out here," I blurt. There is no way I'm passing up this offer.

7

A LOUD COMMOTION IN THE COURTYARD JOLTS ME AWAKE. I shake off the haze and recall how I curled up in the country chic living room to gaze out the giant picture window, overlooking a beautiful green pasture. I must have fallen sound asleep. A man's voice barks orders at the grooms as if he owns the place. Already taking ownership of the guest house, I bounce up to find out who's making all the fuss.

"Maggie! Make sure they weed whack around the fountain too," a short, bald man shouts to my trainer.

"Well, here she is," he beams, as I meander out onto the wooden porch. "I'm Bud Burkhart, proprietor here at Chanticleer," he hustles overextending his hand. "Apologize we haven't met before, but glad you're here. Glad you're here." His greeting sounds Santa Claus jolly, but his interest in actually saying hello only half-hearted. His eyes dart constantly over to the courtyard. He is dressed clearly in his barn attire. The brand-new work boots, jeans and western belt look like a costume on a man that surely spent his entire life in suits and ties.

"You, over there, we need these walkways swept," he shouts to a groom leading a high-strung horse from the paddock to the stables.

"What?" the young man motions to his ears that he can't hear his boss.

"Got a TV team staying with us. We need this place pristine," Bud continues, oblivious to the fact that the groom can't hear him or the fact that his commands irritate an already nervous horse whose prancing could easily trample a foot.

"We got a lot going on around here," Bud says, as he edges a few steps closer to the porch to give the frisky horse a wide berth. "I better get back to business. You make yourself at home." He seems positively giddy over the "TV team" despite the stables having little to do with the story.

"Thank you very much," I manage to offer before he hustles back off toward the barn. I feel bad for Maggie, who's already at her wits end without this added turmoil.

At least half-a-dozen cars also arrived during my nap and are parked on the opposite side of the drive at the main entrance. Grooms busy themselves bringing horses in from the turnout to tack them up for morning lessons.

"That's her over there." I barely catch the words as the whir of the weed whacker starts back up. Covey, the blonde groom from last night, stands at the outward facing door of the west wing, pointing in my direction. I hustle over as he darts back inside. I follow.

"Sometimes the smartest move is to keep a low profile." A raspy woman's voice says as I approach. It's Sperry Davis. She stands by the grooming stall securing her long, wheat-blonde hair into a braid as she talks.

"Looks like we've got company," she says, announcing my arrival more like an outlaw from a western movie, than a debutante. As she turns, I'm caught off guard by her beauty. Her skin glows with a warm, golden tan accented with a light sprinkle of freckles. Her frown indicates I'm not welcome in the private quarters.

I plan to introduce myself, but Covey jumps in.

"This is the reporter I told you about, Callie Kinsey. Channel 5 News." He turns his attention my way. "Great coverage last night. I made it back in time to see that second report."

"Thank you," I say to Covey. "It's a tragic story. We try to be fair and sensitive."

I extend my hand to Sperry, uncertain of how it will be received. "As he said, I'm Callie Kinsey and yes Channel 5. I also ride here."

"Sperry Davis."

It's tough not to gush. I want to tell her I know everything about her and the amazing way she busted her cheating husband, or how I admire how she used every dime of the money she won to build a cancer research wing in her mother's name at Memorial Hospital. Instead, I stick with "Nice to meet you."

"I want to apologize about how the story unfolded yesterday," I say. Sperry continues to get ready to ride, more interested in pulling her braid forward over her shoulder after dropping her helmet in place, than listening to me, but I need to win her over. "I take it you knew Mrs. Lang?"

"We call her Tally. She was Sperry's best friend," Covey jumps in.

"Yes, she was," Sperry reaches for her gloves.

"Sperry showed Tally all the ropes in Wellington," Covey interjects again. "She even flew her to a private barn in Germany for a horse upgrade so she'd win a few more ribbons. We can get you in there when you're ready."

"We?" Sperry rolls her eyes at Covey.

"I've told you, I rode with Gunther before you ever met him when I was at boarding school in Switzerland."

"Oh, come on, boarding school now?" Sperry chides the groom, flashing him a ravishing smile. When anyone speaks of Sperry Davis, the description always includes that she's drop dead gorgeous and full of life. The reports don't do her justice. She exudes cool. A sexy, carefree confidence that would make rock stars trip over themselves to get a date with her.

Covey appears enamored enough that he does not mind Sperry calling him out on telling a tall tale.

"I practically grew up in Palm Beach and let me tell you, it's all about the who's who and Sperry shows them all how it's done," Covey continues.

"Aren't you kind." Sperry taps the groom on the fanny with her riding crop. "Will you take Rollo down for a light lunge? Make sure he's sound after that long haul."

"No worries," Covey says. He grabs a lead line and heads off to the horse's stall.

"Ever hear of delusions of grandeur?" Sperry whispers the minute he walks away. "That's our Covey. Has been everywhere, knows everyone, done everything. It's my fault he's here as a tag-a-long. We had a little fling last year and he charmed all the women off their feet. Now we're stuck with him." She lets out another light chuckle, the way you would over the antics of a precocious child.

Sperry divulges her personal life like she's announcing plans to go shopping this afternoon. I could never be so casual when talking about sex – or even dating for that matter.

"When he gets to know you, he lays off the bragging and he's actually quite fun. He's well-read and has excellent manners. You can take him out to a nice restaurant and never worry that he'll embarrass you. Oh girl, and does he know some moves. Honestly, he's one of the best boy toys I've ever had." I shift my eyes as if that could avoid the candor. I have very little personal business, but what I do have is kept on the down-low. She looks out the door where Covey lunges a very frisky horse. In a T-shirt, jeans and dusty boots, he exudes cowboy sexy. "And, bonus, he's a hard worker," Sperry adds. It's as if she lists the attributes of a pet. Maybe I need to think about dating differently.

"He has his hands full right now," I watch the horse buck and play at the end of the lunge line while Covey expertly guides him around the circle with a long whip.

"We thought Rollo was going to be a great jumper prospect, but he didn't cut it in the Grand Prix ring this winter. I'm going to back off and try him in some lower jumper classes this summer on the local circuit."

Maggie says I'm excelling after only two years, however the terminology and training approaches remain out of my reach. It sounds like Rollo isn't athletic enough for the big leagues. I don't know how that's possible. He looks plenty powerful to me. I'd say he belongs more in the bronc division of a rodeo.

"And you ride him?" I hope I don't sound too naïve. Sperry weighs in at a perfect petite, size two, max. I don't know how she'd ever control Rollo.

"I ride all my jumpers. I've ridden since I could walk. My mom was a rodeo trainer turned hunter/jumper breeder. She put me on all the tough ones. This one's actually quite simple, he just needs to get a little energy out before we start."

"Well, I don't want to keep you," I say. Then with the grace of a colt learning to walk, I do a very abrupt cha-cha. I nearly forgot my purpose of trying to snag an interview. "Before I go, I want to apologize. I got off to the wrong start with all of you yesterday. Is there any way you could do a quick interview when you're done? The chief says it's extremely important to find witnesses right away. A plea from a good friend is always better than from the authorities."

Sperry makes me wait it out while she zips and snaps her tall boots.

"I'm sorry we were so rude yesterday. We were in shock. We didn't know who you were or how you could possibly think Tally was found dead. It's the least I could do. Anything to catch this creep."

"She was an amazing person. A great wife, great friend," Sperry says. As promised, she appeared at the live truck when she finished riding. We didn't have time to pre-tape, forcing her to go live on the noon news. She takes it in stride. We set up in the courtyard at Chanticleer rather than out near the road where the body was found. She glances off to one of the paddocks filled with shiny, dark bay horses. "She loved her pets and was kind to all animals. Now someone needs to be sympathetic to us and come forward if you know absolutely anything. Someone had to have seen something." Sperry's shoulders begin to shake, her stoicism wanes. "Please," she breaks down. You couldn't script an emotional plea any better.

"There are no words to describe the heartbreak experienced here as news travels of Talia Lang's murder," I add, nodding to indicate to roll the footage Ben shot at the scene earlier. "Investigators scour the area for clues, but they say the most useful information would come from a tip from the general public. If you think you saw anything related to this crime please call the Crimestoppers tip line at 1-800-SPEAKUP or call the local police. Sperry Davis, we know this wasn't easy for you. Thank you for joining us. Reporting live from Oak Grove Township. Callie Kinsey, Channel 5 News. Back to you in the studio."

I haven't even been cleared by the director when I am nearly knocked over by someone rushing at me from the sidelines.

"That was awesome. I knew you'd be here today. I came as early as I could," Bunky Bidlow bounds into the situation with a zest reserved for few humans. Sperry sneaks off. Bunky, completely unaware she chased my guest away, continues without taking a breath. "I heard you moved into the guest house. I wanted to see what I could do to help you out." The offer comes out more like, 'can I help, can I, can I?' Bunky Bidlow represents the people version of a Jack Russell Terrier. She practically pants, impatiently waiting for a response. Short in height, the robust woman's signature plaid flannel shirts hang like a tent, her top-heavy bosoms serving as the center pole. Bunky works dispatch at the county sheriff's department. There's a slim chance she could provide an inside scoop. I still need to ask her what she knows, but the sad truth about Bunky is she'll keep coming back if I throw the ball even once. I made the mistake of trying to be friendly with her when I first started riding. Now I maintain a friendly distance. I let Bunky idle while watching Sperry join the rest of the Divas, who start to cluster the way they did yesterday. I still need to ask them about the missing person's report.

"I could use your help," I take Bunky's arm. "Could you meet me in George's office? I want to talk to you, but I think we should keep it on the down low. You head over first. I'll follow in a few minutes."

"No worries." Bunky takes the bait. Her extreme eagerness almost makes me feel guilty, but I need to take a run at talking with the Divas without her in tow. I no sooner reach the main entrance when, like football players breaking from a huddle, the Divas disband and scurry in different directions.

"True friends don't judge," fires the bleach blonde, as she storms off to a white Range Rover.

Seeing me approach, Sperry slowly shakes her head and waves me off. I'll settle for talking with Bunky.

8

"I PLANNED TO INTRODUCE YOU OUT THERE, UNTIL I SAW the ruckus," Bunky says. She sits in the only chair. I lock the door the same way the Divas locked me out yesterday, then lean on the desk. Gut instinct tells me involving Bunky has disaster written all over it, however, at this point, I have few options. I need to understand the cast of characters in Talia Lang's inner circle.

"I appreciate your help," I say, "but let's keep this on the down low."

"I'm an employee of the sheriff's department. This could be construed as conflict of interest," Bunky says. I should be thrilled with Bunky's intention to be an off the record source, but the gleam over her entire face says the chance of maintaining confidentiality is doubtful at best.

"So, help me understand exactly who makes up the so-called Divas," I say.

"This is perfect," she says, strutting over to a large, white write-on wipe-off board hanging on the wall. Used to track horse management, the matrix lists each horse in black marker, along with the assigned stall, feed, turn-out pasture and owner contact information. Bunky positions herself like a teacher at a blackboard to school me on the who's who.

"The first three horses belong to Sperry. Obviously, you know her story, so let's start with Monarch." She picks up a marker off the ledge and taps the horse's name. "You know Tab Chandler, right?"

"I know *of* Talbot Bates Chandler, old-money trust-fund heiress."

"The family never had any boys, so her mother named her after both grandfathers. Arthur Talbot, Detroit Bank and Trust, and Wilfred Bates who has some kind of patent on automotive transmissions. That's where the real money comes from. I think the transmissions are still used by the Big Three today. That family is rolling in money." Bunky lowers her voice and takes a good look over both shoulders. "You didn't hear this from me, but word is Tab's *addicted* to donating money to charities, and I'm not being facetious. I hear it's as bad as an eating disorder."

I cannot fathom how giving money to charities could be on par with binging and purging.

"Who else do we have up there?"

"Next is Dublin," she says, again tapping the marker on the horse's name for effect. "He belongs to Lydia Mullholland."

"I'm familiar with the Mullhollands," I say.

"Word at the county is that Cameron Mullholland took a long list of defaulted properties with him when he left the prosecutor's office," Bunky says. "That's how he made such a killing in commercial real estate."

Bunky turns back to the board, skipping down a few lines. "Here we go, there's Boo. Super cute bay horse. If you haven't heard of his owner, Christa Muldinaro, she'll be disappointed. She hired a publicist this winter to make a name for herself, including trying to get one of those crazy reality housewife shows to film in Detroit."

"She's the tall, skinny gal that was with the others?"

"Yes. She's obsessed with working out. And watch out for her going ballistic on you. She likes to brag she has mafia connections."

Bunky gives the remaining names on the board a once over. "That covers the core group. The others aren't really part of the tight-knit circle, they simply are rich enough to board in the west wing."

"What about the blonde that stormed off?"

"I almost left out Halle Frankel. We call her 'the Blonde Bombshell.' Right now she's leasing Comet. She comes and goes depending on whether or not she's married."

"So she rides when she has someone to pay her bills?"

"Not just anyone. The same guy, Alan Frankel." Bunky goes on to explain that Halle met the retail clothing tycoon, her on again off again husband, when she worked as an international flight attendant and he was on a buying trip. They're engaged again right now. "You should see the rock. Six carats I hear. This will be the third or fourth time they've gotten married to each other."

"Seriously?"

"You can't make this stuff up. She's been the *Bland* Bombshell lately. She even left the girls and flew home early from Florida this winter, claiming she didn't want to be without him." Bunky taps the marker on her open palm like a nun tapping the ruler in Catholic school. "She didn't want him to worry that she was hanging out with that wild crowd."

Wild is not a word I expected to hear associated with these sophisticated women. I take it with a grain of salt.

"Let's see if I've got the Divas straight. We've got "Tab" Bates Chandler, charity addict diva; Sperry Davis, divorce millionaire diva; Lydia Mullholland, marriage wrecker diva; Christa Muldinaro, wannabe mafia diva; and Halle, a blonde or bland bombshell diva, depending on the day." I'm running out of wind as I complete the list. "And of course, Talia Lang." I want to call her the dearly departed diva. I refrain.

"She was amazingly kind diva." Bunky says slowly. She looks sad dragging the marker past a horse named Johnny Rocket. "The others have all pissed someone off somewhere. Talia Lang was nothing but nice. Supposedly she was having marital trouble, but compared to the others she was a saint."

"That's what I'm hearing," I say. It suddenly strikes me as odd that no one has tried to reach me since we signed off the air. I grab my phone from my pocket. Eight missed calls. Three text messages from the station all saying URGENT in caps. I forgot to turn the ringer back on after I signed off the air.

"Bunky, I'm sorry to be rude, but I've got to go." At least I could tell the truth to make my escape.

"I haven't even gotten to Clive Kasserman yet. You're going to want to hear about Florida," Bunky blurts, trying to keep a foot in the door. "I don't think Halle came home because she wanted to."

"I really have to run," I say, reaching to unlock the door.

"I'm telling you, Callie, none of those women have been the same since they got back from Florida." Bunky isn't bothered that I am halfway out the door.

I turn back to Bunky so she'll know I'm sincere. "I promise we'll catch up later. I really do want to hear the rest of your story, but I've missed several urgent calls." Simultaneously, I notice a smaller, blank write-on wipe-off board on the ground leaning against George's desk. I tuck it under my arm and turn to take off.

"Remind me to tell Maggie I borrowed George's blank board," I yell as I jog down the aisle. "I'll return it."

"Something went down between them. Mark my words!" Bunky won't relent, calling after me with complete disregard for who may hear her.

Ben charges from the north to the south wing as I bolt for the main entrance.

"Over here!" I yell.

"Where have you been? The station has called a dozen times," Ben says, keeping pace as I continue to power walk toward the guesthouse. "Dale Lang has been trying to reach you."

"I've got six missed calls from a private number and two calls from the desk. I knew something major must be going down," I talk as I thumb through my phone. "These must be calls from Dale Lang." I open another screen. "No voicemails. You fire up the truck, I'll call the station. Let me grab my bag."

"Oh yes, we've spoken to him," Obstinate Al sounds more ornery than usual. "He's non-stop trying to get a hold of you. He left three numbers." Al rifles off the first number.

"Thanks," I say and hang up.

Dale Lang answers on the second ring.

9

"THIS IS MY FAVORITE CHAIR. WOULD IT BE OKAY IF WE set up here?" Lang asks. Ben and I stand in awe in the great room of the Lang's massive English Tudor. Floor to ceiling two-story windows overlook a gorgeous, wooded lot. Without waiting for an answer, Talia's husband collapses into the chair, as if answering the door and guiding us in depleted his last bit of strength.

"I've been interrogated for the last twelve hours. I am physically and mentally exhausted, but I want to talk to you," Lang says. I knew about the questioning from our initial phone call. Dale Lang did not sound happy with the interrogation methods. I called the chief after he said he wanted to do an interview. The chief insisted he send an officer over with us. I knew there was no way Lang would agree to the interview if we showed up with a cop. Knowing the man is volatile and a prime suspect, we allowed a squad car to wait down the street. I have the officer's cell number on speed dial and promised to call immediately if anything goes wrong or if Lang confesses.

"Looks like we'll have plenty of natural light," I say, trying to keep the conversation light.

"Yes," Ben agrees, "this will work great."

We exchange uneasy glances. I can't put my finger on it, but Dale Lang's behavior is clearly odd. For starters, even though he is moving very slowly, as if he's in physical pain, his eyes dart fast and furious around the room.

"Callie can sit on the couch," Lang instructs. That's another thing.

People don't normally direct the seating. They usually wait for us to call the shots.

"Is there anything you want to discuss off the record before we start?" I ask, as I open a notebook and get myself into position a few feet from Lang's chair. I always try to ease in with a little conversation before we begin an official interview.

"Nothing we need to discuss ahead of time," Lang responds firmly. "I'd like to get it all on record."

"Then you'll need this," Ben says, leaning in to clip a mic on Lang's tailored striped shirt.

"I wasn't too pleased with the intrusion last night," Lang starts, "but then I realized at least you cared enough to investigate all sides of the story. Those other channels, hell even my local paper, never tried to get a hold of me."

"We owe it to you to at least ask if you want to speak. When you said no, we respectfully left as quickly as we could."

"You didn't have much choice," Lang retorts with a hint of a smile. "I had a 12-guage in your face."

"That did hasten our departure." I say, cracking a little smile myself.

"Okay we have speed," Ben announces, meaning he's officially rolling and recording. I prepare to ask the first question, but Lang takes over before I utter even one word.

"Talia, my wife, was a great lady," he starts. "She contributed not only money, but time to this community with many volunteer efforts." After listing a number of attributes, he transitions all on his own to the night of her disappearance.

"I had a late evening meeting with clients, so she had attended a charity dinner alone. She never returned home." The story mirrors exactly what he reported to police.

"Her friends didn't help matters insinuating she was having an affair." Dale Lang breaks his gaze from the camera, and for the first time turns to acknowledge that he is speaking to me. "I'm sure you heard that at the stables."

"Actually, her friends haven't said anything," I say.

"They act loyal on the surface, but they're cutthroat at the core."

Lang hesitates, as if he's unsure of his choice of words.

"The police mentioned a polo player. Have they found him for questioning?"

"They're only looking at me. They don't care whether Tally got mixed up with the wrong crowd from South America."

Lang stops and takes a breath.

"Her car is missing. They impounded mine. They told me they'll scour it until they find necessary DNA to prove I killed her. Like vultures on roadkill."

My notebook remains blank.

"They think they're so smart, but they aren't piecing the details together quite right. I've called you here today to tell you exactly what happened and to get it all on the record. The public record, not a private interrogation room where they can twist my words any way they want."

I watch Ben out of the corner of my eye. Arched over the camera, the master storyteller slowly presses the zoom button for a close up. A tight shot on the middle-aged man's face captures the worry lines of anguish, the tears of pain.

With no additional prodding, Lang continues.

"I want to set things straight, then have my peace. Where I'm going I'll have nothing but time to rest and contemplate," he says.

I force myself to breathe at even paces. *Listen, just listen*, I tell myself repeatedly.

"Tally and I had been having trouble lately. I've been putting in a lot of hours trying to secure a new business deal. Like I said, I met with clients the night she… she, well, anyway, on that they were right. She *had* been getting dressed up and going out with the girls, dancing and carrying on, even before Florida. And they *are* right. I didn't like it."

A chill runs up my arms and down my spine. It's suddenly understandable why police are not pursuing any other leads. This guy is going to confess. Lang stops, the next words seem to stick in his throat. He chokes the emotion back. Silence overwhelms the room. I don't budge, afraid to even swallow. This shocking admission will end life as he knows it. I can't help but have empathy for this man. Caught up in the moment, I lean forward to hand him the box of tissue from the end table. Lang raises an arm in self-defense with the power and precision of someone well skilled in martial arts. I quickly retract.

"I was going to hand you a tissue," I say.

"Stay where you are!" Lang's voice becomes as commanding as his actions. No longer crumpled and exhausted, he sits up straight, reaches down the side of the chair and pulls out a gun. A black, sinister looking handgun points at me from less than three feet away. My eyes lock on the pistol. The interior of my lungs screech, unable to inhale a breath. As his finger rests on the trigger, every pore on my body flares with an icy chill.

Ben carefully rises from behind the camera in slow motion. "Take it easy," he coaxes, "It's okay. Callie is just handing you a Kleenex."

"Just like they're ready to hand me a life sentence," Lang says, wielding the gun in Ben's direction now.

"You're handing me tissues because you can't wait to hear the big confession. You know this will make you famous. You captured the bad guy. I see how excited you are."

Ben holds his arms away from the camera as if to prove he's unarmed. I stare at my lap.

"That's right," Lang says. "It was a trap. Sit over here." He uses the gun to direct Ben to join me on the couch. Ben follows instructions.

I lament over insisting the cop park so far away. I even told him the interview could take over an hour. We're way in the back of the house. No one will hear gunshots.

"Before this gets ugly," Lang says, "I want you to know one thing and one thing clear. Is that camera still rolling?"

Ben nods.

"I loved my wife. My wife loved me. We didn't have children, we only had each other. Yes, we hit difficult times." Tears take hold of him. "But I don't need you outsiders getting involved in our business." Lang leans forward, moving the gun even closer to the two of us.

I stare directly into the barrel of the deadly firearm, mesmerized at how perfectly round the cylinders are constructed. I've covered a couple of hostage situations over the years, but never at the receiving end of a gun. My thoughts wander to ridiculous places, including hearing Bon Jovi's "I'm wanted, (bam, bam), dead or alive," playing softly in my head.

Lang sees the dazed look on my face. "We're losing her," he says to Ben and raises and lowers the gun up and down to bring me back. His hands now remarkably steady.

"Keep me here, but please let Ben go," I plea. "He and his wife have a new little baby."

"You two know nothing about life!" Lang thunders. He pushes the gun in a little closer. Sweat beads form on his forehead. "The cops, the news, the public," he pauses, "you only care about crimes and *how* they happen. What about *who* they happen to?" Lang uses the sleeve of his free arm to wipe sweat from his brow.

"It doesn't matter whether I brought this on myself or not, the anguish is unbearable. You don't realize how precious life is until it's gone. Are you sure that's still on?" he asks Ben, pointing the gun at the camera.

"Yes sir," Ben sounds defeated, outmuscled by a one-pound package of gun metal. You'd think Lang would want the camera turned off to avoid evidence. I guess when you're already facing a life sentence, two more murders won't matter. I remain utterly silent. A blood curdling scream will only speed up his actions. He turns his body straight to the camera and clears his throat.

I grab Ben's arm preparing for the worst.

"My name's Dale Lang. No one will ever comprehend the depths of my grief, but you can see what lack of compassion leads to." He pauses, stretches his neck, then raises the gun in the air.

I'm not sure which is louder, him cocking the pistol or the huge gasp of air I suck in. A thunderous explosion follows, and then a smattering of blood.

"Ben!" I scream, sure he was shot first. We slam into each other as he lunges to shield me. I look back over at Dale Lang. He sits slumped in the chair.

"Call for help!" I shout.

Ben stumbles as he pushes numbers on his phone. I am no help. I stand to grab my phone from my bag, but plop back down on the other end of the couch. I brace for a minute, then wobble my way to the kitchen where I find a roll of paper towels.

"The police are on their way," Ben says as I walk back into the room. He's powering the camera down. When he pulls his hand away, it's covered in blood.

"Here," I say, winding a long length of white sheets into a wad.

"They're going to want the tape," Ben says. The blare of sirens announce police arriving. "We've got back up on the hard drive." It's instilled in us to protect at least one source of the footage. I don't have the energy to protest. Someday we may need the footage, right now I'm playing the scene over and over again in my head. The more I contemplate Lang's final tirade, the less it makes sense.

"What was that rant about?" I ask Ben. He remains silent as he makes his way to open the front door. "Ben, seriously, I don't get it. Was Lang guilty or innocent?"

"You are turning pale," Ben says. "We need to find you a medic."

"They're on the way." The guy stationed in front of the house stands in front of us, his two-way radio blows up with one call after another sending emergency response to our location.

The officer surveys the room. "I think you two should wait outside." He grabs my arm and helps me to stand.

"Please check Ben, no one has checked Ben," I plea.

Outside, I do the only thing that makes sense. I call the station.

"It's Callie. I have an emergency." It is 3:05, start time for the afternoon story assignment meeting. Before I can say the call is confidential, Obstinate Al plops me on speakerphone. Routine, but completely inappropriate for the topic I need to discuss.

"Rick, you need to go to your office and call me immediately. Privately." Rustling and murmurs create a clear picture of the reporters and producers looking at each other wondering what is going on. "Right now," I add and hang up.

10

A FLURRY OF ACTIVITY CONSUMES THE NEXT HOUR. STATE and local investigators pass Ben and I around for questioning. When they finally release us, we head back to the guesthouse to decompress. As I step out of the shower, my phone rings. I am finally getting noticed by the network, but not as planned. The attorneys are not pleased with the incident or the request to air the footage.

Luckily, my mom calls next, right when I need some comfort. She offers to bring a fresh business suit out to Chanticleer for that evening and additional clothes for the next few days. A visit to the crime scene may help her believe I've been working the past few days. She's still punch drunk with her own theory that I suddenly have an active love life. A slew of text messages arrived earlier today, including a morning *"where ya been???"* with a wink face and another about an hour ago saying *"he must be quite a special guy"* with two wink faces and an eggplant. I don't want to know how she learned to use *that* symbol. She shifts to full mom mode when she hears about the nightmare we've been through.

Within minutes an SUV swirls up the drive. Ben bounds out to greet his wife.

"I was so worried about you two," sweet Brianna comforts both of us as she enters the guest house. Ben clings to his wife with one arm and holds baby Jake with the other. Brianna was my first college roommate. You'd think I'd get credit for fixing them up, but the truth is, I tried to keep them apart. Brianna came from a small-town church family. Ben, on the other hand, was a bad-boy football player. After a few starts and stops, Ben and Bri became a steady couple. I stood up in their wedding a few years ago and now they have Jake, who turned ten months old on the fifth. Our friendship has remained tight, which is unusual in the world of television news, where job scarcity often scatters friends to affiliates all over the country. We worked at a small-town station together in northern Michigan and then somehow both got hired at Channel 5 within a year of each other.

I can't admit it to anyone, but I've been a complete wreck since Jake arrived. I'm about as single as I've ever been. Even the dating site that I loathed joining didn't provide a single legit match. I don't need a baby yet, but having someone special, especially during this type of crisis, would be nice. My phone rings, saving me from crumbling at Ben's family reunion.

The call lasts less than 30 seconds. I quickly relay the news. "After much ethical debate at the local and network level, the network agreed to allow Lang's final comments to be shown," I quote the general manager's exact words. "They're even going to allow the sound of the gun being fired, as long as the screen goes black first." Even though I'm relaying the news, I remain a little in shock over the decision.

"That means I have to get to work," Ben says. He hands off the baby, and kisses Brianna on the forehead. "I'm going to grab a coffee, then head out to the truck to edit."

My mom arrives and instantly seeks out baby Jake. She's got the soul of a tree-hugger, and I have the drive of a career woman, but physically, we're twins. Her crazy, curly, brown hair bounces with enthusiasm as she coos at the baby, never stopping to put her purse or keys down.

"Hi. Your real baby is over here," I say, anxious for a hug. My mom excels at coddling. She shifts her attention and holds me tight, smoothing my wet hair.

"Oh my, sweetie, how do you get wrapped up in these things?" My mom wears her signature yoga clothes, leggings and a long tunic top. This particular coordinating set happens to be eggplant, but she owns similar outfits in every color imaginable.

"It was awful," I start to tell my mom, but I am distracted by the big screen television above the field stone fireplace. Our promotions department is already hyping the story coming up on the evening news. I break out of her embrace to turn up the volume.

"The socialite slaying takes another deadly twist. Our Callie Kinsey witnessed the horrific event. It's a story you'll see only on Local Five at Five. Tune in for a full report." Studio news anchors will read variations teasing the upcoming story at each commercial break.

"Darling, you are not safe out here," my mom says.

"Mom, I cover murders for a living. Do you think it's any safer downtown?"

"It's just all this death is so bad for your karma, honey. The doom and gloom is affecting your personal life." She looks over at Brianna and baby Jake. The hint couldn't be more obvious.

"Don't worry, Ben will be staying with her," Brianna pipes in. Ben looks up from the coffee he's stirring and gives a consenting shrug.

"Here?" I ask.

"There's plenty of room. It's not like we haven't all roomed together before."

The small house has three master suites with three full baths, palatial compared to the college apartment we shared back in the day and way bigger than the confines of the news truck that we share now. Ben and I usually spend full days driving around in the tight quarters of a front seat divided by no more than an armrest.

"So, Bri's assigning you to bodyguard duty?" I tease Ben.

"We are going to be out here for a stretch. That drive back and forth is ridiculous," Ben says.

"I have a bad feeling about everything going on around here." Bri turns extremely somber.

"What's wrong with all of you? Why is a murder out here so different than the ones we cover every day everywhere else?"

"Ohhhh, maybe Callie wants a little privacy," my mom pipes in with a smirk. There it is. I knew even the shocking news of witnessing a suicide wouldn't keep her from prying into my presumed private life.

"Mom," I huff, "I've been working."

"Right," she says to Brianna, with a knowing nod of the head.

"I don't have time for any of this," I say. "I've got to get dressed and get to work." I blow kisses at both women and head into my new first floor master suite to change.

"Okay honey, I need to head out too," and there she goes. In a snap my hippie mom shifts out of maternal mode. She began getting edgy minutes after arrival. "You know I can't miss my body and mind purification class. I don't understand why they've limited the session to one evening a week."

From that moment forward, we barely have time to breathe. We start with live shots recounting our ordeal. "While authorities say they are sad to hear of Mr. Lang's death," I tell viewers, "the murder investigation of his wife, Talia Lang, continues – and they will not confirm her husband or anyone else the guilty party until the investigation is complete."

In between newscasts, Ben and I face a second round of police interrogations, along with interviews with three different newspaper reporters and two radio stations. Even Gavin Phillips from Channel 8 asks to do an interview.

It is almost midnight by the time Ben and I drag ourselves back to the guest house. We are both surprised to find Brianna and Maggie waiting for us. Baby Jake sleeps soundly in his car seat on the floor in the middle of the room.

"Look what Maggie brought over," Brianna says, pointing to a pot on the stove.

"Homemade chicken soup," Maggie mutters softly. The woman, who survives primarily on white bread and cold cuts, looks a touch embarrassed at displaying her homey side. I'm not complaining. I plop on the sunken couch and cozy up with a mug of soup, anxious to allow the warm broth to help me recover from the mania of the day.

"And look what else we made!" Brianna's exuberance shatters the stillness and jolts my very tender nerves. The hot soup splashes in the giant mug, but thankfully doesn't spill. Brianna produces the whiteboard I borrowed from the barn, now filled with magazine photos.

"I know, these aren't the real people," she says, "but it was all I had."

"You're making a collage?" Ben asks in disbelief.

"It's a crime board," Brianna says defensively. "Look," she points to the center, "here's our victim. A stand-in photo obviously. You need to insert the real deal. Over here," she points to a column on the left, "is where we'll fill in the suspects." Dale Lang's name is at the top. 'Polo player' with a question mark is listed under Lang.

"Honey, we are not the police," Ben says.

"On this side we'll track motives," Brianna rolls right along, ignoring her husband's sarcasm.

"That is why I snagged the board," I offer. "I'm not trying to solve the crime, but I need to track leads."

"Finally, being a primetime widow has paid off for me," Brianna says. "I watch at least one show every single night of the week. I could run a crime unit. I used a combination of evidence boards from *Law City* and *Chicago Vice*. Maggie helped me fill in the names." She positively beams over her accomplishment.

I wish I could share her enthusiasm, but this is no made-for-TV drama.

11

MY MIND WHIRLS IN CONFUSION AS I PULL OUT OF THE station parking lot. Rick pulled Ben and me in for a visit with the station psychiatrist to ensure we didn't suffer any post traumatic issues after witnessing a suicide. No one would want to go through that type of experience, but the truth is the intensity of covering the stories keeps any repercussions at bay. Anxious to stay on top of the investigation, I call the usual suspects: the lead investigator, Chief Zurn and the medical examiner asking for updates. All three give 'nothing to report' replies.

Preoccupied, I accidentally turn right on Lincoln Avenue, heading on autopilot toward my condo. You have to be pretty absorbed in thought to forget you're staying at a luxurious guest house. The accidental detour gives me a thought.

I pull over, scroll through the contacts in my phone, hold my breath and hit call. Fifteen minutes later, I pull through the giant wrought iron gates of a premiere lake front home, A long, white, one-story ultra-modern ranch. True to most lakefront architecture, the back faces the road. The entire front of the house captures stunning lake views on the other side. Michigan is called the Great Lakes State, conjuring images of mighty freighters, like *The Edmund Fitzgerald* on the ocean-sized lakes. The real gems are the hundreds of absolutely gorgeous inland lakes that populate Detroit suburbs, each garnished with multi-million-dollar houses.

Sperry Davis waves from the front door as I pull up.

"I left the gate open for you," she says. "You can pull up right here along the curb." I do my best not to gawk as I park alongside a fenced-in tennis court.

The inside of the home mirrors the outside. White kitchen, white furniture, plush white carpeting, even a white baby grand piano sits by an entire panel of floor to ceiling windows. The deep blue of Pebble Lake, surrounding trees and sky, provide the spray of color for the room. Along the back hall, large black and white photos hang in uniform black frames.

"Are you looking at the photos?" Sperry asks. "Those belong to my second ex. He's a big-time Hollywood producer."

I interview celebrities from time to time, but no one that compares to the heavy hitters smiling at me now.

"He's worked with them all," she says, taking in the photos herself as she speaks. "I love this one of Cher pinching his ass, and look how young Bobby DeNiro is in that one."

Anyone that won an Oscar or has thought about winning an Oscar poses with Sperry's very tan, very handsome ex. Sperry is even in a few. I can't wait to call everyone I know and tell them about this house and these photos. I feel like I'm thirteen, wearing braces and standing next to the most popular girl at school. In other words, at a complete loss over how to respond to someone as super cool as Sperry.

"That's amazing," I finally speak. "I don't mean to be rude, but what did your most recent ex-husband think of these pictures hanging around?"

"Oh, we didn't live here," she says, in that matter-of-fact, nothing is private tone. "I moved into his home." She purses her lips and shifts her eyes like a naughty Playmate and glances toward the water. It's around the bend on the lake," she points out the window. "I can't help it, I love this neighborhood. Luckily the lots are big, the mature trees block the view, I don't boat, and this ex flew the coop back to LA. After my most recent divorce, I snuck back down here. I never see either of them."

"And the Hollywood ex didn't mind you moving back in here?"

"Now that's a wild story," Sperry lets out a husky laugh. For a petite, beautiful woman she has a deep, raspy voice. "Can you believe it? I think he completely forgot he bought this house. Come on, sit and enjoy the view."

"It seems kind of hard to forget," I say as I take a seat on the fancy white sofa.

"I know, right?" At least she gets how crazy this sounds. "People in Hollywood think there are only two places on the planet, LA and New York. They broaden their horizons a little when they're in search of a vacation, but even then they only venture to a handful of resorts, like the Ritz in Maui, Villa d'Este on Lake Cuomo, a few chosen places in Miami, Aspen, Cabo or Monte Carlo. They don't go for the unknown, and yet they wonder how the paparazzi always know where to find them." She shakes her head in mock confusion. "Anyway, he probably totally forgot Michigan exists. I pay the property taxes and utilities to ensure no reminders pop up on his radar."

"Unbelievable. Even if I won the Powerball jackpot, I wouldn't forget that I owned a gorgeous lakefront home," I say.

We chitchat about Sperry's life and exes a bit more. Like me, she was raised by a single mom. But instead of hanging out at communes and Indian reservations with poor people, her mom sold horses to the prestigious hunter/jumper show crowd. Between her striking looks, golden hair, perfect figure and riding ability, Sperry waltzed right into the privileged world.

Eventually I shift to the topic of Dale Lang and the unanswered question.

"I don't want to be insensitive, but I know you were best friends with Talia. What do you make of all this?" I force myself to ask.

"I have no hesitation in saying Dale could never have killed Tally," Sperry says. "He killed himself because he could not fathom life without her. They were truly best friends. I mean, that's why she came back for the benefit. She was sick of all the drama going down in Florida. She was only trying to make him jealous." Sperry presses her right hand on her forehead as if she could make the memories stop.

"And then something went horribly wrong," I say.

"I really don't know you, Callie. I don't even know why I trusted you enough to have you over today. I'm lost. Talia and Dale were family to me. Our friendship outlived all my marriages. I don't know who to turn to or how to help," tears bubble. "I guess it doesn't matter. Nothing will bring Tally back. Or Dale."

"Hopefully you can help police catch the killer," I offer. "What about that polo player? Dale said something about his wife getting involved over her head with a bad group of people."

"That's what's frustrating. The police keep asking who she was having the affair with. They don't believe it, but Tally was all talk and little action. She played the guys against each other and kept them all at bay. The whole time all she really wanted to do was make Dale jealous enough to come running to her rescue. He would have, too. He was trying to let her have some fun while he was busy with this big merger, and it got all out of whack." Sperry lets out a big sigh. "Tally didn't know what the hell she was doing. The whole mess would actually be funny, if it wasn't so damn tragic."

Sperry now squeezes her temples as if her brain feels like a pressure cooker.

"By all means, I don't want to make you relive it," I turn to face her more squarely. "I was feeling kind of lost, too. I've never been emotionally part of a case before. I wish I knew how to be of more help."

"Be our champion." Sperry perks up a bit. "Ride the police until the right person is in jail," she says.

"I will," I accept the call to action from my new hero. "I called every agency on the way over. So far nothing. While we're on the subject of calls, I'm trying to reach Covey. Do you have a number for him?"

"Oh, please don't contact him." Sperry's plea comes out like a wail. "He told you he was with Tally the night she disappeared, didn't he?" For such a big talker, Mr. Covey left that little detail out of our conversations. Luckily, Sperry is worked up and doesn't wait for me to answer. "You heard him the other day. He has to be in the know on everything, even when he's not. Oh, God." She presses her palm on her forehead again. "I know this is so wrong, but I threatened him, saying he better not talk to you or anyone from the media. You had to have noticed already, he has no self-restraint. Please don't tempt him to start talking by asking him even a single question. God knows what he'll concoct," Sperry says and looks at me for a reaction to her near hysteria. In the same manner the station psychiatrist graciously dealt with me earlier, I pass no judgment. Partly I get where she's coming from, mostly I'm caught off guard with her being so forthcoming.

"Here's the thing," Sperry goes on. "Tally flew him up as a pawn. One more trick to get Dale's attention. Kasserman didn't work. The polo player didn't work. So she tried carting around a boy toy. And trust me, Covey doesn't get that he was being played." I make a mental note to figure out who Kasserman is. Sperry gazes out over the lake while spewing this information. "Or maybe Covey did know but he went along with it trying to make me jealous. The truth is, he doesn't have a clue about what was really going on. If he is suddenly in the spotlight, can you imagine the story he'd create? It would be 99-percent fabricated to keep himself at the center of the investigation. We'll never unwind the truth from fiction."

"So he flew up from Florida for the benefit?" I play it cool, careful not to reveal that she just gave me a couple of giant new pieces of information.

"Yes, we used the guise that Covey needed to come up to prep before the horses were shipped back from Wellington. The truth was, Tally didn't want to go to the stuffy party alone, so she brought cute Covey to make Dale angry. When Dale didn't charge in raging with jealousy, she got mad and called me to say she was going to fly down to see Enrique, her polo friend. We thought she was in South America all this time."

"Where did Covey go?"

"He dropped Tally off at home, spent the night in our locker room at the barn. In the morning, he took a cab to the airport and flew out on the first flight, like he was supposed to. I picked him up at the Fort Lauderdale airport. Tally's the one that veered from the plan." Sperry's eyes drop to the white carpet. "Or she was intercepted."

"The police need to know about Covey."

"Oh, we told the police. They know he flew up with Tally, and even that he gave her a ride to and from the party. He was here for less than 24 hours. I would never stop him from talking to the authorities, but when he became enamored with you, I knew his story would grow and grow and grow to grab your attention." Even if he won't be a reliable source, I can't wait to talk with the blonde groom, especially now that I know he spent time with Talia Lang right before she disappeared.

I arrived at Sperry's feeling lost about where the case was heading. As she walks me out to my car, I find myself leaving in far worse shape. She sent a million new facts fluttering around in my head. Unfortunately, like a mass of dollar bills freefalling from a tall building, I swipe at thin air, unable to grasp any.

"Obviously I'll call you if I hear anything," Sperry says as I open my car door. "And thanks for understanding the dangers of our dear friend Covey."

"Maybe you shouldn't keep him on the payroll."

"Ah, he's entertaining, and it's only money," Sperry says. "And technically, it's not even my money." I like this gal. "Do you play tennis?" she asks, eyeing the courts on the opposite side of the drive.

"A little."

"Now that we've got decent weather, I'll have you over to hit a few."

"I'd love it," I answer in disbelief. Hopefully I'll have a chance to brush up on my tennis game before the invite. "About Covey," I return focus to the story, as I toss my purse into the car. "I totally get that the kid's a piece of work, and I might have to weed through some tall tales, but he was with her at the party. Maybe he would have insight on who could have been angry enough to kill her."

"Suit yourself," she says, taking the request better than expected. "Be careful," she winks. "He has his sights on you and he'll charm the pants off you -- literally."

12

A CALL TO MY AGENT GOES STRAIGHT TO VOICEMAIL. Whether my job is on the line, or whether this story continues to bring national attention, I'm going to need her. It seems no one is in the mood to talk today. At least that means I get a little down time. The entire drive back to the guest house I daydream of the down-filled king-sized mattress and oversized down pillows. The spring weather drew in dark, puffy rain clouds making me long for afternoon for a nap. When I pull into the parking lot, it's obvious there will be no rest.

Parked a few spaces from the main entrance of Chanticleer sits a Channel 2 news car. The large front stable doors are rolled wide open, allowing me to clearly see the unmistakable blonde head of Leslie Littleton. She stands inside the doors, a cameraman in tow.

"Now what?" I ask the *The Twins* as they meet me on the gravel drive. *The Twins* being a polite name for Maggie's holy terror Jack Russell Terriers, Spunky and Spanky. They weren't from the same litter, but they share an identical knack for getting into serious mischief. She keeps them locked up while people are riding. The rest of the time virtually every boarder at Chanticleer helps shoo them away from trouble.

Their protective nature provides a bit of a comfort. They take the job of guarding seriously, keeping pace at each side of my ankles like miniature centurions. Their brown spots worn as badges of honor. All three of us gaze steadily forward and confident as we march toward the competition.

"Here's Callie now," says Tab Chandler, dressed in one of her exquisite riding outfits including polished tall boots and spurs. She confidently greets me at the door and motions me to hurry in, as if I'm Chanticleer's director of public relations. A complete shocker. I have never formally met this woman and I don't think I'm on any better terms with her than Leslie Littleton. Evidently, she does not intend to let the Channel 2 reporter in on that secret.

"What's going on?" I play dumb, even though it's clear the enemy reporter has descended on my home-turf looking for interviews.

"We're following up on the story," Leslie says. I wonder why the reporter uses a sing-song voice trying to sound as innocent as possible. As I walk through the door the problem becomes evident. Leslie and a middle-aged cameraman stand with their backs edged up toward the massive doors, while five women dressed in riding clothes form a human wall, intent on pushing them back out into the parking lot. It's the Divas, minus Sperry Davis who I just left at her house.

"You've been informed that this is private property," Tab tells them. I keep a careful watch on the faces of the fellow boarders, hoping they don't betray the fact that I'm not entirely welcome either. To my surprise, Lydia Mullholland, Christa Muldinaro, and Halle, the Blonde Bombshell, all seem pleased to see me.

"And we told her they're the press of a button away from us calling the cops to have them removed," Bunky Bidlow says, popping her short frame forward from behind Christa. It's becoming clear why the famed Divas eagerly welcome me as the new spokesperson. The alternative is Bunky. While I try to formulate a plan, I watch Spunky and Spanky inspect our guests. Spunky, leery of the camera, backs up cautiously. Spanky, on the other hand, moves in for a closer look. He circles slowly around the guy's ankles. I pray he doesn't bite. After sniffing the cameraman's leg with interest, he stops, lifts his leg, and takes a leak on the poor guy's jeans.

"Uh oh!" Bunky shrieks, as she watches the cameraman jump back. He hikes his equipment above the spray and scoots out the doorway. Good ole Spanky expedites the eviction process for everyone.

"I'm so sorry!" I exclaim, stifling a laugh as I follow him out. Leslie runs on tiptoes behind us trying to negotiate gravel in high heels.

"Are you okay?" I ask, inspecting the jeans. Only a trickle hit the mark.

"Let's use this as an excuse to scoot you two out of here," I whisper in a hushed tone, like I'm on their side. "These women are very sensitive right now. I ride here, and I don't even get interviews." The Twins follow along emitting low growls.

"You could at least call them off," Leslie says, as she continues to walk on the balls of her feet, protecting her ankles from becoming a target for the dogs' teeth. The mighty mini-minions successfully chase the competition off the property, leaving me to go face the usually more formidable opponents -- the Divas.

"You handled that beautifully," Tab says, reaching out for a handshake as I walk back in the door. Even in barn clothes she comes across quite businesslike. I watch over her shoulder as the Channel 2 car rolls out of the lot slowly, hesitantly, almost as if they realize they've been duped.

"I don't think we had a chance to formally meet. Talbot Bates Chandler. Please call me Tab." Her skin glows with the sheen of routine facials and expensive skin creams.

"Callie Kinsey," I return the introduction. "Most people call me Callie."

"Of course. Any news this morning?" It's her turn to look over my shoulder, probably wondering where the giant news truck lurks. To the best of my knowledge, Ben stayed home after his visit at the station.

"My sources are all saying nothing to report."

"Nothing reported at dispatch either," Bunky interjects, smoothing the front of her oversized plaid shirt, intent to stay in the mix. "But I heard a news flash here," she adds triumphantly. "I hear you're looking for a new horse!"

"Now that's premature," I say. Maggie did say I might be outgrowing my beginner horse several weeks ago, but I would not say we are horse shopping.

"Are you thinking of buying local or going to Europe?" Tab asks. Lydia, Christa and Halle move in closer, anxious to hear details of where I intend to find a new mount. Maggie warned me that if we begin horse shopping, to keep the activity on the down low or it would become everybody's business. As always, she is right.

"I'm not even close to really start looking," I say with intent to wiggle out of the conversation.

"Honestly, you don't have to go to on an extravagant European boondoggle," Bunky says. A two-time local junior champion, faded ribbons from days-gone-by still adorn her tack trunk. She knows horses and, brought up in an average working-class family, she also knows the strains of limited finances. Bunky mucked stalls to earn lessons back in the day. Now as an adult, she works two jobs to afford to keep her horse at Chanticleer. "Focus on the horse's attributes and if it suits you, not where it came from or what its ancestors accomplished." Constantly trying to prove herself to herself, Bunky routinely makes it her mission to try and instill some type of higher equine knowledge to anyone who will listen.

"I respect what you're saying," Tab says, "But you can have both. You must shop from someone you trust. I'd only use Sperry's broker, Gunther. He has quality horses, plus his business gives ten percent of every sale to the European Sport Horse Retirement Coalition."

"And 90-percent of the overpriced profits to himself," Bunky whispers to me.

"In fact, Maggie asked me to give you the contact info." Tab grabs me by the arm to lead me away. "I have some info for you in my locker. Come on, I'll get it for you."

"I'd love that," I say, knowing Tab's offer is as much of a charade as the European breeder donating profits from the sale. Tagging along behind the socialite, we plow past the others and head alone toward the inner sanctuary of the West Wing lounge. I may finally have an opportunity to ask some plaguing questions, particularly what happened between the women down in Florida.

Tab carries the horse shopping act out all the way through slowly opening the combination on her locker. So much so, I start to wonder if she is really going to give me horse brochures. She's so deliberate, I can't help but pick up on her combination as she spins 26-4-32. Once the locker swings open, she looks over toward the door to make sure the area is clear.

"Have a seat." She points to the wide bench next to her locker.

"Thanks," I plop down.

"I was stalling. I wanted to make sure we weren't followed." Tab steals a glance of herself in the mirror inside the locker door. She gives her short, brown hair a little comb through with her fingers. "I need to take you into my confidence," she begins. I don't know Tab, but she seems tense. "Have you noticed Halle acting strangely?"

"I've never met her," I say. "In fact, the first time I saw her was here the other day. I did see a little disagreement with you all in the parking lot."

"Disagreement? That was a full-blown meltdown. The woman is on edge. First, she tore out of Florida, now she's been beyond distant. I feel like I don't even know her."

"I keep hearing about Florida. What happened down there? What do you mean *tore out*?"

"Let's just say she made a hasty departure a few days sooner than scheduled."

"Do you think it has something to do with Talia's murder?"

"There's one way to find out. Why don't you see what she knows under the guise of interviewing her?"

"It doesn't even need to be a covert operation. I would like to interview all of you."

"Timing is of the essence. I think you better start with Halle," Tab says. She peeks out the door assuring there are no lookie lous hovering. She turns and lethargically shuts her locker.

It sounds like Tab is accusing Halle of being involved in Talia's murder. She and Sperry both referred to trouble in Florida. Dale Lang seemed suspicious of Halle, too. Given Tab's edgy state, I won't overreact to the accusation. So far, I'm being told versions of the truth. I need facts.

"I am a little confused. Was Halle also close with the polo player?" I ask.

"Not that again," Tab sighs. "The police are following the wrong thread. We had a few drinks with Enrique and company. We didn't know them well enough for Tal to go visit. That was a giant bluff to get Dale's attention."

"Now that you brought up Mr. Lang, what's your take on why he killed himself?"

"They were the most in love couple you'd ever meet," Tab Chandler quickly agrees with Sperry. "I can't believe his distress led to such a horrific outcome."

"So you think the disagreement in Florida had something to do with Talia's death?"

"How much do you know about that?" She turns swiftly toward me, as if she's been waiting for this topic.

Suddenly, I wonder if I'm caught in a ruse. These women are crafty and Tab is the ring leader. Could this locker room bench be the hot seat and a ploy to find out how much I know? Will they try and keep me quiet, like Sperry is doing with Covey?

"Almost nothing," I say. "Halle flew back from Florida early." I pause. I don't have to worry about what I say, because I honestly don't know anything. "But I don't know why. Did she have a falling out at the horse show? Did something happen between her and Talia Lang?" I consciously use first and last names to maintain a professional stance.

"You seriously haven't heard what happened?"

"No. Dale Lang briefly mentioned trouble in Florida. That's all." Bunky and Sperry did too, but I keep that to myself.

"Halle ran into more than a little trouble down there." Tab shudders like a breeze blew through her.

"That doesn't give me much to go on. Can you elaborate a little?"

"I can't share specifics. Halle was sort of busted, and she was mortified over the incident, hysterical really. I don't know what length she'll go to keep Alan from hearing about it."

"Alan?" I ask, not wanting to give any indication that I've been briefed.

"Her fiancé, Alan Frankel. She's terrified he'll call their engagement off." Tab twists her own wedding ring. "I'm terrified what she'd do to maintain her secret."

A distinct coolness lingers in the dim tack room from the long winter months. I grab my forearms bracing against the chill. I recall the blonde's anger the day before in the parking lot.

"What made her blow up at all of you yesterday?"

"That's the thing. Nothing really. We were discussing who would handle the details for the Langs' services, and she went nutty, accusing us of being busy-bodies. I totally get how outrageous this might sound," Tab bites her lower lip. "I know this dirty little secret, and that might put me in danger. I have two beautiful daughters and a lot of responsibility," she says. "If God forbid, she's created some type of a hit list, I can't be on it." Tab visibly shakes as she tugs the handle to secure her locker door.

"I'm torn between betraying a friend and fending for my life," Tab continues. She seems as rattled as Sperry did earlier. The secret must be a whopper to create this type of strain.

"I'm not even sure we should involve you," Tab continues. "I don't want the guilt of getting you in the mix with her. Can you anonymously make sure the authorities know she has something to hide? And please, please don't mention me."

"I need a little more info," I say. "What was she busted for and what happened in Florida?"

"I can't share. I'm worried sick about my safety. We have this place practically bugged. We've been listening in on people. I cannot be the one caught talking."

Bugged? So that's how they overheard my call the other day.

"I'm making it sound over the top," she continues. "It's not high-tech. It started out as fun. We bought the silly little Ear like you see on TV. It seemed like a clever gadget to spy on the polo players at the bar. Then we started playing around with it at the stables to hear if anyone was talking about us. In fact, Halle was chasing you around with it on the other day."

So that's how they heard my call. I vacillate between feeling violated and wondering why I haven't tried using something like that before.

Tab continues her train of thought.

"My question is, how did she know who you were? Or that you were talking about something worth listening in on?"

13

I MAKE THE FAIRYTALE WALK FROM THE HEAVENLY stables to the lush guest house. It took all of two minutes to acclimate to this luxurious lifestyle. I stop in my tracks and a smile lights my face. Cute Cop rocks on the white wooden swing chair on the big wraparound porch.

"Business or pleasure?" I ask. I hope he can't hear my heart binging right out of my chest as I approach.

"A little of both," he replies with that incredible smirk. Perfect white teeth, wavy brown hair and his physique make him pure underwear model material.

"Want to come in for a minute?"

"That was my plan," he says. I pray I can pull it together enough to open the door.

"The chief says you left a distressed voicemail earlier."

"I did leave a rather emphatic voicemail." I try to make light in case the chief told him I sounded paranoid.

"We're all a little worried about you after the Lang incident."

"I'm okay. I was forced to go to the station for grief counseling today."

"I also wanted to tell you that I felt bad for peeling out the other night," he says. Troy pulls out a barstool and makes himself at home at the counter, dropping his athletic frame onto the seat.

"I assumed you had to get back to work."

"That's a good way to word it. Let's say I wasn't feeling too business-like, and that was a solemn scene, so I left."

The chemistry between us whips up internal combustion all over again giving me a new understanding of being weak at the knees. Mine may melt. The situation calls for a glass of wine. Luckily, I did a little shopping this afternoon. The groceries are still in the car. Troy offers to help unload.

"I'm on a budget," I say as I hand him the 4-pack caddy of wine bottles. "You get an extra 10-percent off when you buy four."

"A wine-o that eats meat lover's pizza. I think this could work," he says, tapping me on the hip with the wine as we make our way back into the house. I'm thrilled Ben is gone tonight, yet a bit nervous at the same time.

Troy masterfully pops open a bottle of wine. We spread pita chips and a couple different dips on the coffee table, plop on the comfy couch and talk and talk and talk. Troy tells about how he served as a Navy Seal, then in an arm of the CIA, and now he owns his own security equipment company.

"I don't get why you're working at the local police station. It seems small potatoes after all your other adventures," I say.

"I tell people I like to stay busy. But the truth is I've had a little trouble readjusting to civilian life. And getting back into socializing," his jaw tightens. "Actually, dating. I use this job as an excuse to be busy on Saturday nights."

After a glass of wine, I'm a bit tempted to ask Troy if he knows about Halle's big bust, but I'm enjoying his company. I don't want him to think I invited him in to pick his brain about the case.

"Your mom sounds like quite a character," Troy says while casually refilling our glasses.

"I can't believe you heard her 9-1-1 call."

"Who didn't?" he says with a seductive smirk. For a guy against dating, he sure has some suave mannerisms. "How does your dad deal with her?"

"I don't exactly have a dad," I start slowly. "Or at least not one that my mom has owned up to. She's a self- proclaimed, full-fledged, free-love hippie. She raised me on her own."

"That's pretty rad," he says, imitating a stoned hippie. "Do you ever want to know who your dad is? You turned out great with a single mom, but are you curious about your father?"

"My mom's idea of a great bedtime story was to tell a tale about a princely man that might be my dad." I take a sip of the wine. "When I started school and we began learning geography, she thought it would entice me to study more if I thought I was from whatever region we were studying. When we learned about Mexico, my dad was Mexican. When the class studied Germany, he was German. In fourth grade when we reached China, I finally pulled the plug on the gag. I mean, I was old enough to know I didn't resemble a single person in the photos."

Cute Cop belly laughs at my story. My whole life I've wanted to meet someone that can genuinely laugh at my family dynamics the way I do.

"You poor thing," he puts his glass on the table. "Let me give you a hug." He gives me a great bear hug. "You feel pretty good," he says. The smell of his cologne permeates my soul.

"You, too." I'm going all gushy. I set my glass down to reciprocate, when a mood-shattering A/C D/C ring tone ruins the moment.

"I have to get that. It might be an emergency." I give him my cutest, scrunched, *I'm sorry* face. It's Sperry. I walk the phone into the kitchen. In the open floor plan, it's not completely out of ear shot, but it gives me a little privacy just in case.

"I'm so glad you answered," Sperry sounds tired. "I'm a mess."

"What's wrong?"

"Are you alone?"

"Ironically, no," I say, kind of proud that I have a guy over.

"Act natural!" she orders.

"Are you okay?"

"I said act like everything's fine. Who's there?" she demands.

Not wanting to offend Sperry, I play along.

"A friend stopped by for a glass of wine."

"Okay, listen. Act normal, but listen to what I'm telling you." I *am* listening and Sperry sounds groggy or drunk.

"Of course."

"Our conversation today made me start piecing things together. Everyone's been afraid. We all know too much. But I'm telling you, when I wasn't expecting it, a light bulb went off in my head. I *know* who did this."

"Wow," I barely utter. There is no way I can act natural after that revelation.

"I know what you're thinking. I need to go to the poleesh," she says with a slur. "I can't come forward until I am absolutely shertain."

"The sooner the better." Part of me wants to motion to Troy for backup, but I don't know Sperry that well, and she definitely sounds out of it. She could be drinking or worse on some kind of sedative and hallucinating.

"I know I'm right," she sounds frantic. "This killer has access to all of us."

"We have to act right away."

"I can't. I won't be vertical much longer. I took a schleeping pill."

That explains why she sounds loopy.

"It doesn't matter what type of crisis you're facing, never sacrifice sleep, Callie. Under eye bags are the quickest way to show your age," Sperry says. I find it hard to believe she's more concerned with getting a good night's sleep than identifying the killer. There's no telling whether the sedative has made her whacked out or if she's really got some type of lead.

"I can have the detective come to you."

"I want to talk to you feirst. Okay. I'm in bed now."

"Let's meet up first thing tomorrow," I give in. From the sounds of it, she'll be passed out by the time anyone drives to her house anyway.

"One o'clock?" she asks.

I'm watching Troy. He played it cool at first, but he moves to the end of the couch and is leaning toward the kitchen trying to listen.

"One seems a little late. Can't you make it sooner?"

"It's all I've got."

"Okay." I surrender. "See ya at one."

"What was that all about?" Troy asks immediately.

"One of the gals I ride with called to set a time up to come out here tomorrow."

"What time is she coming out?" he asks, as if he hadn't been listening.

"One. That'll give me time to get some work done in the morning and do a live shot for the noon news."

"Hey," he says, "look at me. I think you're cool. I've had a really nice night. We're not off to a very good start if you're not being honest with me. Say it's bad timing and I'll hit the road." That Navy Seal training. I thought my story seemed super plausible.

"You didn't know I was stopping by tonight," he continues. "I didn't even think to ask if you were dating someone else."

"What?"

"Sounds like you've got company coming over a little later. I'm guessing it's someone that gets off duty at midnight down in the city."

"No, *tomorrow* at one," I say before catching on to his misguided logic. "Oh no, you thought I had a booty call coming over? You sound like my mom."

"You are being guarded over something."

"Are you going to make me confess to being a pathetic workaholic who never dates?" I punch him. "If you give me one more of those great hugs, maybe I'll tell you who called."

"A half hug," he says as he stretches out one arm to pull me back to the couch.

"It was a woman from the barn," I say, pulling away from Troy's arm. "Talia Lang's best friend, Sperry Davis. She thinks she might have a tip on the case, but she took a sleeping pill and sounded so groggy I don't know what to make of it. We are meeting at one o'clock tomorrow. I'm sad to report, no booty call."

"We could change that," he says.

"Tempting," I say, looking away.

"But not a good idea." He dips me backward to force me to look at him.

"Why did you come waltzing into my life in the middle of all this?" I ask. "It couldn't be worse timing."

"I know," he says, as he plays with my curls. "We can keep it cool until this case is solved.

"You better not go disappearing again, mister," I poke him in the belly.

"I won't. I have a confession." He takes me back into his big strong arms. "I knew I liked you when we met in the moonlight. When I heard what happened at the Lang estate, I wanted to rush right over and make sure you were okay."

"I'm glad you came over tonight," I say. I haven't had anyone care about me in a long time.

14

"WHY DIDN'T SHE GO TO THE POLICE?" BEN ASKS FOR THE third time.

"I'm telling you, she took some type of sleeping pill. She practically passed out while we were on the phone."

Ben and I sit on high top stools at the kitchen countertop of the guest house. I attempt to bring him up to speed on the unusual call from Sperry Davis the previous evening.

"Where is she now?" Ben asks with a huff.

"She said she'll be here at one." I try to remain calm. It's my fault Ben is frustrated. Between butterflies in my belly (Troy) and bats in my belfry (exasperation over this story), I didn't sleep a wink. At sunup I tucked my red-plaid flannel pajama bottoms into a pair of boots and meandered out to feed mints to Cassidy. Then I tried to keep myself busy by strolling around the path that leads out beyond the pastures. Two nosey chestnut horses followed along the inside of the fence line trying to keep me company, but they didn't provide enough distraction, so I caved in and called Ben. I told him there was a development in the case and hung up. I knew the suspense would get him moving. I didn't take into consideration the ramifications that would ensue after he arrived.

"And you had me rush back out here because?" he asks.

"I couldn't stand being out here alone," I confess in a mouse-like squeak.

"Why didn't you go for a ride?" he asks.

"With our jobs on the line?"

Ben rolls his eyes.

"First, no one was out here that early. And honestly, I have too much on my mind to even think about riding. This story is creeping me out. I'm sorry I hauled you out here so early, but this will give us a chance to prep something good for the noon news."

"I'm on afternoons," he barks.

"Rick already said he'll sign any overtime requests."

"Where's that stupid board from the other night?" Ben asks. I had forgotten about it.

"Right here," I say, and grab it from its hiding place behind the couch. Thankfully Troy didn't see it.

My phone dings. It's my mom. One of my other attempted distractions earlier was texting her that I met a cute guy.

'*What happened to one from earlier this week?*' she responds.

'*This one's better.*' I send the reply quickly so Ben doesn't ask about it. If I continue to try and convince her I wasn't with anyone last week, we'll bounce back and forth for an hour.

"We might as well start tracking some of the names you keep tossing around," Ben says.

I place the board on the dark granite countertop between us and grab a wipe off marker.

"Let's start with one I haven't had a chance to tell you about. Tab Chandler pulled me into confidence yesterday, to say she's concerned about a gal named Halle Frankel. She's the blonde that rides with them. I guess she's been acting odd." I say. "We need to add a photo of a blonde." I uncap the marker and add Halle's name to the suspect column. "Dale Lang and Sperry mentioned her too."

"That sounds like mean girl gossip. The chief said this is likely a crime of passion. I think we need to stick with the men in their lives. Who's the other guy Sperry said Talia dated besides the polo player?"

"Covey came up to take her to the benefit." I add the kid's name to the list.

"No, there was someone else," Ben says.

"Tab and Bunky mentioned a guy from here that they hung out with in Florida. Some wealthy tycoon." I twirl the marker, unsure of whether to put the guy's name on the board. "Kaufman, or something like that."

"Put him on there," Ben instructs.

"And we already have the polo player," I say as I point to his line. "Now we need to focus on motives. That column is almost empty."

"Tab said Halle was busted for something down in Florida and she wants to keep it a secret, but I don't know exactly what happened." I follow a line from Halle's name over to the motive column and write 'busted' followed by a question mark.

"I don't want to sound sexist, but do you really think one of these ritzy gals committed murder?"

"Maybe not with her bare hands, but we covered two big murder-for-hire stories last year." I stare at the name, perplexed over the notion that anyone could resort to killing someone to solve a problem. "I have a lot to ask Sperry. It's why I'm so anxious for her to get here."

My phone dings with another text from my mom.

'*Shaman Richard gave me cleansing ritual to do with you after witnessing violent death.*'

'*I showered!*' I reply. That will raise her feathers. My mom takes her Shamanistic practice very seriously.

'*He says the trouble is not over. You are in danger,*' she quickly writes back. That's not good. As much as I like to tease my mother, Shaman Richard is gifted with seeing the future. His third eye never fails.

'*I'll be careful,*' I type back. Her warning does nothing to settle my nerves.

Luckily, I have a full day's work to keep me occupied. We spin through the noon news in record time. There are no tape feeds, no interviews, just a quick update from the scene where I inform viewers that the police are hard at work. Once again, I make a plea for witnesses to come forward and give the Crimestoppers number.

Now we sit waiting for Sperry to arrive, and she takes her sweet time.

"Knock, knock." Maggie lets herself in the front door. "What's going on?" she asks as she looks at our newly populated crime board.

"Playing detective," I say.

"I was going to ask if you wanted to go for your first trail ride. The weather is gorgeous and," she says, pausing to create intrigue. "It's the Divas that are heading out. They said it was okay if I asked you to join them."

"I'd love to, but I'm waiting for Sperry Davis."

"Sperry?" Maggie laughs. "Good luck with that one. That woman is never on time, if she shows up at all." Maggie has a point. I was supposed to be introduced to Sperry a half dozen times over the past two years and it never happened.

"She called me. It sounds rather urgent."

"Ah, to do with the story," Maggie says with a soft Irish brogue. She studies the board. "Who's Kaufman?"

"Some guy Talia Lang had a fling with in Florida I guess," I answer.

"Oh, you mean Kasserman and you mean *all* of the Divas," Maggie says, stressing the *all*. "One at a time, mind you. Come to think of it, they all flew down on his private jet. Word is he flew back without them. From what I understand, the ladies were quite irritated over having to fly home commercial." She raises her eyebrows. "You'd see his estate if you go on the walk --" her voice rises with enticement.

"Ben is out in the truck and I really should wait in case Sperry shows."

One o'clock comes and goes, then one-thirty. At nearly two, I walk over to the stables and find Maggie.

"Sperry said she had a couple of important meetings today. Did any of the ladies mention where she is?"

"She'd consider the plastic surgeon an important meeting," Maggie says, pulling the girth tight on a saddle. "Or maybe she had a nooner," she whispers, so the other women don't hear.

"Have you seen Covey yet today?"

"The new blonde kid? No. He won't stay with the rest of the grooms and makes a point of saying he doesn't report to me. Says he's staying at 'an estate'," she gestures with air quotes. "Perhaps he's being served breakfast in bed by a butler."

Chanticleer's grooms live in two mobile homes on a lot near town. The places are clean, however, judging by first impressions, Covey would not rough it in a mobile home park.

"With his charm and his way with women, he probably did meet someone who's putting him up," I say.

I go back to the main door and peek out to the parking lot. Still no Sperry. Maggie follows me.

"You're going to drive yourself mad," she says. "That woman is so unpredictable. Go throw a saddle on Cassidy and take your mind off all of this for a while. If she shows up, I'll call you immediately. These gals don't go too far or too fast. They'll walk you around the Kasserman estate and you'll be back in an hour. Now go on."

"Do I have a minute to change?"

"Sure. I'll tack Cassidy up for you myself." Maggie gives a big grin, proud of herself. "Now hurry!"

I obey Maggie's orders and am back outside, ready to ride in mere minutes. The women wait patiently as I mount Cassidy. Tab conducts a polite reintroduction to Lydia, Christa and Halle. Then she imparts a few rules of etiquette, including delegating the particular order the women and horses like to follow.

"Callie, we're going ask you to stay at the back," Tab requests. Not being a trail veteran, the Divas choose the rear as the safest place for Cassidy, tucked well behind the giant backend of Lydia's mount, a Thoroughbred Percheron cross named Dandy. With a cluck we hit the trail leading to the back of the property.

The women couldn't be nicer, nor their pace any slower. For women that are veterans of the show ring, they are extreme chickens on the trail. Lydia isn't even riding her own horse. Dandy, a deep dapple gray, is one of Maggie's safe schooling horses.

Once again, I find it difficult to comprehend that anyone would use the word *wild* to describe the Divas. All four exhibit mannerisms consistent with retirees working as docents at the Metropolitan Art Museum. First, they recount the history of the Chanticleer property, including a little story of how one former owner lost the deed in a card game and another to bankruptcy.

"See that white house on the left?" Tab asks. "That's Gloria Aldridge's place. She still comes here on weekends. She made the first chocolates in a copper kettle on the stove that's still there today."

"Now her drugged-out daughter probably uses it to make meth," Halle pipes in. Gloria's chocolate truffles are sold nationwide, and her candy factory takes up about a square mile near the Detroit International Airport. She's a local celebrity, and her daughter has made the news a handful of times for cooking up trouble.

"Oh no!" yells Tab.

Lydia turns around to lend explanation. "He piled up logs on us again. We can't get through. Now we have to go the long way around."

"Who?" I ask.

No one hears me as they pull up their horses to turn around on the very narrow path. The horses let out a few choice whinnies and give a handful of nips, as they cram into each other. The tight confines cause quite a traffic jam. They're not enjoying being forced into a trail mate's tail, as they spin from east to west like weathervanes.

"We have to enter at the far end of those fields, but we can still get there," Christa offers. The destination looks miles away.

"That seems a bit out of the way," I gently suggest. I don't want to be gone more than an hour and this pace is ungodly slow.

"Maggie said you wanted to see Kasserman's estate," Christa says. "We can get there by going around Winkler's Pond."

"God forbid we disturb O.J.," Lydia snarks.

I only know of one O.J., and if this person is anything like him, it can't be good. It sounds like they're worried about disturbing an ogre that lives in the swamp.

"Who is this guy?"

"Clive Kasserman. Heir to the frozen concentrate juice fortune," Tab says. I've come to realize that nearly everyone in tippy-top income brackets is referred to by their fortune.

"His great grandfather owned over half the orange groves in Florida," Lydia adds. The fact that his name has an alternate meaning, gives me a little sense of relief.

"What brought him to Michigan?" I ask.

"He's a Michigan native. Plexagate Plastics. All of our great and great-great grandparents invested in Florida back in the day. Mine built condos in Fort Myers," Tab says.

"So he's not a bad guy?" I ask, not ready to admit I heard his name mentioned in conjunction with the trouble in Florida.

"Well, we run in the same circle with him but," Lydia says.

"He does have a bit of a temper," Tab turns in her saddle to look me in the eyes. "He built this amazing estate out here in horse country and let's say he's been a tad bit possessive over protecting it."

"A tad?" Lydia pokes back at Tab.

"Nothing for you to worry about, Callie. We have a bit of a hall pass. Mostly he goes after landowners in the area and people from the local hunt club."

"He gives a whole new meaning to O.J. when they enter his property," Lydia says. "Supposedly he runs after them, leaping over logs and chases them off with a shot gun. The name does have a bit of a double meaning."

"His property butts up to the far side of Chanticleer, right where Talia was found. Has anyone mentioned this to police?" Silence fills the air again. I know firing warning shots is a far cry from how Talia met her demise, but the notion seems worth investigating.

Through a clearing, I finally see an expanse of dark, gray roof tiles stretching over a building the size of an apartment complex. "Is that his house?" I gulp. The magnitude is completely bewildering. Similar to the equestrian center there are also a number of smaller matching outbuildings surrounding the mansion.

"Yes. That's his primary residence," Tab says. "Ladies let's err on the side of caution and avoid him today. We don't need him roaring up in that super-charged golf cart, shooting at us."

"I thought you were friends of his?"

"Can we just say 'it's complicated' to that one?" Lydia tries to play it off.

"I'd say it's beyond that," Halle seems to pop out of a daze. She catches herself spilling a little too much and falls silent. Come to think of it, she has seemed a bit absorbed in her own thoughts, or distant as Tab mentioned.

"So he doesn't like horses on the property, that's his prerogative," Tab tries to fluff off the gossip. She turns once again in her saddle to look directly at me. "I know it sounds crazy that someone would buy a compound in the heart of horse country if he doesn't like horses, but I went to school with him. He's not that bad."

"He's a hot head and unpredictable." Lydia won't relent.

"That's plenty enough," Halle, now fully engaged in the conversation, all but scolds Lydia to stay quiet.

A soft breeze carries a spring chill. I know they all had some type of fight with the guy in Florida. Evidently the Divas aren't quite as forthcoming with gossip when it involves themselves.

"You don't run around shooting randomly without finally hitting something or…" I hesitate, "someone." Another stretch of silence makes me realize I'll have to take my questions about Kasserman elsewhere.

We enter a magnificent trail that leads into the woods, and along with it comes another dip in temperature.

"Do you guys remember the time we took this path over to Dharma's for champagne brunch, and Tally got the bright idea to hop off and pick wildflowers on the way back?" Lydia reminisces a short while later on the trail. The others begin laughing.

"She went to mount back up on one of the fallen logs," Lydia turns to face me. "She put her foot in the stirrup and first the log rolled, then the whole stack. When she tried to leap into the stirrups, the whole saddle rolled under Monarch's belly." Lydia spouts tears from laughing at the recollection.

"She was lying flat on her back and the mare took off," Christa adds.

"The part that was the most hilarious," Tab stands in her stirrups and turns around to me to include me, "was when the mare came trotting back. We honestly think she didn't know how to get back on her own."

"Did Tally get hurt?"

"No, we had about a bottle of champagne each, Tally just rolled to the ground." All four women howl with laughter. Even I find myself laughing at the visual of it all.

"We should have brought a little bubbly for the ride today," Lydia says.

The laughter turns sullen, and I leave the women to their silent memories of a dear friend. I lean back and gaze up at the patterns made in the trees as the sun peeks through the leaves. The walk through the woods is truly spectacular and ends with a great surprise – a giant log jump that leads to a nice, open farm field of mowed down corn stalks.

Fox hunt fences pepper the countryside. I can't resist trying one out.

Thankful to be at the back of the pack, I ease Cassidy up a bit to let the others get well ahead. I ask him to pick up a trot, then a canter, and up and over the tiny two-foot log we go.

Cassidy, who has been docile through the woods, lights up over the jump, then celebrates by bolting clear past the pack, farting and bucking as he gallops down the side of the field. Apparently, I'm not the only one fed up with the leisurely pace.

The other horses, not seeing what sparked the incident, fear the worst and take off following as if they are being chased by a pack of hungry hyenas. By the time I realize the rest of the group is far from enjoying the gallop, we have already reached the other end of the cornfield.

"You could have killed one of us," Tab snaps. I circle back to find four sets of very angry eyes glaring at me. I consider making up a story about the horse taking off, but it wouldn't explain my half seat jockey position, as I encouraged Cassidy to gallop on for most of the length of the field.

The horses huff and puff.

"I'm so sorry," I offer. "I really thought I could pop over the log and settle right back into a walk. I didn't mean to cause trouble."

"And you went the wrong way," Tab adds with a sigh. "Our trail is over there." She points catty corner, clear across the empty field.

My seat bones ache, numb from pain. At a walk, that corner is at least a half hour away. Pure agony. And we still need to make our way back home at some point.

"I really am sorry," I say. "I didn't realize how far you were going. After the trouble I've caused, why don't I head back to the barn? I have to get ready for work soon."

"Great. She turns toward home, and they all go crazy again trying to follow back to the stables," Christa says without acknowledging me.

Tab assures the others it will be okay for me to head back. We part amicably. They even show me a trail that leads directly to a dirt road to take a short cut home.

Once on the trail, I find my bearings. Cassidy and I wind around the opposite end of the pond from the crime scene. The close proximity to the murder plays tricks with my psyche. No matter how hard I try to look away, my eyes sweep the pond area. With pure horror, I spot a corpse, except the body I'm seeing isn't buried in mud and this time the woman has long blonde hair. A super charged golf cart roars off through the woods. I grab Cassidy's mane to hold my balance. These aren't hallucinations. There is a woman's body lying dead about a hundred feet from where we stand.

I abruptly turn Cassidy around. The women are about halfway up the corn field by the time we come charging up from behind at a full gallop, sending the horses into a whole new frenzy.

This time I offer no apology. This is an emergency. I need help.

15

WE CALL AUTHORITIES IMMEDIATELY, THEN AGREE TO get the horses safely back to the stables. Determined to arrange coverage, I hold the reins in my left hand, while keeping the cell phone pushed against my right ear as we hustle back to Chanticleer. The horses pick up speed as they near home creating increasingly louder booms with the sound of twenty hooves repeatedly hitting the ground simultaneously.

"You sound like you're being trampled," the six o'clock producer yells into the phone. I'm hesitant to admit I've been playing hooky on a trail ride, although they wouldn't have another exclusive story if I hadn't.

Hearing the commotion, Maggie meets us in the drive. She calls for grooms to take the horses. I run straight for the West Wing tack room. I feverishly scan the lead line hooks. The space reserved for Sperry Davis sits empty. It had been there. I collapse against the wall and slump to the floor. The body was face down, but I know that is Sperry Davis lying out there. Her murder was premeditated and it happened while she was on her way out to see me.

"Callie please tell me this isn't true." Maggie catches up with me as I put my saddle and bridle away. Next I wander over to check the latch on Cassidy's stall door, falsely searching for some sense of safety amidst the turmoil. Maybe even stalling from facing reality.

"I wish I could," I mutter.

"Then we better get back down there," Maggie musters much

needed strength for both of us. "Someone is going to have to guide police to the area."

"No," my own resolve returns. "You stay here."

I snatch my purse and car keys from the top of my tack trunk.

"Where do you think you are going?" she asks.

"I've got Ben."

Hysterical shrieks from the Divas echo down the aisleway.

I have no more desire to return to the scene than I have to subject Maggie to danger.

"The most important job for you right now is to protect the ladies," I say to Maggie as she follows me to the door. "Take them to the guest house." I start to walk away, then turn back. "And lock the door."

"I'll be fine. I'll be fine," I keep repeating to myself as I ease my way down the narrow path off Kings Road. No sign of a police vehicle yet. I told Ben I would confirm the body's location while he fetches the camera. Yellow tape marking the area where Talia Lang was discovered flaps about 100 feet off to the right.

"Odd how bodies keep finding you," Troy quips as he approaches from behind. I nearly wet my pants. I'm so engrossed surveying the crime scene I never heard him.

"Are you okay?" he asks.

I'm not. I keep that to myself.

"You wonder why he didn't drag the body another fifty feet over to the swamp," I say as I survey the area. Cattails and six-foot-tall phragmites grow in the boggy ground around the edge of the swamp.

"That pond is definitely deep enough to submerge a body," Troy admits. I had wondered the same thing when I found Talia. This time I have a little more insight. Halle was beyond distracted since joining the group. Maybe the bodies remain in the open because *she* wasn't strong enough to drag them that far. A shiver races right through me. I recollect Tab's nervous shudder. Could a fellow equestrian be capable of such a horrible crime?

"I've got to cordon off the area," Troy says, then quietly begins unfurling spools of official yellow tape. I can't help but watch him.

Ben slams the back of the truck door.

"Before you completely rope me out, can I get one more look at how she died?" I ask Troy.

"Official answer, no," he says. "But you beat me to the scene. You could have taken a look before I got here." He holds the tape in the air for me to slide under.

"I noticed one of her horse's lead lines was missing back at the barn. My guess is she was strangled like Talia Lang, but I don't see a leather lead. What do you think?"

Troy uses my shoulder to balance as he leans forward to make his own inspection.

"Nothing telling," he says. "What were you doing out here anyway?"

"We were on a trail ride." I flag my arms to grab Ben's attention. "A few women from the stables were going to take me to the Kasserman estate, but we never made it."

"What do you mean?"

"The first trail we took was blocked by a pile of logs. The other trail was locked off with a gate. Then I discovered the body, and we bee-lined it straight back to Chanticleer."

"Yea, but you weren't in search of the estate. You are on it."

"No, his house is a couple of fields over."

"He owns all this surrounding property too."

"Wait a second, the women say he has quite a temper," I squint, trying to follow the trail. I heard the golf cart earlier. "Are you saying both women were found on his property?" Troy continues working as if my question is rhetorical.

Ben consults with Troy on where to set up the camera. Within minutes, the state investigator rolls up, along with a few CSI folks from the Lang scene in tow. Chief Zurn and the Medical Examiner arrive shortly after. The area buzzes with a new case. It is only a matter of time before the other news stations pull up, as well.

"Callie, come take a seat in the squad car for a moment," Chief Zurn instructs, pointing me to his cruiser. He opens the back door and I take a seat, unsure of whether to scoot over to make room for him. Awkward to say the least. He shuts the door like a limo driver and heads to the driver's door. Then state investigator, Detective Sergeant Kowalski, hops in the passenger side.

"You're not under arrest," the chief says immediately. He adjusts his burly frame so he can watch my saucer-size eyes through the rearview mirror. "However, we do have some serious questions for you."

"Hi Callie," Kowalski says. He's far more average-sized than the chief and can actually turn around to address me in the backseat. "Thanks for cooperating." I can't claim I'm being cooperative. I was tricked. I've known the Detective Sergeant for a few years. Normally, I'm chasing him with questions. He drives me crazy when I'm in a hurry because he ponders everything. Even the simplest question leads him to gaze off into space while he meticulously formulates an answer. I can't fathom that he'd toss me into a squad car like a criminal. In fact, he is usually amenable to the press. When a college student was killed by a hit-and-run driver on the campus of the University of Michigan last winter, he asked us not to include the vehicle color in our coverage. He didn't want to alert the driver that they were closing in on him. In return for the favor, he tipped us when officers moved in for an arrest.

"Whatever I can do to help," I say, trying to sound as sugar-sweet as possible.

"At this point our discussion is purely procedural. You know the drill."

I want to believe him, but I'm sitting in the *back* of a squad car. The chief continues to watch me in the rearview mirror.

"You seem like a nice gal," the chief takes over. "But you have to admit it's a bit odd that you found both bodies."

"Officer Kirkpatrick mentioned that you noticed a leather lead line missing from the stables this afternoon," Kowalski says, checking his notes.

"I didn't see it on the body," I say.

"What would make you suspect that piece of equipment was involved in the crime?"

"Er, well, really, I guess I'm guilty of playing amateur detective." I wonder if my potential new honey inadvertently landed me in this predicament. "The chief mentioned a possible horse connection in Talia Lang's case. I made a quick check of the tack room and noticed her lead line was missing." I pray revealing the chief's insight doesn't land me in more hot water.

"It's troubling enough that you had the wherewithal to check, but what's really bothering me is that the strap was not visible at either scene." Kowalski gives me a long look; I can't tell if he's waiting for me to squirm or contemplating where to go next. "Callie, I'm not prepared to release any details, but the leather straps were hidden under the bodies in a way that only the person that committed the crimes could have known about them."

I can hardly breathe.

"I assure you I never saw them. I'm sure you visited the tack room, it's pretty obvious that the hooks are empty."

"We know your station is in flux. That would put you in undue stress to get a good story," the chief says.

"I would *never* commit a crime to get a story," my voice shrieks with hysteria. "I hope you are not insinuating such a horrible thing."

"And yet, here you are, back at another scene, camera at the ready," the detective says.

"Detective Sergeant Kowalski," I employ every formality possible. "You can't seriously think I had anything to do with these deaths." Ben paces between the live truck and the tripod. I check my phone, it's 4:30. "That's our photographer over there. Please talk to him. He's been with me all day."

Kowalski slowly and methodically looks at his phone. "It was shortly before airtime that the first body was discovered as I recall."

"I worked an early shift that day. I was out here to ride my horse."

"What would you think if you were us?" the chief asks.

"I certainly wouldn't be thinking I did it." The chief puts both hands on his belly and sighs. He knows I'm right. I don't know why they're applying muscle. "This second murder clears Dale Lang. There are still other suspects."

Both men turn to see what I know. "You have me nervous to admit

I poked my nose in any further." I pause. They continue to watch me. "The women say they're friend Halle has been acting strangely. She held up the ride today by arriving late. And I've heard they've had issues with a guy named Kasserman. The bodies were found on his property. Surely those are better leads than looking at me."

Ben widens his pacing circle to scour the area. He checks his watch.

"Please," I finally say in a desperate tone. "We go live in twenty minutes. I have to get to work. At least you know I'm not going anywhere."

"We'll let you go," Kowalski finally says. "For now. We've got one final question for you," the detective turns all the way around in the seat and raises his eyebrows, as if he is playing a trump card. "Why did Sperry Davis call you after midnight last night?"

"She said she thought she knew who the murderer was. I begged her to call you. For some reason she wanted to meet with me first."

"Why didn't you tell us about the call?" the detective asks.

"I don't know," I answer. "She called late at night and didn't sound coherent. She said she took a sleeping pill and was about to pass out. I didn't know how serious to take her. If she really could identify the killer, I couldn't understand why she wouldn't call you right away and why she wanted to wait until one the next day to meet with me. It didn't make sense."

"She said she knew who murdered Mrs. Lang?"

"Yes." With all my might I fight back tears punching to escape. I lose the battle and now try to capture the droplets before they cascade.

The chief hands me his handkerchief. Kowalski seems ready to hand me a pardon -- for now. "Did she give you any inclination of who she suspected?" he asks.

"She was slurring terribly. She insisted on talking in person. She was coming out here to meet with me," the notion makes me sick. "Do you have any idea what time she died?" I ask.

"The medical examiner needs to make the official determination. For now, we're going to let you go. And please, let us do the job of investigating," the detective says firmly.

"I will." I fumble to open the backdoor before realizing, like any common criminal, I can't. There is no interior handle.

Without uttering a word, the chief opens the back door and helps me to my feet. I hand him back his hankie. Then I walk straight over to the news truck where Ben hands me a mic. I have very little time to pull my thoughts together before we go live.

"Two prominent women are now dead, and although police are not ready to link the murders, the bodies were found in close proximity out here in a very rural area," I launch into the story. I hype the fact that police need leads to help solve case. The detective didn't say so, but it's clear both women were killed by the same person. Knowing it's not me, any of us could be next on the hit list.

16

"FOR THE SAKE OF ARGUMENT, I'M ADDING MY NAME TO the list of suspects."

"That's ridiculous," Ben says while attempting to swipe the makeshift crime board away. I stretch it out of his reach.

Ben and I sit perched at our new hangout, the kitchen island. We monitor one news channel on the big screen over the fireplace and another on the smaller television in the kitchen.

"I'm tracking the same suspects as the cops, and if they're questioning me, my name goes on the board."

"Since when did it become our job to solve the crime? Our only job is to report on the investigation."

"Two well-known women are dead. They're going to put someone behind bars quickly. Trust me on that one." I point to the last column on our board. "We've got to start zeroing in on a motive and work backward from there."

"That alone should clear you." Ben offers.

"I wish. They accused me of trying to get a good story to keep my job."

Feeling strange, I write 'needed story' on the board.

"The forensics report will save me. Sperry said she wasn't coming out this way 'til one. When the medical examiner concludes the time of death was after 10 a.m., I'm clear. I was with people the entire time."

"Don't they usually determine time of death at the scene?"

"They usually ballpark it. This case is too high profile. The detective said they're going to let the M.E. handle it." I drag myself from the stool to the fancy built-in-the-wall espresso machine to whip up a cup of coffee. The Nespresso whir mimics the frenzy going on in my brain.

I look out the front window. Riding is the only thing that will take my mind off the case for a little while. Plus, I want to spend some time in the West Wing and going out to see Cassidy lends the perfect excuse.

"Whoa!" I yell as Cassidy veers left, ducking out in front of a small red and white striped vertical jump.

"If your heads not in it, your body should not be on a horse," Maggie yells.

"I thought this would help. I'm way too distracted." I trot Cassidy back toward Maggie.

"Not your usual form today, but certainly understandable," she responds. "Don't let's end on that. Trot if you have to, but let's have one up and over before we call it quits."

Maggie's comforting Irish brogue calms my nerves. I circle back, pop over the low pole and prepare to pack it in for the day.

"I don't understand how two people from such privilege could end up murdered," I say to Maggie. She walks alongside Cassidy and me back to the barn. "I never met Talia Lang, but Sperry had such a great spirit, I can't see anyone ever wanting to hurt her."

"Ah, you were under the introductory magic charm. Eventually she'd cross ya," Maggie says. She clutches my calf in the stirrup iron as she often does with riders when she wants their attention to make a point. "Don't get me wrong now," she pauses to intentionally choose her words, "the Divas are good clients and keep me in business, but I make it habit to stay an arm's length away from their personal matters for a reason. A lot of secrets are piled behind the walls of that West Wing. I'd dare say it's filled with as much scandal and secret oaths as any highfalutin private men's club."

That old cliché *if only those walls could talk*, could never ring more true. Those women have a lot to hide. I need to get a look behind those walls to see if anything significant strikes me. To do that, I need to ditch Maggie.

"I've got it from here," I tell her as we reach the grooming stall. I circle Cassidy and hook him to the crossties with his head facing outward. "I'll spend some good quality time with my boy," I pat his big bay neck. "I owe him some extra treats for dealing with me being such a complete mess today." I snag a couple of carrots from a bag hanging on the wall. "And by the way, speaking of the West Wing, Tab Chandler asked me to grab some paperwork out of her locker for her. Is the door unlocked?" I make the story up as it comes out of my mouth.

"Paperwork?"

"Something for one of her non-profits." The explanation seems plausible. I untack Cassidy as I talk, hoping to encourage Maggie to head along on her way. "Tab says she can't bear to step foot on the property this morning. You know how dramatic they are. I offered to scan it and email it to her."

With that, Maggie gives a whistle to gather up The Twins.

"I'll take the little terrors with me," she says. "They've been on the scent of a rabbit all morning. They should be ready to collapse by now."

I swiftly put Cassidy back in his stall, then creep down to the West Wing. Not a soul lingers near the stables. Still, the shakes set in as I open the door to the Diva's private area. In one swoop, I shut the door behind me and distinctly feel all the oxygen sucked from the room. With no windows, daylight quickly extinguishes too, forcing me to turn on the light.

It's completely rotten to betray Tab's trust so soon after earning it. But this mini-crime will be in everyone's best interest if I find anything that leads to the killer. And besides, she all but showed me her combination. At this point, I've broken into the room and I'm already twirling the numbers on the combination lock. There better be a payoff. I give one last heave of hesitation before opening the narrow door. Breaking and entering suddenly holds a little more weight than I expected. I crack the door open slowly, as if the killer might jump out.

I search for signs of drugs. None. Telltale pictures from Florida. None. Maybe a news article about Halle from a Palm Beach publication? Nope. A saddle sits covered on the saddle rack. Tab's helmet and polished boots occupy a sparse lower shelf. Wicker baskets on the top shelf hold a few items like gloves, a hairbrush and hairnets to use under the helmet. Not so much as a loose horse hair laying around.

"Callie!" A shout erupts in the hall.

Oh no, it's Maggie.

"Callie!"

"In here," I respond.

Luckily, Maggie jogs by, shouting as she stays her course through the barn. "Those menaces stole an entire uncooked chicken off the counter and ran this way. Have you seen them?"

For two tiny Jack Russells, The Twins manage to pull off some pretty big stunts. I slam the locker door shut and search the area frantically for anything that looks like *paperwork*, in case Maggie pops her head in. I check two cupboards, rows of matching coffee mugs, water glasses and an assortment of crystal stemware. I reach for the drawers, all lined with serving sets in neat rows. No junk drawer. Not so much as operating instructions for the high-end coffee machine or a USEF handbook in sight. I check the hand-painted horse and hound hunt scene wooden garbage can sitting at the end of the mahogany bar. To my surprise, one rumpled piece of paper lies at the bottom.

"They're at the end of the aisle way. I'm going to need you!" Maggie shouts and hustles back past the West Wing door. She may be distracted, but I am not leaving this room empty-handed. Maggie is street-smart. She will subliminally harbor suspicions about my fabricated task if I don't materialize some type of paperwork. I snatch the crumpled paper from the basket.

"Coming!" I respond, limping as I iron out the wrinkled paper on my thigh while heading to the door. I pick up a jog. Sounds of the dogs growling as they tear into the carcass, leads me right to the scene.

"I've got Spunky. You grab Spanky," Maggie orders.

"Okay, but I think we're a little late to save the bird," I say, as I place the measly paper up on one of the higher plank shelves, like it's a document worth protecting. With a quick lunge, I successfully catch the dog from behind.

"At this point I'm trying to save a vet bill from having their stomachs pumped," she shrieks. "Look how they've torn into it!

They've managed to eat their body weight in raw chicken."

The poor ripped up carcass lies covered in dirt on the ground. I place Spanks under my left arm where he does his best to wriggle free, while I stoop to pick up what's left of what would have been Maggie's dinner.

"Where shall we dump it?" As the words tumble out of my mouth, accusations of Chief Zurn and Detective Sergeant Kowalski flood my brain. The thought unhinges me. I could never be capable of disposing of a body. "I'll handle it," I blurt, anxious to make an escape. I drop the dog, take the paper and make a run for the guest house. The ratty chicken dangling at my side.

The chicken carcass brings a deluge of reality to the situation. Dale Lang made a good point. For protection it is easier to focus on a crime and not the people who are violated. Someone dumped two beautiful women in a ditch. I need to do everything possible to help find the person capable of such horrific violence. I dump the contents of my purse on the counter looking for a small, white napkin fragment with Covey's phone number on it. It might take a little effort to sort truth from fiction, but I firmly believe the groom will shed some light on who the women may have angered and perhaps what went down in Florida.

"We're sorry this call cannot be completed. You have reached a device that is temporarily out of service." I recognize the standard recording of a prepaid cell phone.

It should come as no surprise that a fly-by-night groom would use a throwaway phone, and even less of a shocker that his minutes are used up. There will be other ways to track him down. In the meantime, I have another important call to make.

17

"HEY, IT'S CALLIE," I TRY TO SOUND NONCHALANT AS CUTE Cop answers on the first ring.

"I figured shift change would be a good time to catch you."

"Yep. Got off fifteen minutes ago."

"Well, it's a little awkward, but I didn't get to talk to you before I left the scene the other day and it sounds like the detective didn't appreciate that I made another discovery."

"I wanted to talk to you about that, too." Questions. Will he be asking them as a civilian or a cop?

"Are you sure it's a good time? I don't want to bother you."

"Actually, I hope I'm not bothering you."

"What do you mean?" I suddenly feel like I'm back in junior high. "I called you."

"Look out front," he says. I walk toward the front door. "I'm the one walking up the steps."

My entire insides bungee off a bridge.

"Hi!" I gush as I swing the door open. Sometimes I wish I could keep my exuberance a bit more in check. He flashes that awesome smile, I grin back. If he thinks I'm guilty, he's awfully nice to criminals.

Once inside, we step all over each other in conversation, me trying to clear my name, he trying to make sure I know he didn't turn me in.

"You told the chief that I was looking for a lead line."

"You can't leave out a single detail when it's a homicide."

"It was just educated guesses to piece the case together. I never realized my investigation could be construed as incriminating," I admit.

Troy maintains a professional silence. I can't blame him.

"Did you hear about the fundraiser tonight at the Tip Up?" he finally asks. The Divas are throwing an impromptu fundraiser at the local bar to collect reward money.

"Yes, we'll be there. We're going to preview it at six and go live again from the party at eleven."

"And then will you be off duty?" Troy asks.

"We cannot be seen hanging out in public."

"I'm sure I can buy you a beer without raising too much suspicion."

As usual, my phone interrupts a nice moment. Sperry's sister Lucy agrees to do an interview, which means I must send Cute Cop packing.

"Why in the world did you cram this in?" Ben asks. He has the pedal to the metal as he eyes the clock on the news truck dash.

"It was the only time she could make it."

I want to say Lucy McCauley, Sperry's sister, was more than accommodating at fitting us into her schedule. That was not the case.

"I had to beg for this interview," I say and check my makeup in the visor mirror. "We need to talk to someone outside the pack."

Lucy lives in the heart of Detroit's suburbia. We are racing for a four o'clock interview, then we'll have to fight rush-hour traffic to get back out to the country for our six o'clock live shot.

We pull down Montcalm, a street lined with mature Oak trees and dozens of identical small, square red-brick ranch homes with white aluminum trim. We zero in on the address and roll to a stop in front of one of the many homes with updated windows and siding, and a meticulously kept lawn. A woman pops a storm door open along the side of the house and waves us up the short driveway.

"That must be Lucy," I say. She's a robust woman, wearing a flowing orange and blue kimono over black stretch pants.

I help Ben lug our gear up the driveway. Lucy motions us in, mouths "Palm Beach," and signals for us to wait on a tiny back landing one step down from entering the kitchen. With the air of Liza Minnelli, she paces in her bare feet, back and forth, kimono fluttering behind her.

"How long is she gonna keep us waiting?" Ben asks. He shifts his weight from one foot to the other. I don't bother trying to answer. I'm still taking in her full evening makeup, including eyeliner and thick false eye lashes.

"I'm not asking you to rearrange your schedule for a month," she says. Lucy's hands flail as she pleads her case. "Just one day." I can hear a man ranting on the other end of the phone. "I understand you run a busy salon."

From what I can piece together, Lucy is on the phone with a hair stylist who expresses reluctance to shuffle appointments in his very packed calendar to meet Lucy's request.

"It's not like I have a whole lot of days to choose from. I'm overwhelmed myself and it boils down to can you make it or not?" Lucy huffs. I can't believe what I'm hearing. Lucy seems more the Super Cuts and home coloring type than one who flies a stylist in for an event. One thing seems for sure, Lucy McCauley certainly isn't grieving.

When she finally hangs up, Sperry's sister makes no apologies. Instead, she grabs a full size yellow legal pad and jots a note on a multi-page to-do list. She flips through two- or three-pages scanning line items. Sighing, she turns her attention to Ben and me. Hopefully, we are the next item on the massive agenda.

"I'm sorry to keep you waiting. Come on in," Lucy says. She creates a sweeping gesture causing us to gaze around her small home. "As you can see, my sister was the have, I'm the have not."

As we make our way to the living room, I immediately recognize a strong family resemblance, especially in the blue eyes.

"Let me tell you what that phone call was about," Lucy sighs again. A wedding party photo sits on an end table in the living room. Sperry, looking radiant, stands out.

"Look at this," Lucy says. She sits in an armchair and lifts a thick document off the neighboring end table. The papers are folded in thirds, but there is no way they ever fit in a standard letter envelope. "This is one portion of the last will and testament left by my sister. You would think a directive of this size would contain large donations to charity, maybe account for every last cent to be dispersed, but no – this portion strictly contains exact instructions for how she should look in the casket!" Lucy pauses, shaking her head. "You wouldn't believe the details. She could have another wing of a hospital named after her for what this funeral is going to cost."

Lucy slumps back in the chair. Grief returns to the forefront. Ben looks over for direction, unsure whether or not to roll. I shake my head no. This overwhelmed woman clearly needs a private moment.

"The undertaker is working with a plastic surgeon to quote 'iron out every last wrinkle' before the showing. I mean, she probably thought she'd be 80 or 90 when she died, so I guess that one makes sense. I just ordered a brand-new Chanel suit. Lucy points to exact the wording which reads *the very latest couture design from the Paris runway show*.

"She has a makeup artist appointed, one that only applies make up with an airbrush. And you heard it yourself. We have to fly her favorite hairdresser up from Palm Beach. And rather than act honored, Raul is demanding payment for every appointment he would miss, plus a first-class ticket to get here. Wait 'til he finds out there's no Ritz out there in the country where he'll be staying. All this drama to have my late sister's hair coiffed postmortem."

"She has left you with a lot of work," I say.

"If she were sitting here right now, she would laugh it off," she adds. "She always looked fantastic, and acted like it was effortless."

"She was beautiful."

"She worked it. Sperry liked men and the men liked her. Our mother used to say, 'she always had suitors and that suited her just fine.' She loved being the center of attention, and let's face it," she says, looking at me with the same devilish demeanor of her sister, "she had a zest for life."

"That's why I'm here. I've spoken with the women at Chanticleer. I'd like a family member's perspective on what her life was like."

Lucy jumps in describing yachts, jets, champagne, and five-figure shopping sprees, all funded by the open wallets of a myriad of men. I'm shocked Lucy has no filter.

"Did you know anyone from the horse world? Clive Kasserman?" I ask. I don't really need this on tape, but I'd like to find out if she knows anything about the multi-millionaire maniac.

"Is he O.J?"

"I believe so."

"Not my sister's style. I'm not saying she never had… what shall we call it?… *interactions* with him. But he's been around the block. She preferred conquests outside the local social set."

"And did you ever meet a friend named Halle?"

"Va va va blonde? Oh yea, I know all the gals. I spent two weeks with them in Florida."

"Would you say Halle was the Blonde or Bland Bombshell during your visit?"

"There was nothing bland about that woman when I was visiting this winter. She flitted in and out the entire trip and was always dressed quite saucy."

"Do you recall hearing of her getting busted for something down there?"

"Well," Lucy has the same husky laugh as her sister. "She probably *busted out* of one of those tops. She packed herself so tight in a shirt one night, I warned her not to hit the brakes more than a touch or her girls would arrive at the restaurant before us."

"I think this bust was a bit more serious," I say.

Lucy purses her bright pink lips into a pout.

"No, but they hit it hard this season. I'm not surprised the partying and antics caught up with them. I warned Sperry, everything comes at a price. Whether they meant to or not, those women left a trail of broken hearts wherever they went," Lucy says. The sparkle fades from her eyes as she realizes that the lively lifestyles she enjoyed recounting, may have led to the Divas' deadly demise. She fights through. "I'm telling you, Sperry and her friends were never out to hurt anyone or take advantage. Those women could pay their own way. Their free spirits should have never led to their --" Lucy searches for the right word, "murders." She holds her hand up to stop the camera. "Stop. Please."

"Of course," Ben and I say in unison. We have plenty in the can already.

"Off the record, that's not rolling, right? I'm not going to lie, there has been drama with Sperry before, and the night before she died was no exception. Sperry called me quite late to tell me something important.

I called the detectives, but I couldn't tell them much. She was slurring. Evidently, she had taken some sleeping pills. She kept saying either *it* or *he* turned on them."

"Could she have said 'she'? I don't want to spread rumors, but I've heard more than one person question Halle's state of mind."

"Hhmmm." Lucy tilts her head listening to an imaginary recording. "Could've been *she*. Sperry was almost incomprehensible."

I debate whether to tell Lucy that I had the same type of call from her sister, and decide against it. It won't bring any comfort to know that neither of us learned more about Sperry's suspicion or could have saved her from a gruesome fate. Secretly though, I am thankful to know Lucy's story corroborates mine. That will be helpful in getting the detective off my case.

"While we are off the record, I have one more delicate question. Did you meet or hear about any polo players while you were down there?"

Lucy's face lights up. "The Latin Lovers?"

"Was there an Enrique?"

"I don't know. They hung out as a team. Up until this last divorce, Sperry was a one-guy-gal. But after the cheating scandal, she grew jaded and began playing the field in a big-hitter Palm Beach crowd. She was getting mysterious gifts and trips from dignitaries she would only call by code names like *Beach Boy* or *The European*. I've told the police about them, but the nicknames don't give us much to go on, do they?"

When I realize it's nearly five, we bid quick goodbyes to Lucy and prepare to race back to the country for our evening newscast.

"Lucy gave me plenty of questions to ask the remaining Divas when we cover the fundraiser tonight," I tell Ben on the way back.

"Watch how much you poke around," Ben says with the sternest voice I've ever heard. "Playing guessing games may have gotten Sperry killed."

18

WITH LESS THAN TEN MINUTES TO AIRTIME, I RUN UP THE giant log steps of the Tip Up Bar two at a time. Tab Chandler happens to be standing at the front door tying balloons on the door handle.

"Hey there. I didn't have a cell number for you. We're going live in a few minutes and I thought it would be great if you'd join me for a quick interview."

"Right now?" she asks. The urgency catches her by surprise. I throw an apologetic smile.

"It's all we've got. We need to head over right away," I say, as I turn and begin leaping back down the steps. Thankfully she follows.

For a little added anxiety, the interview with Lucy McCauley came up so suddenly this afternoon, I ran out with nothing but my purse. I have no laptop, no iPad, no notebook. I'm not even sure I have a pen.

"I'll meet you at the truck," I yell to Tab as I pick up a little jog. "We literally go on in four minutes!" Searching my purse I find a pen, but to my dismay the only semblance of a paper is the crumbled mess I found wadded up in the trash bin of the West Wing earlier. I am too frantic to go on without at least a few notes so I pull it out. The paper has some type of racy bikini ad on one side, so I quickly fold it in half to hide the photo. I write *police confirm murders are related* across the top, then jot the three key names, *Talbot Bates Chandler, Talia Lang and Sperry Davis*, before I walk over to the mic. I know from experience when I'm frenzied, even the most obvious words, especially names, can elude me when I'm on the air.

"Thanks for doing this," I say to Tab. "We were at Sperry's sister's house this afternoon and traffic was awful getting back."

"Oh Lucy," Tab says and smiles. "Those two were best of friends."

"Sounds like you knew her. Were they close?"

"They were so different in so many ways, but that family bond ran deep. They always had each other's backs. I wish my sister and I had a tenth of what they had."

Interesting. That means the portrayal of fast women that liked to live life out loud were truth and not portrayals from an envious sister.

I keep the interview and fundraiser preview short and sweet. The big news of the day is that the police confirmed that the two murders appear related. That means Dale Lang was likely innocent and a killer remains at large. After we sign off the air, Ben and I pack the gear up and ascend the stairs of the Tip Up together. Our plan is to eat dinner, then leisurely shoot video for the later broadcast. A much earned break after the busy afternoon.

I look forward to showing my buddy the cool horse bar. The impressive log cabin lodge was a luxurious private hunting lodge back in the industrial heyday. It was sold and converted to a restaurant probably before I was born.

"You laid the Lucy McCauley footage on a disc for me, right?" I ask Ben as we reach the top of the stairs. It's been a long day, and I suddenly feel like we're climbing a mountain.

"Yes, ma'am. There's no way I'm running back down to Mason Heights in rush hour traffic again," Ben assures me. "It's safe and secure."

"Awesome. Next order of business, please make me stick to some kind of salad. I'm so exhausted, all I can think about is devouring a big juicy cheeseburger and a giant plate of fries." We heave the massive wooden doors open to reveal a hefty-sized crowd for a Wednesday, milling loudly around.

Not too surprising, Troy Kirkpatrick sits waiting for us at the bar. Our eyes meet.

"Nice tactic," I whisper to Ben while he surveys the room. "So, chance meeting that we run into you, huh?"

"It happens everywhere else, why not here? And look at this, there are two seats available," Troy says. Ben takes immediate advantage of the openings.

"Close enough to talk to Guy, the bartender," Troy continues, "opposite side from the band, which can be a bit loud, and front row to the dance floor. Trust me, there's always a show."

"How far from a cold drink?" Ben asks. With that, Guy comes over to formally introduce himself, treating us like local celebrities.

"Bud? IPA?" the bartender asks.

"A Coke," Ben looks at me. "Until we're off duty."

When we're settled, Ben turns to whisper, "So what do you call him? *Cute Cop?* Are you sure you've been that lonely out here?"

"You sound like my mom." I pop a menu open to block my reddening face from view.

"We've been working round the clock," Ben says, as he takes the menu from the bartender. While Ben is distracted, I try to get a few words in with Cute Cop.

"You look pretty handsome in street clothes," I say. He's wearing a great pair of jeans and a light blue designer striped shirt, with cuffs turned up to reveal a contrasting paisley print. Even when he's sitting, I can tell his ass looks great, making me feel ridiculous in my dowdy business suit. He not only looks good, he smells heavenly. Sitting next to him through dinner makes keeping my mind on work a challenge. Good thing I only drink iced tea while on the clock. Any amount of alcohol might melt my resolve.

"What an odd place for the equestrian elite to hold a fund raiser," I say between bites of salad.

"It's the only game in town, which always leads to an interesting mix of people," Troy explains. "When you belly up to a guy in a plaid shirt at the bar, you'll never know if you're sitting next to a plumber or a multi-millionaire. Everyone mingles with each other pretty well around here."

"Hey Troy," a deep, husky voice approaches from behind. I turn to get a glimpse of the baritone. The proverbial tall, dark and handsome just strode in.

"How's it going?" the stranger asks. Before waiting for an answer, he shifts his view to drink me in with a once over. "Obviously pretty well, you're sitting with a lovely lady."

Troy offers a swift, garbled introduction. I can't hear the guy's name over the pheromones exploding like fireworks between us.

"Nice to meet you," I say, extending my hand.

"What brings you way out here to God's country?" he asks. He's tall and slender without being skinny, dressed in jeans and a t-shirt, with a Gucci belt and loafers.

"I ride over at Chanticleer." Holy cow. I can't believe my response. I should have said we're covering a story. In fact, we're covering the fundraiser happening right now, at the bar. Instead, I tell him where I ride with the express purpose of making sure he knows where to find me down the road. I couldn't be any more fickle if I tried.

"I'm from this neck of the woods myself," the guy says. "We'll have to trade contact info."

"Sure," I say, then quickly push my barstool back to stand.

I have to excuse myself. I wait forever to meet a nice guy. I finally have one sitting right next to me, and before our first official date, I'm already challenged in the monogamy department. There is seriously something wrong with me.

"If you two can excuse me a minute, I need to find the ladies room." It looks like the men are going to wrestle over who is going to escort me. They let me escape peacefully.

I douse my forehead with a little cool water in the bathroom sink to pull my thoughts in check. I have plenty of questions for the Divas after the visit with Lucy, and I really need to find out what happened in Florida. First, I need to get Ben moving to shoot footage of the event. When I return to our seats at the bar, Tall Dark and Handsome is notably missing. I can't help but wonder if Troy bullied him away.

"Where'd your friend go?" I ask.

"Unexpected departure," Troy responds.

"That's odd," I say. "He seemed prepared to hang out a while."

"Until he found out who you are."

"Who I am? What?"

"You know who that was, right?"

19

UNDER THE PRETENSE OF HEADING OVER TO VISIT WITH the divas, I race from the table and scour the room. I can't believe Tall, Dark and Handsome is Clive O.J. Kasserman, the maniac I keep hearing about. I finally spot him – pinned up against the wall by five-foot-two Halle. The Bland Bombshell holds Kasserman, at least six-three and weighing in at a hundred pounds heavier than her, in place by poking him in the chest with her finger. Before I can make my way over, he picks her up at the waist, places her to the side and storms toward the front door.

"You better watch who you're pushing around," I hear him say. "Or I'll send you on a trip to visit your friends."

Yow. Clive Kasserman, orange juice heir, has quite the temper.

"I'm not afraid of you." So does his blonde sparring partner.

I turn to avoid eye contact with Halle. Under that Marilyn Monroe blonde hair and cleavage, this woman appears fierce. I saw her blowup with her friends in the parking lot the other day. It seems wise to steer clear.

The unexpected U-turn plops me right in front of the official Diva table, where luckily I receive a warm greeting from Tab, temporarily abandoned by her cohorts.

"The tech guy at Lydia's husband's company made a website site for us this afternoon, so we trashed the original flyers. We're going to use these," Tab says as she pats the stack. The 8x10s have photos of both Sperry and Talia, a giant Crimestoppers 800 number printed across the middle and the web address to the new site across the bottom.

"Perfect." I take the top sheet off the pile. "I'll refer to it at eleven."

"That's great. I don't think we need to make speeches and all that." Tab beams and references the packed room with her arm. "Of all the great restaurants and nightclubs we've visited, this was always Sperry's favorite," Tab says, sipping a grapefruit martini.

Sperry was first and foremost a horsewoman. She was named after one, raised by one and became a phenomenal rider herself. The rustic Tip Up represents a piece of horse heaven. The old wooden ceiling beams are covered with riding equipment including antique saddles, helmets and riding crops. Hundreds of photos featuring the local horse-set cover every inch of wall. Photos of prestigious guests, like Edsel Ford, visiting Tip Up when it was still a hunting lodge, give the place extra panache.

"Speaking of Sperry," I say, as quietly as possible to break the harshness of my question. "Her sister said today she was dating a few different men in Florida. Do you think any were hurt enough by her or Talia to retaliate?"

"You *know* what I think," Tab says under breath. She casts her glance sideways at Halle approaching the table. Clive Kasserman is gone. Halle still has fire in her eyes. I'm beginning to see the possibility.

"Ah, you've seen the new flyers," Lydia says, also returning to the table.

"Got one right here," I flash the latest copy. "Am I in your seat?"

"No, you're fine. I need to trouble you though," Lydia says, surveying the table. Halle has turned her attention to a couple of women from Chanticleer gathered at the opposite end. "I have an idea for a banner out front. Come with me. I want your opinion," Lydia uses her champagne glass to motion me away from the table.

"I can't believe they serve champagne here," I say as we walk outside. "Is it decent?"

"We keep a secret stash of Veuve Cliquot behind the bar."

"Here, hold this a minute," she says handing me her glass. She leads me straight to the front door where she takes an abrupt right turn, onto the massive wooden porch. I twist the heavy flute in my hand. It's real crystal. With shaky hands, Lydia pulls a cigarette and lighter from her small clutch, lights up and takes a long puff.

"I'm a mess," she says, taking another long drag. "Old habit from law school," she says, examining the cigarette in her hand. I know Lydia's back story. She was not raised with a silver spoon in her mouth. She met her husband while interning at the prosecutor's office and caused quite a scandal by breaking up his marriage. Not that smoking is a socio-economic or intellectual indicator, but I'm not that surprised she's a smoker.

"Look, I don't know if I'm doing the right thing. I have to talk to someone, so I'm taking you into my confidence," she reaches for the champagne glass and takes a swig. "This is tricky," Lydia says between sips and puffs. "Here we are doing all this hype, looking for witnesses that might solve this murder, and I might have information that will help, but I'm too scared to come forward." Her eyes shoot back toward the front door to make sure she's not overheard. "If anyone comes out here, we're talking about making a giant Crimestoppers banner to spread across this porch."

"Got it."

Lydia closes her eyes, tilts her head back and inhales the night air as if it's valium.

"It's Halle. She's edgy. She's covering up something that's really bothering her. I've been suspicious of her behavior for a while, but tonight she's really scaring me. I not only think it's possible she hurt my best friends," Lydia says, leaning against the wooden railing for support. "I think I could be next."

"Is there a possibility she's shook up from the murders?" I ask while I process what I'm hearing. Evidently Lydia does not know Tab harbors the same suspicion. They both came to me in confidence, so it's definitely not my place to reveal anything.

"We all are upset. She's showing signs of rage, not grief. You're an outside observer, you've seen her. What do you think?"

"Have you shared this with your husband?" I try to redirect with a question. "He could find a discreet way to have her investigated."

"When he hears she's on drugs, he'll start asking all sorts of questions about where she's getting them." Lydia tosses her cigarette over the edge, sets the champagne on the railing. "We all use the same source."

"What kind of drugs we're talking about?"

"The usuals," she says, as if I surely take the same. "Prescription level stuff: Xanax, Valium, maybe a little Adderall or Ozempic when we want to drop a few pounds. You and I know it's nothing harmful. As the former prosecutor, Cameron doesn't like to be associated with impropriety of any kind. The last thing I need right now is for him to confiscate my stash when I need it most." Lydia gives her bag a little rattle for effect.

"I'm telling you Halle seems really strung out," Lydia continues with the topic at hand. She turns to check the front door yet again. "Now that it's coming out of my mouth I can't believe what I'm saying. Yet, with Tal and Sperry laying in a morgue, I have to protect myself."

Lydia seems almost as strung out as the Blonde Bombshell she's accusing. She fumbles around inside the tiny bag again, this time producing a round, white Mentos which she pops in her mouth.

"Most of me trusts Halle with my entire being. Part of me is afraid to turn my back. What should I do?"

"If you don't feel you can go to Cameron, I guess I can discreetly ask investigators to observe her."

Lydia nods in approval. What I don't share with her, is the request had already been made earlier that day after Tab made the request. To ease Lydia's paranoia, I offer to let her walk back into the Tip Up alone. I go the long way around to the edge of the parking lot, where I pretend to check on the news truck.

The crowd has grown noticeably thicker as I try to make my way back in through the front door. Ben sees me approaching and gives me a thumbs up, indicating he's already rolling. I throw my hands up indicating I'm doing my best to make my way back, when I'm blindsided by a shove. Christa Moldinaro has Halle by the arm, neither woman notices that they bumped me during the altercation.

"What are you doing confronting him?" Christa pulls her wannabe mafia act on Halle. "Are you trying to set him off so he'll go ballistic on the rest of us? Not smart Halle. Not smart." Before Halle can reply, Christa notices me standing beside them. "And don't you try to go listening in on something that has nothing to do with you," she says to me.

"I have no idea what you're talking about," I say. The two lean toward me. I feel pinned against the wall, like Halle had done to Kasserman earlier. Evidently, Christa saw Halle confront Kasserman and she's not happy. I have no intention of crossing either woman.

"I'm trying to make my way over to the photographer," I say. "I am strictly here to cover this event."

"That's how she operates," says Covey, appearing out of nowhere. He slips his arm through Christa's to physically hold her at bay.

"Right," she snaps at him. "That coming from the biggest user on the planet." Christa pulls her arm away from his grasp. "You need to go back to Florida to find your next Sugar Momma. You've run your course with this group." Christa points at Covey. "I'm warning you," she says, then points to me. "And you, too!" Then she storms back to the Diva table.

"I'm sure she's harmless," I say.

"She's not. She's always threatening to go crazy on someone," Covey says. He puts a protective hand on my shoulder. "Don't worry, I can tell you are good people. I'll protect you."

"I tried calling the number I had for you this morning. The number didn't work and no one seems to know exactly where you're staying."

"I let very few people in the private inner circle," he says with a suave wink. He releases the grip on my shoulder and lets his hand graze along the entire length of my arm, as he backs a few steps up preparing to depart. "You and I both know I couldn't possibly stay at a trailer park."

"I've got a couple of important things to ask you about."

"Absolutely, I'm all yours" he says. I know he's playing me, yet I'm tempted to fall for it. "Let's wait and talk in private. We don't need these women getting concerned that I'm talking to you." His reassuring manner makes me feel protected. The guy is smooth, too smooth. I understand why Sperry cautioned about keeping an arm's distance. "Make sure I get a good working number from you before you leave tonight," I say. I start to push toward Ben, when I notice a commotion at the Diva table. Christa, Halle and Lydia now all stand hunched toward each other over the table. Tab raises both her hands, trying to hush the conversation and keep the gals in check. Judging by the strained necks, fist punching and finger pointing the women are arguing.

"Callie, Covey, somebody, get Jimmy!" Tab simultaneously calls toward me and then in the opposite direction over to Covey, who just reaches the door. I have no idea who Jimmy is. I look around for bar management. It's impossible to tell who's who in the packed crowd. Tab points to the phone on her ear. "He's on his way," she mouths, as if that will fix everything.

"Come on ladies," Tab tries one more time to break up the fight. "Enough already. Jimmy's on his way in, pack up." Within minutes a large man in a black polo shirt, black slacks and black dress shoes stands by Tab's side.

"We're all on edge," she tells the man. "Let's get them out of here."

"You got it," the husky guy replies and reacts like he's been given a military command.

"Jimmy's been with me forever," Tab informs me. "Best driver and confidant on the planet, and on occasion," she pats him on the back, "bodyguard and bouncer."

"Hey, what's going on over here? Are you causing problems?" Troy bounds over. Ben follows at his heels with the camera.

"I think the Divas had a few too many," I whisper. "Tab's driver is escorting them home." The main table now sits empty.

"We've got plenty of footage. You going to put a piece together?"

"Might as well. I think the action is done here for the night."

I stall a moment, allowing Ben to head out so I can say a proper goodbye to Troy. In all the commotion of the evening, I hadn't given Cute Cop much attention.

"Don't worry, I know you're working," he says reading my mind. "Meet you back here at, let's say five after eleven?"

"Of course," I find myself saying as butterflies swirl in my belly.

The evening blew by with no time to go back to the guest house, so I use the same crumpled piece of paper to refer to key facts that I had earlier in the evening. It seems like three days have passed, rather than twelve hours, since I plucked it from the trash bin. In a day and age where we're expected to go on the air with an iPad to look high tech, I am wielding not one, but two 8 x 10s. With one hand, I refer to my notes on the crumpled paper, with the other I show the Divas' new full-color flyer. Once we're off the air, I notice that I folded the paper with my notes backward, and inappropriately flashed the bikini image to our viewers. In a swoop, I also notice that it's not a swimsuit ad at all, but a lewd photo for an escort service. I tuck the paper as quickly as possible in my suit pocket. I can't believe I didn't notice how racy it was sooner. I peel away from Ben to call the station.

"Hey, it's Callie. I want to make sure no one was bothered that I didn't refer to my iPad for notes during the live shot." I won't let on about the impropriety of the photo if I don't need to. I head back to the bar as I talk. I'm more than a little anxious to see Cute Cop.

"You held up the flyer," the late-night producer sounds confused.

"Yes, I also had a few key notes scribbled on a crumbled piece of paper, just making sure the lack of professionalism didn't ruffle any feathers." Troy waves me over as the producer promises to listen in for any scuttlebutt about me during the post show meeting. I decide it's best to order a beer -- or two -- while I wait to see if the crude image will get me suspended, or worse yet, fired. Cute Cop and I no sooner toast when we're ambushed from the side.

"There you are," says George, Chanticleer's manager. Retired from the Marines, George still sports a buzz cut on his silver head and, when he's not on probation, runs the stables as if managing a military outfit. Even the horses snap to attention when he raises his voice.

"You know George," Troy whispers to me, as if that would explain the intrusion. I wonder if I should call Maggie. George is supposed to be regaining sobriety so he can come back to work. I watch him try to catch his balance in order to join our conversation.

"I've been watching your reports," George says. He squints trying to focus in on my face. "I'll tell you a thing or two about those gals."

"Now George," Troy tries to appease the guy who is in no condition to carry on a conversation. There's a brief lull while George braces himself on the bar to take a sip of his beer. I angle myself sideways to keep further conversation at bay.

"Serves 'em right!" he pops in between Troy and me, again spraying a little spit with his slurs. "Sluts. They were both sluts."

"Now George let's be respectful," Troy says. I wonder how Troy even knows George, then it dawns on me our usually stoic barn manager has become the town drunk. Troy's efforts to pacify the man fall in the line of duty.

"You know better than anybody they got what they deserved," George continues slurring. He punches his fist in condemnation and loses his balance. Catching himself on the edge of the bar he continues. "Out to pull men into their web. They danced with the devil and had to be taught a lesson."

Troy whispers something to George and leads him away by the arm. Rather than escort George out of the building, Troy simply leads him to the far end of the bar where he orders him a Coke and sits him down in a corner chair.

"Where's your man?" Ben asks as he takes a seat at the bar.

"He's over there, putting a grownup on a time out."

"So you're admitting he is your man?" Ben's smile grows wide.

"I apologize for George's poor manners and rough language," Troy says, as he takes his seat back at the bar. AC/DC chimes. I look at the caller ID. It's the station. I pray it's the producer giving me the all clear.

"I've got to take this," I say to Troy, then mouth 'station' at Ben. I walk with the phone to the back patio where I know it will be quiet. The producer assures me no one mentioned the paper. Temps still dropping to the 30s on spring evenings, leaves the back patio deserted. I can finally take a minute to examine the lewd photo. How did something this trashy land up in the West Wing?

In a flash, I find myself strangely gasping for breath. It takes me a second to register that an arm, covered in a rough burlap coat, wraps around my neck in a choke hold. Pungent breath, reeking of alcohol, spew from grunts before my assailant finally speaks. When he does it registers with a familiar slur.

"What's a pretty lady like yourself doing out here in the dark?" he asks tightening his grip. "You think you're too good to speak to me? Are you going to walk away? I see what you're doing, trying to put the moves on that cop," his voice escalates as he launches into an outburst. "You're no different than those other women and as such, you will meet the same fate."

I try to fight back. I'm no match for the strong biceps holding me from behind. Images of Kasserman, Halle, a mysterious polo player and Dale Lang flitter through my mind. I know now how misguided we were to accuse any of them. What I'm not sure of, is whether I'll get out of this situation alive to expose the real killer.

20

"HE SEES THE DEVIL WHEN HE'S DRUNK," GUY, THE bartender, says. He huffs while tackling my assailant. George attacked from behind. He holds my head face toward the ground. Pinned down in a strong hold. A pair of work boots and one pair of tennis shoes scuffle dangerously close. From what I gather, the observant bartender ran out the back door to wrestle me from George's grip.

George fought in the Gulf War and is packed with muscle from manual labors with horses. Even drunk, he puts up quite a fight. George fends Guy off with one arm, holding me in place with the other, while I frantically kick, punch and squeal. From the corner of my eye, I see Guy plant the palm of his hand up under George's chin. A quick spray of blood flies out of George's mouth, indicating he probably knocked a tooth out. George flinches long enough for Guy to pry his arm from my neck. I gasp for air.

Troy races in behind Guy, arriving in time to grab George.

"I'm not even going to make a call, I'll haul you in my pickup," Troy says as he pushes my assailant toward the back door.

"Check to make sure Callie's okay while I get this guy outta here." Troy defaults to cop mode. "Sorry, honey, I have to run. I'll stop by later."

I can't help but register the word 'honey.'

"Are you okay?" Guy asks.

I am still on my feet in the exact spot I was when the altercation began. I remain bent over for a few minutes taking inventory of my body parts. Nothing seems broken, everything hurts. I stretch up and gently touch my throat, afraid to speak. If there's damage to my larynx, I'm cooked professionally.

"What happened?" Ben asks as he arrives at the patio doorway. I can't let him know I had a close call or I'll get pulled from the story. Thankfully my crazy curly hair hides how disheveled I really am.

"It's stupid," I attempt a laugh. My voice box feels bruised. I speak softly so it doesn't betray me. "I was out here in the dark on the phone and literally ran into George, the manager from Chanticleer. We startled each other. I think we're all paranoid with the murders." I use the dark to my advantage and elbow Guy. He gets the message.

"Hey, busy night, everything seems fine now, I've got to run back to the bar."

My throat, neck and shoulders throb. My rib aches where George elbowed me after I kicked his shin. Reality sets in like the loud thump of a gavel on a judge's desk. I might be dead by now if an amazingly observant bartender hadn't acted so quickly. I straighten myself up and take a shallow breath, attempting to look as pleasant as possible. Complete pretenses for Ben. I can fall apart later.

"For the eighth time, please let me take you to the hospital," Troy pleads. Afraid that the late night visit will wake Ben, we huddle in throw blankets on the rocking chairs on the front porch of the guest house. The cool air feels soothing after the trauma. Troy finished the business of locking George up, and now he turns his attention on me.

"I hear your voice getting weaker, there may be internal damage."

"It's just bruising," I whisper. "Station management flipped out over me witnessing a suicide. I can't imagine what action they'd take if they found out I was attacked. There's no way I'm getting pulled from the story."

"We only booked George on drunk and disorderly. If you don't file a report, he walks free in the morning."

I gently touch the injured area on my neck and picture myself lying lifeless in the ditch, in the same gruesome manner I found Sperry.

"No. He tried to kill me and I'm sure he killed Sperry and Talia. You have to hold him."

"That's up to the prosecutor. You have to report the incident for her to file charges."

I stop rocking.

"There's no other way?"

"I saw the tail end of the altercation," Troy shakes his head as he speaks. "It seemed pretty violent. Usually, when he's drunk, George wants to be heard by people, not hurt them."

"He's on probation for a violent outburst here at the stables a few weeks ago too. We think PTSD is making him dangerous."

"All the more reason for you to act."

"The bar can file charges."

"He didn't damage the bar."

"The altercation happened on Tip Up property."

"You're a reporter, you know how it works. Any physical altercations have to be filed by the individuals involved. If you don't file a report, basically there is no victim and that means he won't be charged."

"At least he's behind bars for now."

"It's not going to last long. We have to follow due process. I sent the detective a text alerting him to the scuffle. We can't hold him if you don't come forward."

"I can't," I squeak. Troy is right, my voice is becoming weaker. I pray there's no permanent damage.

"He may now be a suspect in the murders. However, the DNA processing could take months."

"Physical altercation charges won't hold him that much longer," I whisper, trying to keep the word count to a minimum.

"Touché. I should have been there for you," Cute Cop says and slides his rocking chair closer to mine.

I hope what I'm feeling is real and not a result of being isolated out in the country in a vulnerable situation. I fight off the emotions by staring over at the gorgeous Chanticleer stables. My biggest concern right now is making sure I don't get pulled from this story.

21

I LAY IN BED, AWARE OF A GNAWING PAIN PULSATING IN my neck before opening my eyes. It wasn't a nightmare. I really had been attacked the night before. With great difficulty I attempt to swallow. Everything in my throat feels swollen and damaged. I'm terrified to attempt a sound. I can't think of anything but the condition of my vocal cords. I pray they aren't seriously injured. When people tease me about my constant babbling, I always joke that at least I get paid to talk. I don't want my career to come to an end at the hands of a psycho.

Silently, I pad in fuzzy zebra slippers from the bed to the bathroom, then down the hall for coffee. Sunshine beams into the kitchen. Ben greets me wearing tattered old football shorts that were once bright orange and an equally faded t-shirt from our college days.

"How ya feeling?"

I nod, acting extra groggy so I don't have to speak and hit brew on the coffee machine. Ben won't expect a reply this early in the morning. As coffee trickles into the brown mug, I inspect the damage to my neck in the reflection of the microwave door. It's probably best that the tinted glass makes a poor mirror. George's thumb gouged the side of my neck toward the back. The marks won't be noticeable to a casual observer.

I plop on the couch. Out the window, horses munch peacefully on grass in small groups completely unaware that horrific violence has been taking place around here.

"How did you sleep?" Ben asks. He stands with his arms crossed in front of his chest next to the couch, a bit menacing for this early in the morning. The strong stance and my paranoia make it difficult for me to maintain the self-imposed vow of silence. I sense he's wise to something.

"What do you mean?" I ask softly.

"The chief called this morning." I don't respond. He paces in a small two-foot space in front of me. "You left your cell on the counter. He rang three times in a row. I thought maybe there was a development in the case, so I finally answered." Ben waits for a response. Every muscle in his body, from his jaw to his arms clamp tight, signaling me to stay clammed up. "Evidently the development occurred last night, right under my nose."

I curl my feet up underneath me on the couch. Our makeshift CSI board lies next to me on the floor. I pluck it and the marker. *Afraid to talk*, I write.

"You should be terrified."

I give a no big deal shoulder shrug.

"This is a big deal. The chief called to let you know that George McNabb will be released this morning."

"What?" My voice proves stronger than I expect. "Already?"

"He was popped for a minor drunk and disorderly. The prosecutor has nothing substantial to hold him on unless you come forward." Ben plops at the other end of the couch, giving up his tough guy approach. "I didn't want to let on to the chief that I'm in the dark. Here's what I pieced together so far. There was more than a bump into each other in the dark last night. George must have attacked you. Your buddy Cute Cop hauled him in. Do you think he killed the other women?"

"Look at my neck," I squeak. "They found their man."

"The chief says they spent hours trying to get a confession out of him. The questioning led to nothing. For now, there's not enough evidence to hold him. In fact, the chief was very specific at saying we better not associate George McNabb's name with the murders in our coverage." Ben stops pacing and faces me directly. "What I don't get, is why you didn't go to the police station to file charges?"

"Where's my phone?" I ask. Every ounce of my body aches, as I swing my head to look back at the counter. I wince and grab my neck.

"Look at those bruises," Ben says. "The even bigger question is why aren't you at the hospital?" Ben tosses my phone at me as if he wished it was a punch. "Why did you lie last night? First, you were hurt and second, this is a development in the case. What's going on with you?"

"Ben," my voice falters, forcing me to whisper. "For God's sake it's only 8 a.m. I set my alarm so I could follow up first thing this morning. Troy and Guy both saw the attack. George was going to jail no matter what." My weak vocal cords create some weird dips as I speak. "I needed time to think about the repercussions." My phone rings startling us both.

"Hey, it's me," Troy says, sounding winded. "I snuck outside to give you a heads up."

"I heard already."

"It's what I tried to tell you last night. George has a bad rap for misdemeanors, but a deadly attack isn't his M.O. There's not enough to hold him on."

"Tell that to my neck."

"That's the other reason I'm calling. I could lose my job for this. Kowalski asked me if you provoked him."

"Are you kidding me?" My voice cracks.

"Coincidences are not stacking in your favor."

"Unbelievable," I say.

"You can barely speak young lady. You have to get to a doctor today."

"I'll try. Listen, I'm sorry, Troy. I really can't talk right now. Thanks for the heads up." I drop the phone on the couch, pick up the marker and circle my name on the suspect list. Then I write 'staying silent for awhile' across the bottom. Ben starts to speak, then stops.

"This is ridiculous," he finally blurts.

"I know. If I was a guy I wouldn't be in this predicament. We'd be hyping the fact that the prime suspect attacked me. Because I'm female, I have to be worried about being put on probation for my safety."

"I'm going out for a run. We are going to talk when I get back."

The minute Ben steps out, I find myself wandering out the front door and pacing up and down the fence line of the paddocks like an agitated horse. I call my emergency hotline.

"Hey, honey."

"Hi, Mom." Calling my mom is so routine, I forget about my throat.

"What's wrong? You sound terrible."

"I had a little incident last night." As the words spill out, I crumble. I'm glad I made the call. She listens with compassion as, at a whisper, I fill her in on the whole story.

"I can't let Rick or anyone at the station find out what happened."

"He should pull you off the story," my mom says.

"When did you become a sexist?"

"Death doesn't care if you're male or female."

"There's no way I'm giving this up." The rolling pastures come more alive with green each day. I take a seat on a large boulder.

"You're staying out there to be near the Cute Cop."

"Mom," I whine. I pick myself up off the rock. "Track with me here. I have a huge predicament on my hands and no one to mentor me on how to handle it. I don't know what to do."

"Shaman Richard was talking about you again yesterday. He says this is your year," my mom continues. "He says love and money find you." The shaman at the Enlightened Spirit Shamanic Center primarily offers holistic cleansing and healing, but he also possesses psychic tendencies.

"Shaman Richard. He's the perfect one to help me," I say eagerly. "Maybe he can lead us to evidence to prove George is the killer."

"Now Callie, you know the shaman strictly counsels matters of the heart and soul."

"This is serious. I want to live and if I do, I don't choose to spend the rest of my life behind bars. The police honestly have me on the list of suspects. Could you ask him if he'll help me?"

We end with my mom sending love, but no commitment to talk to her shaman. There's a nice horse trail that stretches around the borders of Chanticleer's ten-acre parcel. Rather than pace the fence line like a frenzied horse, I set out to power walk the loop around the giant hayfield. A crop of winter wheat stands about knee high. Interestingly, I don't feel like a victim. I feel like a survivor given a second chance at life. I plan to live it well. To do that, I have to clear my name. They say the best defense is an offense. I call Kowalski.

"I understand you heard about the altercation last night," I tell him.

"We did and I'm going to have to ask you come in for questioning."

My first instinct is to defend myself. I take a breath. "No problem," I say.

"We also got a report which shows your phone pinging to cell towers in the vicinity of the crime scenes at the times both murders could have occurred," Kowalski says.

"Of course it would. I've been out here covering the story."

I agree to meet the detective later that day and head down the final leg of the trail which leads right to the back side of the stables. Cassidy has not been turned out yet, so I swing in the side door for a visit.

"What's the matter big guy?" Cassidy looks as if he knows he's missing out on a beautiful day. I grab his lead line off the door and head for the courtyard. "You can graze for a little while," I tell him as we hit the grass. He seems happy to be going anywhere but stir crazy in his stall.

Maggie scurries from the stables to her house on the other side of the drive, her signature pink flowered mug of hot tea jostling in her hand. She looks far too rushed to notice me. Not in the mood for conversation, I slow down and hang back for a minute. The morning tranquility only lasts a few minutes. A truck, going a little too fast, flies up the drive sending gravel spewing, dust flying and Cassidy into a prancing fit. George steers his black F-150 recklessly toward us. Raw panic shoots through my entire body.

I tug at the lead line to lift Cassidy's head from the lawn and turn back toward his stall. I fumble with the latch and manage to toss the horse into his confines. I could hide out in there with him, but the 10 x 10 enclosure seems risky. The killer is coming after me in broad daylight, proving he's getting bolder by the minute. I'm sure George saw me with Cassidy as he parked the truck. He'll check the stall first. There's another side door at the opposite end of Cassidy's wing that leads directly to the guest house. If George enters through the main door of the stables, I can slip out and escape at the opposite end. I scoot across the lawn, barrel up the front steps and slam the door. With a poof, every ounce of resolve vanishes. I've heard about people that can't dial 9-1-1 in an emergency. Similarly, I physically cannot make the deadbolt lock turn. I peer out the window. The gruff, burly drill sergeant comes back out to the parking area. He looks directly at the guest house as he marches around the back of his truck, surely en route to finish me off. With almost eight hours to sober up and his strength, this crazy man could pull off a silent strangulation with minimal effort. Meanwhile, Maggie has disappeared into her house. If I had working brain cells, I would have gone in that direction. Ben will be out running for at least an hour. With shaky fingers, I manage to dial his number. I hear the phone ringing in the bedroom. I swear I can hear George's steps crackling on the driveway. It's hard to tell above the pulse beating in my ears. I peek out the front window again. The twins run down to greet George. Tails wag as they circle his black work boots. No clue they're befriending an enemy. George keeps stride, never glancing down at them. His vision remains focused ahead, intent on his mission.

I desperately want to call Maggie, but I hate to put her in danger for trying to help me. I know not to hide under the bed or in a closet. That stunt is for movies. In real life, those are called dead end places for a reason. I head to the kitchen to look for a weapon. I grab a knife and go back to the window in time to see George do the unexpected. He continues around the bend in the drive, heading toward the house where Maggie retreated moments ago.

"Hey," a voice behind nearly knocks me over. I shriek. Covey, the elusive groom, stands a few feet away in the kitchen. "I told you we'd find some private time together."

I have no idea where he came from. "How did you get in?" I vacillate between feeling enraged at the break-in and lucky to have protection.

"I definitely owe you an apology, Miss Callie," Covey says. He's dressed in the same jeans and a checkered shirt I've seen before. He puts both hands in the air, "but let's put the knife down first." I'm embarrassed. Staring out the window, clenching a knife, I must look like a crazy woman.

"With everything going on around here, you can't be too careful." I gently place the knife on the counter.

"I heard about last night. That's why I'm here. I came to see if you are okay. No one answered and the door was cracked open, so I let myself in to check on you," Covey says, then places his right fist over his heart, followed by a small chivalrous head bow. "I also confess that I used your facilities, which is why I startled you from behind."

"How did you hear about last night?" I ask.

"I'm staying down the road. I couldn't sleep, so I went back to the bar for last call. Everyone was talking about all the action."

Maggie and George walk along the drive. Maggie hands George an envelope. He probably came for a paycheck. A minor relief, but I'm not leaving the house until he's gone.

"As long as you're here, there are a few things I'd like to ask you about," I say.

"Sorry, Miss Callie, I ran out of time for a social call at the moment. The ladies are meeting here any minute. I need to be on duty before they arrive."

"I just want to ask you about Halle Frankel and what happened in Florida." I'm cautious not to use the word busted. I'd like to hear his perspective.

"Ma'am, I am not at liberty to speak out of turn about my employers." I hadn't noticed before, but Covey possesses a slight twang and deep southern formalities. "I assure you they are all in good standing. I apologize that I have to rush off. I look forward to getting to know you better. This was simply a wellness check. We'll plan a little more time for the next visit."

Although Covey exits through the front door, it feels like the groom vanishes into thin air again.

22

I RETURN TO THE WINDOW IN TIME TO SEE MAGGIE MOTION for George to follow her to the stables. He responds like business as usual. I wish I had some way to warn Maggie. She won't be so anxious to have him around when she hears what happened last night. George veers over to the paddock and gives a chestnut horse a rub on the neck. The ability to compartmentalize behaviors must be the sign of a true psychopath.

A parade of Range Rovers begin pulling in. The Divas arrive. With this many people around, I figure it's safe. Time to head for a much-needed shower. I have one foot planted on the imported tile floor about to enter the warm water when my phone rings. I wrap a towel around myself and reach for my phone off the counter.

"Where did you sneak off to?" It's Maggie. "I saw you with Cassidy. I thought we were going to have a wee hack this morning."

"I took him out for a little fresh air."

"Ah yes, that's why I'm calling. A little diversion will do you both some good. How would you like to go and explore a little more of God's gorgeous countryside?" Before I can answer, she continues. "This will be a good chance to get back out there and clear your mind of that awful discovery. It's a spectacular day, and I'm sending you out with an experienced horsewoman."

Clearing my mind is the least of my desires. I'm far more concerned about keeping my distance from George McNabb, who remains on site.

"Thanks for the offer, Maggie. I've got a lot of work to do."

"Don't go," a male voice whispers from behind the bathroom door, making me practically jump out of my skin. I pull the towel tighter and open the door a crack. Once again Covey stands uninvited in the guest house.

"What are you--"

"Shush!" he cautions and points to the phone.

"Maggie, I have another call coming in."

"Then throw your breeches on and meet us over here."

"I don't think I can." Click. She's gone, leaving me with the intruder.

"For the second time, my apologies Miss Callie," he says, laying on the southern charm. "I overheard Christa Muldinaro looking for a trail mate and Maggie mentioned you. After watching Miss Christa bully you last night, I have to advise against it. I came to tell you it's in your best interest to bow out. Don't trust her."

"I gave you my card. How about calling?" I say, closing the door. "Or knocking would be another excellent option."

"You and I both know she's certifiable. No telling what she'd do if she saw me over here, especially if she knew I was trying to protect you. The only option was to slip in around the back again. I'm warning you. Keep your distance from Miss Christa. I don't want you to get hurt."

"Hey! Where are you?" It's Ben, returning from his run. Great. How am I going to explain being found naked in a towel with an incredibly good looking blonde in the hallway?

"Oh, good," Covey yells back, heading toward the living room. "I saw the front door open and, with everything that's transpired around here, I came over to make sure everything is okay."

"Callie should be here," Ben says, sounding a little worried.

"You're right. I think I hear a shower running." Covey's voice trails as if he's already heading out the front door. "Can't be too safe these days. Glad everything's okay. Sorry to have troubled you." Wow this kid is good. He sounds completely believable. No telling how many husbands and boyfriends he's skirted.

I quickly turn the shower on. I'm not sure I want to be in cahoots with the sneaky Casanova, but it beats having to explain anything more to Ben. As I'm wrapping my hair in a towel, the phone rings again.

"Where are you? Christa is waiting for you."

"Maggie, that woman hates me. There's no way you told her I'm the one you're planning on sending out."

"She was planning on riding out alone. I'd prefer to have a buddy system, especially with everything that's transpired around here."

"I have to stay here. We may have some developments in the investigation." I'm immediately remorseful for using the word *developments*, given Maggie's inclination to snoop.

Despite Covey's break-in, the bathroom provides a sense of safety. I close the toilet seat and convert the room to a makeshift office. First order of business, I text Ben and ask him to secretly get some footage of George if he's still on the property. Next, I mentally prepare to call Rick to fill him in on the complications of last night. I practice a few scenarios in my head and realize I'm at a complete loss of where to even start. I choose to get dressed instead. Procrastination, after all, is a superpower.

As I pull a navy suit out of the dry-cleaning bag, my cell phone and the doorbell ring simultaneously. Ben's name pops up on caller ID, so I assume he's locked out. I haphazardly throw on the skirt with the t-shirt I had on earlier and head for the front door.

"Oh, good, you're here" Lydia Mulholland says. "I want to introduce you to Zari Gold, Christa's publicist."

Zari looks as big city as can be, in a couture charcoal business suit with a matching long, light-weight charcoal coat. She has on expensive sling back shoes with a matching purse. Her dark, shag-cut hair and her makeup both look as if they had been done by a team of professionals.

"Nice to meet you," I say, pulling my t-shirt down over the skirt. Judgment beams from her eyeballs as she takes in my ridiculous get up.

"I'm shooting video of Christa at the barn today. We are *this* close to having a reality deal. A little vulgar in terms of timing I know, but we had strong interest before the unfortunate incidents. We can't let our momentum slow now. You know how fickle Hollywood is," Zari says, then drops her voice to a whisper. "And you I and both know, unfortunately, these murders will help clinch a deal." This gal operates at a pace well past a mere coffee buzz. She gives me another once over.

"We pitched Saks to sponsor wardrobe. They're a solid go. I have an entire rack of clothes and a stylist on site. We're prepping the women for the funeral. You're welcome to take a look at what's left once they've made their selections."

"Our station has a policy against that. Thanks anyway."

"Okay," she sighs. "We do need to talk about coverage. Here's my card. I'm based in New York with a small office in L.A. I'm currently working out of Chicago to be close to my fiancé while we plan the wedding." She holds a three-carat sparkler out for me to inspect.

Stupefied by the encounter, I silently accept the card and nod. I thought Bunky was exaggerating when she told me Christa hired a publicist.

"We'll see you in a bit. By then I'll know who's wearing what."

"And if you can call off the video guy, that would be great," Lydia says. She finally gets a word in as Zari sashays back to the stables, her heels wobbling through the gravel. "Christa stayed back in hair and makeup. She wanted me to let you know she's concerned that being on camera violates her yet-to-be signed contract." Lydia drops her chin and raises her eyebrows, making it clear she's only in charge of delivering the message. "Although on a more realistic note, the big camera is making security uncomfortable," she adds.

"I'm sure we have plenty of footage. I'll tell him to wrap it up."

"You're a life saver!" Lydia calls out as she chases after the publicist.

Ben magically appears as the women leave.

"Lydia mentioned we have security on the property now," I say to Ben as he walks in. "What's that about?"

"Did you tell Rick what happened yet?"

"Here's the problem. The cops think I taunted George. It's going to be a whole he said, she said thing."

"You are stalling," he says. "Luckily for you, I'm prepared to make a trade. I won't tell Rick or anyone at the station about the altercation last night, *if* you go stay at your mom's until this case is over."

"Are you kidding? I'd rather face a firing squad than stay at my mom's."

"Joke all you want, but we both know it's way too dangerous to stay here. And now that you're on George's radar, your place is not going to be any safer than here."

"Let's find out what type of security we have out there."
"Please don't tell me you're referring to the bouncers."
"Bouncers?"

Intrigued, I make my way to the stables. Halle bursts around the corner accompanied by the new security team. Beefcakes would make a better description. Muscle bound men wearing head to toe black. Ben wins. They look like bouncers.

"That completes the tour," Halle sounds winded as the group of muscular men follow her toward the West Wing lounge.

"Wait!" Halle says as she notices me sidestepping out of the way. "This is Callie Kinsey. Channel 5 news and fellow horse owner. She's totally on the approved list and, in fact, Callie, this is Hank. He's assigned to you." I can't decide which is more astonishing, Halle acting like she knows me, or getting a beefcake as a gift.

The entourage reaches the door to the private quarters.

"What do you think?" Tab Chandler asks as she sidles over to greet me. I'm not sure if she's asking about the bouncers or the rather long clothing rack sitting in the center of the tack room. It holds dozens of beautiful suits hanging in clear plastic garment bags. A young assistant takes notes from the tickets on each sleeve, cataloging the inventory.

"Callie, choose an outfit," Halle says.

"She can't," Zari Gold says as she hustles in through the door. "Station policy, right Callie?"

"Right," I answer mindlessly. Between the people and the props, there's not an inch of floor space left in the West Wing lounge.

Hank stands six-foot-ish of solid muscle. He shimmies alongside the clothing rack and positions himself behind me. The other four sets of muscle, dressed identically in tight fitting black t-shirts, black pants and black combat boots, stand arms crossed in a row along the wall. If we weren't grieving such horrible deaths, I'm certain buttons would be flying while these men strip to Donna Summer's *Hot Stuff*.

"How did all of this come about?" I ask.

"Alan hired security detail for each of us," Halle explains. Tab strolls around to the far side of the clothing rack to flash me a roll of the eyes. I do my best to stay focused on Halle. "He's worried sick about me," she continues, "having to come out here for the services and such."

"Okay ladies, we've got to focus on getting this demo video done," Zari says. She pulls a lens cap off a small video camera. "We only have a couple of hours until we need to dress for the funeral. My apologies we couldn't pick a better day. We have to cover as much as possible while I'm in town. Halle, you promised to see Christa off for her ride in this scene."

"Does this mean I'll have a recurring role?" Halle asks Zari.

I follow the group outside to the courtyard for a big Hollywood send off. Christa, wearing an outfit straight out of *Town and Country*, sits mounted in the saddle while they decide why Halle would be sending her friend off rather than join her. Christa straightens herself in the saddle when she sees me in tow.

"Say you wish you could go, but you have a charity luncheon," Tab says to Halle.

"I could feign an injury," Halle says, as she fakes a limp on her left foot. "I took acting lessons. For that level, I need a contract of my own."

"I'll be your agent," Lydia pipes in.

"I like it!" Zari continues to struggle walking around the farm in heels. She balances on the horse's neck while making sure her camera is on. "Why don't you say you haven't been back in the saddle since that fall in Palm Beach, or something juicy like that?"

"Say *anything*. We need to get going," Christa says. She pops open a compact, inspects her makeup and applies more gloss to her already shiny lips. She has a GoPro camera mounted to her helmet. "Boo is getting bored with this."

"Callie, maybe you'd be kind enough to see if this camera is straight," Christa says and motions me over. Surprised, I oblige.

"I saw Covey leaving your house earlier," she says, lowering her voice as I approach. "Do you think you're going to get information out of him by sleeping with him? I meant it when I said back off."

"You are," I want to say certifiable, but I catch myself, "completely off base." I can't believe that I fell for her ruse. Not wanting the discussion to escalate, I turn and walk back to the guest house.

"Come on, let's get rolling," I can hear Christa moan in the distance. "I have to blast around the trails to get footage on this action camera, then get cleaned up for the service."

The only thing I hope the camera picks up is Christa getting bucked off.

23

"THE BEST PLACE FOR YOU IS AT THE STABLES," I TELL MY bodyguard.

"The orders are to stay with you 24/7," Hank says, shrugging his chiseled shoulders.

Ben and I found the guard waiting for me on the front porch as we were heading out of the house. My voice is still ginger. I don't want to use what's left of it convincing this guy to stand down. Tab sees us from over at the stables and points to her phone. Simultaneously mine bings with an incoming text.

'*What are we going to do with your guy? Mine follows like a shadow! Excuse yourself, I have something to tell you."*

"Hank, I'm crossing the parking lot. Stay here, I'll be right back," I try not to sound like I'm asking a dog to sit and stay.

"A ploy if ever I saw one," Tab whispers under her breath as I approach. Hank ignores my request. He and Tab's beefcake chaperone stand at attention at a respectful distance. "Come on, bodyguards? These are either the guys Alan hires for local runway shows or bouncers from some bar." Tab steals a look at the guys. "Don't be fooled for a minute. Halle's acting helpless to Alan and helpful to us. That cleverly puts her in charge of the security detail. Did you notice her guard is the shadiest looking guy? They immediately snuck off for a private meeting. I bet he's the hit man."

A loud uproar interrupts Tab.

"Whoa! Whoa!" a groom shouts.

Maggie joins the mix with a loud, "Steady!"

"That's Boo!" Tab exclaims, pointing to a small bay horse galloping up the field heading toward the gravel drive. A saddle sits on his back. Stirrups flail wildly at his sides. No rider in sight. Maggie manages to approach the frenzied horse and carefully hands the reins to a waiting groom.

"Where's Christa?" Tab backtracks up the horse's path. Ben, Hank and I follow. Christa is not within eyesight.

"I knew not to let her go out alone," Maggie says, lamenting to no one in particular. I feel terrible that I wished ill-fate on the woman.

"Carlos, hop on the four-wheeler and head out. If she's injured call one of us immediately before trying to move her." Maggie's face completely drains of blood. "Kyle, take Boo to the wash rack. Hose him off. Make sure he doesn't have any injuries."

Unbelievably, Zari shoots the whole scene, not asking about or looking for her client.

A white Range Rover pulls in the drive and speeds toward us. The tinted driver window lowers and Halle sticks her head out.

"What's going on? Yousef and I were heading into town to get sodas. We heard yelling and turned back."

Tab explains that Christa's horse ran back without his rider.

"I'll head out in this vehicle in case she needs to be transported to medical attention." With that, Halle and her bodyguard peel out. We all watch as Halle takes a right out the drive, like she knows exactly where she is going. She never asked which direction Christa went. I sense Hank standing at my side. I ignore him. He can do whatever he wants as long as he doesn't get in the way.

Ben heads to the Chanticleer office where Maggie sets up a war room. Unsure of what to do, I follow.

"Of course, no one ever leaves these things on the chargers." Maggie says, grabbing small walkie talkies off the desks.

"We all have phones," I offer.

"You ever try using them out on the trails?" Maggie looks up at me. Her eyes express pure worry. "You can barely get a signal in the driveway."

Ben checks power on the handheld devices. "These will do," he says and motions us to head for the door.

"I heard the groom say he's waiting for you to check the horse before putting him away," Ben tells Maggie. "We'll go back out front and watch for Carlos to return."

The white Range Rover already pulls back in to the parking lot as we reach the front door.

"No sign of her," says Halle, as she hops out of the SUV. "Look who we did find."

Covey hops out of the back seat. "Thanks for the lift."

"Thanks for the effort," Halle says to Covey, then turns to the rest of us. "That kid had the sense to take the shortcut through the woods the minute he heard the commotion."

"I ran the entire trail from here to the Kasserman estate," Covey says, still panting. "No sign of Christa."

"We drove the pipeline up to the pond and back. Let's hope Carlos has better luck on the four-wheeler," Halle adds.

"If she was bucked off, she's not going to be lying directly on the path," Tab says.

"Covey, how wide of an area did you check?" Ben asks.

"I, I don't know." Covey stands bent over like an exhausted runner at the finish line of a marathon. "I heard Maggie and Hector shouting. I saw Boo loose and took off. I was running pretty fast trying to get to her."

"Covey had the right idea hitting the trails," Ben adds, "but Tab is right. If you were running with any amount of pace, you would not have noticed if she was lying off to the side."

"If she's knocked out, she won't hear everyone calling for her," I say. "Let's follow her path again and this time spread out on both sides of the trail. It hasn't been more than thirty minutes since she left. She can't be that far."

Maggie and Tab agree. The two women, our three bodyguards, Ben, Zari and I spread out in search party formation and head up the trail.

"Convenient that Halle reappeared in time to help with the search," Tab whispers to me. I stop abruptly in my tracks. Tab still thinks Halle could be guilty of the crimes because I didn't tell her about George. A deafening thump, thump, thump drowns out calls for Christa. I turn back toward the stables, my eyes frantically search the Chanticleer parking lot.

"Where is George?" I try to sound calm. "I don't see his truck."

"We have enough people," Maggie says.

"Trust me, this is important."

I'm plagued by a flashback from last night of Christa on the dance floor and George watching and cursing her and the other Divas for being lewd.

"It won't make sense right this second," I say, grabbing Maggie's arm to spin her toward me. "I saw George here a little while ago. Where did he go?"

"He left about 45 minutes ago. Why?"

24

"THEY COULD HAVE FOUND SOME REASON TO HOLD HIM while they collect other evidence," I say as Ben and I scour the dirt roads surrounding the barn. The minute I made the George connection, we left the search party and ran for the news truck. We will let the people on foot look for Christa while Ben and I frantically hunt for George.

"He's got to still be in the area. Keep looking for that black truck," I instruct Ben. I sit forward, diligently searching side to side out the front window. "If anything, I thought *I* was the goner when George showed up today. I never thought he would go after a new victim so soon."

"Slow down. We don't know what happened yet," Ben tries to sound objective. Hunched over the steering wheel, eyes peeled on the surroundings, his body language speaks otherwise. "Her own publicist kept the video camera going thinking Christa faked a fall to add theatrics to her demo."

"I hope that's all this is. She would want get back in time to have her hair and makeup done with the others before the service."

"Maybe she is back, and they're in such a frenzy getting ready, no one thought to call."

I send text messages to Maggie and Tab. Both respond in an instant. *"No sign of her yet,"* they say. I sink down in the passenger seat and gently touch my bruised neck. "I can't believe they let him go after what happened to me."

Ben looks at the dashboard clock. "We have to be at the church in less than an hour for the funeral. I need time to set up before people begin arriving."

"Oh no! We missed our meeting with the detective."

"I'm sure he heard about Christa."

"You don't call the police when someone falls off a horse," I say to Ben. With the force of a swift kick, I realize the impact of what I said. I groan.

"What's the matter?"

"How am I going to explain to the detective why we missed the meeting? A rider getting dumped isn't a good excuse. And God forbid anything bad happened to that woman. How am I going to explain why I was here once again when it happened?"

The small, white wooden church at Five Corners looks like the type you see on a Christmas card. It's nestled under two giant old Oak trees where the town's dirt roads converge with the main paved road. With old carved wooden pews and century-old stain glassed windows, the inside of the church is as quaint as the outside. Working with a church representative, Ben sets up the camera in a small vestibule where he can capture the Lang funeral as unobtrusively as possible. While he's doing the manual labor of hauling in gear, I feverishly work the phone.

Neither the detective or chief are responding. Maggie says they still have not found Christa. It's maddening to know that George remains on the loose. Guests begin slowly walking down the aisles, meaning we have to shift our focus to the job at hand.

"We need to capture some footage of the who's who," I instruct Ben on a whim. Women dying near their elite equestrian center has the makings of a national exposé. I wrestle briefly with my conscience over the idea of selling out the Divas to the networks. If I don't pitch the story, someone else will.

Bunky Bidlow slides into the pew next to me. She has exchanged her usual flannel shirt for a dark plum sweater and black polyester pants.

"Here come the Divas," she says eagerly. Hope rises. I pray to see Christa in the mix. Bunky likely came straight to the church from work and doesn't know about the newest ordeal yet.

"I don't see them."

"They'll be walking in," she says, stretching her short frame to its tallest extent to see to the back. "That's Tab's family." We both watch a handsome young man escort two young girls down the aisle. "That's the manny. We all adore him, and he adores those girls," she says giving them a wave. The girls wear matching lilac dresses with small, pink flowers embroidered in the skirt. The *manny*, as Bunky calls him, wears a matching lilac shirt and tie under his immaculately tailored gray suit.

"I thought you saw the Divas?" I ask. My voice, still weak from the trauma, raises several octaves giving away my nerves.

"They'll be sure to follow," Bunky sounds confident. "They probably want to make their own entrance." I disagree. Seeing Tab's young daughters arrive without her is not a good sign.

I excuse myself and head to the back of the church. As I hustle out the beveled oak doors, Lydia marches in. We collide.

"Am I glad to see you," I say, grabbing her arm to keep us both from falling over. "I was just coming out to look for you. Where are the rest of the gals? How's Christa?"

"That woman," Lydia sounds beyond frustrated.

"What happened?"

"Step over here." Lydia guides me away from the open doors where she won't be heard. "Did you hear Zari finally confessed that she and Christa had staged this little production? Christa was going to straggle back to the stables leading Boo and act confused like she had fallen. As you know, somewhere the plan went amuck."

"So, she's okay?"

"Quite frankly, she wasn't back yet when I left, but Zari seems convinced her client is pulling a fast one. By the way, she asked me to give you this list." Lydia reaches in her clutch and pulls out a 3x5 note card. In the midst of the chaos, the publicist managed to create a list of each designer the women are wearing for the funeral service as if it's a red-carpet event.

"Where are Tab and Halle?" I ask.

Lydia lifts a small metal box from her purse, opens it and pops a small yellow pill in her mouth, managing to swallow it without water. "Oh Callie, you are meeting us all at our worst." She lowers her voice to a barely audible level. "I told you I was concerned about Halle. She and that bodyguard peeled off somewhere again. Tab is following them. We're all going to miss our dearest friends' funeral. This couldn't get any worse."

I take a deep breath. It's not the time or place to explain all the details, but I have to ease her concern. "Halle may have issues, but I assure you she's not behind the," I search for an appropriate word, "crimes."

"The police checked her out?" Lydia sounds a touch relieved.

"They have a new lead." The organist changes hymns indicating the service is about to start. "I'll have to tell you about it later."

"Pssst," I hear as I make my way back to the pew. Halle peeks her head in through a side door. I point to the front of the church indicating the service is about to start. "It's important," Halle tries to whisper. The urgency makes her voice louder than intended. I'm forced to hustle to the door to hush her. I check the back of the church and then the front. Tab walks in. No sign of a minister yet.

"The service is about to start," I say.

"You need to hear this," Halle insists. "Remember we left to go get sodas when Christa went missing?" I nod. "It dawned on me that I saw Clive Kasserman go speeding past us. So on the way to the church Yusef and I drove past his place. The truck was in the circle drive covered in mud. The kind of mud could only come from off-roading. What if he hurt Christa?" Halle's teeth chatter. I knew the murders would rock this community. Never did I think they would all turn on each other.

"The police have a solid lead – "I start to say, but Halle breaks loose with a wail.

"It's him!" The entire church turns to look at us. I push Halle out the door.

"The police have this under control," I shush her. I shut the door and hope it locks so she doesn't interrupt the service any further. Gazes return to the front alter and I ease my way back to Ben and the camera.

"Was that Halle?" Bunky's short stature in the packed church keeps her at a disadvantage.

"Yes."

"What was she doing over there?" Bunky asks. I ask myself the same thing. The stunt was contrived to the point of being suspicious.

"Look who just walked in," Ben says, nodding his head toward the back. Detective Kowalski, Chief Zurn and Cute Cop merge single file into a pew and take seats. My thoughts reel over where they've been all day and if they allowed George McNabb to strike again.

Covey walks in shortly after the authorities. His bleached blonde hair slicked back with gel, he dons a very nice navy suit. He nods at the grooms lined up in the last row, then continues to make his way forward. He takes a seat midway up, a respectful distance off to the right side. Clive Kasserman saunters in and chooses to remain standing in the back corner.

"Hey," Tab says as she taps my shoulder from behind. "Please don't catch me coming in late on camera. I was following Halle. You won't believe where she went on her way to the service." I knew where Halle went and why she says she took the detour, but there is literally no time left before the service starts to do any explaining. A speaker takes the podium and asks those in attendance to put their phones on silent. Tab swiftly makes her way to the front of the church.

"Make sure you get shots of the cops sitting around doing nothing while another woman may be missing," I whisper to Ben. Attending a memorial service should not take precedence over working the case and finding Christa -- hopefully still alive.

As the service starts, I find myself solely watching the back of the church. No sign of Christa and Zari. They are well beyond fashionably late.

The reverend jumps right into a sermon about the lives of Dale and Talia Lang. The deep love they shared, the years of happiness cut short due to this tragedy. By this account, they both seem like saints. It seems impossible to believe the woman being so stoically eulogized could have been involved with anything tawdry that would lead to her murder.

"Even for the best of us, the day of the Lord will come like a thief in the night," the minister says. How eerie. I can't help but recall my own brush with death in the darkness at the Tip Up.

"Your actions. How you live your life, will determine whether you spend an afterlife basking in heaven or an eternity in hell," the pastor reaches a thunderous crescendo. I keep an eye on the clock. Fifteen minutes pass. At twenty I can't take it anymore. I believe that Christa would pull a prank. I don't see her missing the service. I have to make my way over to Detective Sergeant Kowalski. Unfortunately, he is on the clear opposite side of the church. Daylight dwindles quickly in April. It's imperative that he knows about this disappearance and can scour the area before dark. I have to act now.

With a surge of adrenaline, I stand in the middle of the powerful sermon and step by careful baby step creep quietly toward the back of the church. No easy task in heels.

From the back corner, I make an attempt to flag the detective's attention. No response. I have no choice but to go in after him. On painful tiptoe, I make my way down to his pew, kneeling next to him to express my concerns.

"This is a sanctuary," Kowalski says.

"It's a *funeral* and there may be another if you don't listen to me."

"We know about the rider," he whispers, staring straight ahead to avoid eye contact. An invisible wall shuts down any further attempt at conversation.

"Give me the mic," I say, my fury palpable even with my weak voice.

Ben follows with the camera. We make our way through the crowd gathered out front of the church, straight to the state investigator as he clears the final concrete step leading down from the entrance. I block his path on the sidewalk and plant the handheld mic with our call letters directly in front of his face. Ablaze, I begin firing questions without waiting to see if Ben is ready or not.

"You've been given strong indication of a suspect, but you're refusing to take the lead seriously, why?"

The detective keeps walking, consumed with taking in each of the people exiting the church rather than answering my question. Ben and I keep pace with him.

"If you were truly a victim of an attack Ms. Kinsey, you would have filed a police report," Kowalski finally says, continuing to scan the crowd as hordes of family and friends exit the church.

"We were on our way into the station when Christa went missing. I pray she's okay, but if she's not it's because the prime suspect is on the loose."

"Your facts are inaccurate and I'm busy," Kowalski says. He turns toward me, grabs my arms holding the microphone and pushes it aside. "So you can get that out of my face."

Ben pulls me away from the detective.

"What makes you think foul play when everyone else thinks she's pulling a prank?" Ben asks as he redirects me toward the truck.

"I can still feel his hands on my neck. I can still smell his breath." I gag at the thought. "Let's face it, if Christa was pulling a stunt, she would be here by now."

I plop my purse and iPad in the passenger seat.

"Wait here," I say. "I'm going over to talk to Kowalski off the record, as a human not a reporter."

Kowalski sits in a large unmarked four-door government issued sedan in the street. The vehicle screams undercover cop. I shake my anger and approach the window as if I'm bringing donuts to a stakeout. He holds a cell phone to his ear, but motions that he'll be off the phone in a minute. At least we're off to a better start this round. The detective hits the button to lower the power window.

"I'm sorry for being aggressive," I spew out an apology, "but George McNabb attacked me last night. I could have died." Although he remains seated in the driver's seat, the detective gives me his full attention. His eyes soften and he nods with understanding. "Contrary to your belief, I am not desperate for a story," I continue. "I'm trying to help. Did you get my message earlier? George was at the barn today when Christa went missing. He knew she was riding alone."

The detective turns and looks directly at me, a true look of concern on his face.

"Ms. Kinsey, I understand you experienced a traumatic incident, however, right now you are interfering with an on-going investigation. I must warn you to refrain from going on the air with assumptions or you will face consequences. I'll call you when there's something to report." He rolls up his window and eases the car up the block.

I pivot, unsure over whether to storm off or turn back and chase after the car. As a news reporter I'm used to being shut down by authorities, but as a victim I want to be heard.

As I make my way back to the news truck, I see Troy waiting to pull out of the parking lot.

I wave him down. He rolls the window down but does not stop.

"Can't talk right now." He keeps the car rolling at a crawl as he speaks.

"Two seconds!" I plead.

"The chief and state investigator called an emergency meeting. I have to go."

"Please! You were there last night. Let them know what happened and help get George off the streets!"

"He *is* off the streets." Troy hits the brakes. "Kowalski brought him in for questioning. He's been back at the station since eleven this morning. Last I heard they were transporting him to a psych ward."

"Wait. Christa didn't hit the trails 'til noon. So she is pulling a prank."

Troy hangs his head. "Christa's body was discovered. I really have to go. We need a full court press to find this bastard before he strikes again."

25

"THIS IS BEYOND EERIE," I SAY AS BEN BACKS INTO OUR usual parking spot.

Completely deserted, Chanticleer resembles the set for a scary movie. The late day casts shadows that look like creatures. The air carries the soft smell of dirt from spring plowing at neighboring farm fields. Silence echoes, with the exception of the occasional distant whinny from a horse or two anticipating the feeding hour. After the Langs' service, the entire Chanticleer family went to the wake. Instead, Ben and I face yet another crime scene. We shot what we could of the area where Christa Muldinaro was found and figured we would edit our story here in peace, before heading back for the newscast.

"We watched Christa take off from right in the middle of this parking lot a few hours ago," I stare at the area.

"That's exactly why we're here." Ben turns in the driver's seat to look me squarely in the face. "This rampage is out of control. I'll edit while you pack. We're heading out of here immediately after the newscast."

I mope through the house tossing my belongings into a suitcase. The country mystique has vanished, but it's still sad to be leaving the beautiful guest house and the thought of being so close to my horse. Even on this fairly warm spring day, a distinct chill fills the air. The A/C D/C ring tone calls out from the kitchen. It's the station.

"Ben!" I yell the minute I hit the front door.

"What?!" Ben jumps out the side door of the van ready to attack.

"I'm okay, I'm okay. We just got an amazing phone call. A network producer wants live shots for Nightly News and that new primetime news show Nation Watch."

"Is the network sending out a bodyguard?" Ben folds his arms in front of his chest and launches into a macho jock stare-down.

"Come on, you know this is a big deal." I'm talking to Ben, but I'm already making wardrobe decisions in my head. Thank God my good plum suit is clean. And I'm going to need some pretty significant concealer to hide the bruising on my neck. The color already creeps to dark purple.

"You can't keep risking your safety for a story."

"You're here."

"I've got to focus on my job. Meanwhile, you're a sitting duck smack in the middle of a psycho's killing grounds," Ben says.

As if on cue, Troy rolls up in his pickup truck.

"What if I find other security?" I ask.

"You pulled up at the right moment," I shift my attention to Troy as he lifts himself slowly out of the driver's seat.

"Talk some sense to her," Ben yells over.

"What's going on?"

"I've been asked to go live on both national news and a new primetime news show tonight."

"*Nation Watch?*"

"Yes, how did you know?" I ask.

"One of the producers called the chief today. They're having him on too."

"This is a big opportunity."

"All this after we agreed to pack up and get out of here." Ben won't relent.

"That's why I'm stopping by. I was going to suggest getting out of the mix for a while."

"You're saying I should stay clear of the lead investigator?"

Troy kicks a little dirt.

"Earlier today we thought I helped catch the killer."

"But you were wrong," Troy says, "and that's not sitting well with some."

"Another reason to pack up," Ben continues. "We have no idea who this whack job is." Ben keeps his muscled arms folded tight in front of him.

"Or who he's after," Troy adds, joining the big brother campaign. "He killed three women in a row. We don't want you to be number four."

"That's what I'm trying to tell her," Ben says. He keeps himself firmly planted by the live truck door.

"What if I drum up Hank? Halle said he's mine round the clock."

"Right. Troy, have you heard about this?" Ben sighs. "The horse women hired male strippers to act as bodyguards."

"No fooling? I don't have any Magic Mike skills, but I'm off duty tonight. I guess if these stories are so important to you, I could hang around in the wings."

"It is a pretty big deal," Ben concedes. I'm not shocked. I knew he was trying to find a way to give his approval without totally giving in. The network doesn't come calling often.

My phone dings with a text message from the national producer.

"Don't either of you get any ideas," I point my finger, more at Ben than Troy, "but could your protection include spending the night here?"

"Come on!" Ben sounds exasperated. "We gave you an inch. We'll do the two shows, then we are still out of here tonight."

"The network morning show wants us live tomorrow morning at six. It doesn't make sense to go all the way back and turn around in four or five hours." Neither man says a word. "C'mon, I need you both. If the killer comes after me tonight, this will be the all-time best sting operation. Troy can take him down."

The five and six PM local news live shots go off without a hitch. As I pop the earpiece out, I notice Chief Zurn standing off to the side of the newest stretch of crime tape.

"Hey there," I call over. "I hear you're going live on Nation Watch tonight."

"I am, but that's not why I'm here." My stomach sinks. "We need to have a little chat," he says. My entire being sinks further. He reaches to his side. I expect him to grab handcuffs, instead he pulls out car keys. "Shall we?" he says motioning to the squad car.

I have no choice. I follow and politely take the back seat.

"It's come to our attention that you left Chanticleer a short time after Christa Muldinaro went missing."

"We jumped in the news truck to look for her after her horse came back without her," I say emphatically to be as definitive as possible that I am *not* a suspect.

Like last time, the chief sits in the front seat with me in the back. He tries his hardest to turn his large torso my way to show me some handwritten notes.

"We have a number of conflicting accounts and timeframes from witnesses this afternoon. But the one consistent fact is that you bolted from the property."

"George McNabb had been at the barn, when I noticed he had left the property I was frantic to find him. Check the time on the voicemail I left you. I called you immediately."

"He was with us the entire time."

"I know that now. At that point I thought he was on the loose. Look at my neck." I pull the blouse back and hope the heavy-duty makeup has worn off or faded to show the severity. "I did not provoke this. I had every reason to be beyond convinced he was your guy. Check your phone. I called you and Detective Sergeant Kowalski repeatedly while we were chasing around looking for him."

"You are also the only one that feared foul play. The other women believed Christa had a minor accident. In fact, they believed she faked a fall for the sake of a video she was making."

"That's because I didn't tell any of them that I was attacked by George. When he and Christa both disappeared at about the same time, what else could I suspect? He had been angry with her at the bar last night." As I recall the afternoon, a thought hits me. "We weren't the only ones to search by car. Halle Frankel went speeding off as well. I told you the women have been leery of her. And I'll tell you something else, she knew to turn right out of the drive and she wasn't here when Christa took off. Maybe the women are on to something. I don't know her well, but she has been acting very odd."

"Trying to implicate others is not a good look," the chief says.

"Well, you are wasting precious time trying to implicate me," I say with a huff. "And this time, I have an alibi. Ben was with me the entire afternoon."

"We are aware of that," the chief says, nodding in the direction of the detective sergeant's unmarked Impala where Ben sits in the back seat.

"Ms. Kinsey, when you consider your proximity to each of the murders, surely you understand the need to keep you -- and what you think you know -- under tight scrutiny."

I emphatically promise to report only the facts and am allowed to go back to work.

"You can only imagine the tension here," I say, when the hosts of *Nation Watch* ask about the atmosphere of back-to-back killings in our midst. "Stop and think about it. Virtually anyone in this area could be a victim, and if that's not bad enough, as few leads trickle in," I pause for effect, "we are *all* potential suspects, as well. Because I ride at the stables and I'm covering the murders, even I have been called in for police questioning." I figure it can't hurt to take a stab at citing how ridiculous it is to consider me a suspect.

The chief acts cordial during his portion of the *Nation Watch* segment. He confirms a third fatality and speaks of the shock and sadness spreading through the small, affluent community.

After the shows, I collect a few kudos from co-workers but and not surprisingly, nothing from my mom who doesn't own a TV.

None of the hoopla distracts me from the continued interrogations by authorities. In fact, it dawns on me that national notoriety likely does far more harm than good. Exhaustion weighs my entire body down. When we get back to the guest house, I drag myself up the front steps.

"I'll set up camp here on the couch," Troy says, dropping his small duffle bag on the floor. Normally, that proximity would have me atwitter. Sadly, I have too much on my mind to consider romance. I wish I could confide in him and get his take on where the investigation is heading. This case was already high-profile enough because of the prominent victims. Now I've gone and added national attention, which will undoubtedly apply even more pressure for detectives to solve the crimes quickly. Afraid to enter any conversation, I bid the boys goodnight and shut my door. I stack the two giant feather pillows on top of each other and plop on the bed with my iPhone, prepared to research the topic I dreaded throughout the entire evening.

"How many wrongful convictions are there each year?" I ask Siri.

"Let me check my sources," she says a little too cheery for my taste.

The first entry makes me slump over like I've been shot.

26

MY ALARM CHIMES AT 4:45 A.M., UP AND AT IT EARLY FOR the 6 a.m. morning show call time. After crying myself to sleep, my face looks like a dumpling. I need some ice to de-puff. I slowly crack the door open and begin a quiet sashay toward the freezer door.

"Well, good morning sunshine!" Troy. He's not only up already, he's dressed and sitting at the counter having coffee.

"Did you ever go to sleep last night?"

"Slept like a baby. I'm usually at the gym by now, but I knew you two had an early call. Thought I'd make sure you're off to a good start before I roll out."

"I'm just, ah--" I reach for the top of my head attempting to smooth down wily hair.

"If you're looking for coffee, that wall machine makes a mean cup of espresso."

"That sounds terrific," I say, as a brilliant idea strikes. I'll grab a cup of coffee *and* an ice water. That way I get the ice without appearing odd. "I'm sorry I can't visit. I've got to get to hair and makeup." We exchange a light chuckle knowing we're a far cry from Hollywood and I'm in charge of getting myself ready. I shuffle back to the confines of the storybook bedroom to start pulling myself together. First order of business, I pluck the ice cubes out of the glass and apply them directly to my swollen eyes.

Moments later there's a light tap at the door. Troy whispers that he's leaving.

"There's going to be a lull in investigation," he says. "The medical examiner is heading to Denver for a conference this afternoon. It's the perfect time to pack up and go home for some rest."

Great. He obviously saw the puffy eyes.

"Troy was trying to put your mind at ease to take some time *off* from the story, not give you one more excuse to keep us from packing up," Ben says. He sounds drained. This unique story is taking its toll.

I told Ben that I would treat him to breakfast when we signed off with the network. Once we were in the truck, I announced we were really heading for the medical examiner's office at the county complex. I've interviewed Dr. Zemenick many times and know the coroner keeps early morning hours.

"I'm doing this for you as much as I am for me," I say. "We were both interrogated yesterday. These cops are developing a witch-hunt mentality. The national spotlight is going to make it worse. We need someone outside their circle to help prove our innocence."

"You sound more unreasonable than usual," Ben says.

"I didn't go straight to bed last night. I was anxious to do a little research and you know what I discovered? Police teams are under so much pressure to solve crimes these days, that wrongful convictions are on the rise at an alarming rate. Right here in the United States, 10,000 innocent people are convicted each year. Do the math. That's an average of 200 people a year per state put behind bars for crimes they didn't commit. Do you want to become part of that statistic?"

"All I want is breakfast."

We hit a drive-thru on the way, and Ben actually accepts our mission by the time we pull into the municipal parking lot.

"Ms. Kinsey, I received your messages, but you know the gig, processing evidence takes time." A decade or two older than my mom, Dr. Eugene Zemenick represents the growing number of hippies hitting senior-citizen age. His long afro locks have turned gray, his diamond stud earring looks a little dull after decades of wear, but his flair for existentialism remains strong and intact. We stand in the lobby of the sterile, all-beige tile government building. Dr. Z, as we call him, meets us at the front reception window wearing his white lab coat over a t-shirt, jeans and brown Birkenstock sandals.

"We've had this chat before," he explains. He leans back against an old gun-metal gray desk as if standing in front of a lecture hall. "Modern science brings us robust elements of testing; the ability to define everything from DNA in the minutest strand of fiber, but with it comes with bureaucratic mumbo jumbo. Process, paperwork and backups, baby. Even the high-profile Laci Peterson case took six months to produce DNA results. Those damn procedural shows have the general public thinking you can wave a wand and a screen appears over the victim's body projecting complete DNA strands immediately. It's ridiculous."

"I understand due process with evidence Dr. Z. I'm really wondering if you determined time of death with the second victim, Sperry Davis."

"It occurred shortly before she was discovered, why?"

"I'm afraid I've become one of the suspects," I say sheepishly, then look at Ben. "We both have."

"Strictly circumstantial I presume?"

"Yes. We've been staying at Chanticleer to provide better coverage of the case, but unfortunately, it's also put us in direct proximity of the murders."

"As you know any news related to evidence needs to come from the law. You've already reported cause of death. That's all this office is at liberty to release. We have a few fragments in for processing, but until we get a suspect," he looks at both of us, "a legitimate suspect, we won't be able to complete comparative analysis."

"The truth will set you free, baby," Ben says, imitating Dr. Z as we head back to the guest house. "In the meantime, you heard the good doctor. This case is going to take time to crack and we're getting you to safety while we wait. No more procrastinating. When we get back, we're packing up and moving out."

I am in full agreement -- until we hit the drive.

"Holy cow, what's going on?" I ask, staring in disbelief at the mob scene swarming the stables. News of a third murder brought a new mass of media down to the latest murder scene. It also seems to have brought mass hysteria to Chanticleer Equestrian Center.

"We've got pandemonium," Maggie says as she greets us exiting the truck. She motions for us to follow her over to the stables. "You've got to see this."

"Follow me around this way," interrupts the booming voice of Bud Burkhart. The Chanticleer owner, dressed in big city business attire rather than his barn duds, whisks passed us as we hit the entrance.

"Watch out for the Lord of Chanticleer," Maggie says under her breath. The short, semi-bald owner uses his arms like a referee to clear Ben and me out of the way, as he leads a flock of men and women in white lab coats across the parking lot.

"We're moving on to the west wing," Bud barks out orders, hands still flapping high and wide as he speaks.

"The local investigation isn't good enough for him," Maggie says. "He's *securing the property*," she says using air quotes. Then she points to the front entrance of the barn where a rent-a-cop sits in a white plastic folding chair. "And don't confuse the on-site security with bodyguards. We all still have our assigned bouncers according to Halle. I've been ditching mine all morning. I need a break," Maggie says and reaches for her forehead like she's got a headache. "I'm heading to the house."

"Who are all these other people?" Ben asks.

"A *private* lab team," Maggie says, exasperation in her tone, leading us all to survey a dozen or more mysterious technicians milling about. "He's starting his own CSI unit. Same outfit Sperry Davis used to catch her husband cheating. They've been fingerprinting and collecting evidence all morning. The gorgeous mahogany walls are loaded with white dust. They must have gathered 200 prints!" Maggie tenses up. "You know they are mostly mine. He's out for blood. I hope I don't get hung before the real experts find the killer. Hate to leave you alone with the mania," Maggie says, "but I need a cup of tea."

We continue toward the stables, where Tab and a few other boarders corner Bud and his high-tech team as they head toward the west wing entrance. Tab has her assigned bodyguard, and the driver I met at Tip Up the other night, flanking her sides.

"Don't forget we want full background checks on all grooms added to this investigation," Tab demands. "Hop on it before they have a chance to flee." Bud nods agreeably and jots a few notes on a small pad he carries in a brown leather holder. "You're a doll," Tab says, "make sure you call me for the Kiwanis fundraiser this year." Chanticleer's owner probably would have been equally on board without mention of a donation. Evidently, even when distraught, Tab continues to give compulsively.

"We've done a complete sweep. I can assure you that no maniac is hanging out in any of the buildings or on the surrounding 20 acres of land," he tells the captive audience. "Chanticleer is secure and will remain that way. Round the clock. I've got more security heading in for a night shift."

Bud corrals his minions inside the wing of stalls.

"No one can do drama like the rich," I confide in Ben once out of ear shot.

"Let's go make sure Cassidy is dealing with this chaos."

A scrawny security guard in a navy uniform rises from the white plastic folding chair as we reach the main door.

"Need to see your credentials," he informs us, holding up a bony hand.

"I ride here," I explain.

"Then I'll also need to see your owner's wrist band."

"It's okay, she's with me."

"Mom! What are you doing here?" My mom, dressed in a blue, yellow, green and red flowing tie-die shirt and yoga pants, turns to the security guard.

"That's Callie Kinsey and Ben Winkler, Channel 5 News," my mom says. Her curly hair bounces, as she turns to give us both a loving squeeze like we're visiting for Sunday dinner. "Give them both media and owner credentials." The guard lifts a clip board from beside the chair, makes a couple of check marks then retrieves wrist bands and badges from an envelope.

"Hot off the press," he says, and hands us hastily made laminated neck lanyards that simply read "MEDIA" and yellow plastic wristbands, similar to those used on hospital patients, that evidently prove I board a horse at Chanticleer.

"Callie, I didn't notice you earlier," Bud Burkhart pats me on the shoulder. He left the CSI crew at work on the other side of the stables. "Your mom's been a big help. Glad to have her here. Come on, we need to catch up with the Shaman," he says leading my mom away. My mom starts to follow. I grab her arm to hold her back.

"Whoa, cowgirl. Not so fast. What's going on around here?"

"Oh honey, I've been worried about you. You sounded so distraught on the phone. Shaman Richard suggested a cleansing. We are smudging. Come on, I'm falling behind."

In the blur, I hadn't noticed my mom toting a white candle in a clear jar. I roll my eyes at Ben, as we both follow along to find out exactly what smudging a horse stable entails. In the center of barn, I spot Shaman Richard facing a stretch of empty stalls. The doors hang open revealing mounds of shavings used for bedding and a few tufts of unfinished breakfast hay left behind by horses now out munching fresh grass in the paddocks. Dressed in blue jeans and a white gauze shirt with strips of white flowers embroidered on the front, Shaman Richard holds a bouquet of dried leaves like a bridesmaid in a wedding party. Except his arrangement sends wafts of light gray smoke billowing above his head.

"There are many forms of smudging ceremonies," Shaman Richard informs us in his smooth cadence. The leaves look similar to dried corn husks. He encourages smoke production by blowing on the stalk. "We burn this offering as blessings to the gods to shield against negative energies."

"Bud has been on board since the moment I called. He set the process up perfectly," my mom says, bubbling with excitement as she holds the candle out in front of her chest. "The lab team collects the evidence section by section, then we follow with a thorough cleansing of all bad energy." She pauses and circles the jar in the air mumbling a few words as Shaman Richard moves on to the next section of stalls. With her head still bowed, she continues the explanation. "I am speaking positive affirmations, asking Mother Nature's pure breath to blow and restore purity through this building and these grounds."

The Shaman, with his dark black hair, olive complexion and handsome looks exudes the youthful charisma of a movie star, but insists on shuffling along like an old man. My guess is the elder act makes him feel wise.

"What does Shaman Richard have?" Ben asks my mom.

Shaman Richard pauses his activities. "We use what the Great Provider has given us as gifts right here in the Midwest. Pine resin and sage," The shaman says. He loves explaining his culture. He cups his hand, encouraging the smoke to flow toward Ben and me so we can smell the scent. "These plants represent the four elements: air, fire, water and earth. Sage represents the cleanest smell of the earth. Our thoughts and prayers are carried on its smoke. It is a symbol of our intentions being carried to the heavens."

"Ready for you in the West Wing," Bud says, his booming voice carries down the corridor.

"We are finishing this middle section," Shaman Richard calmly replies. He acts as if he has never seen a clock. He takes my arm and pulls me away from my mom. "I also brought a special mixture for you, Callie. Your mother and I will conduct a special ceremony for both you and Benjamin when we finish here."

"Thank you. We'll be at the guest house." Even if I didn't want to participate in the ritual, I know not to put up a fight. My mom always wins. I am about to turn toward the door when the shaman tightens his grip.

"And young lady, your session will not be a cleansing. We will be summoning all the forces we can to protect you." I'm not going to fight Shaman Richard either. His intuition is never wrong. I don't need to admit it out loud. He and I both know I need all the protection I can get.

27

HUDDLED IN THE BACK OF THE LIVE TRUCK WITH THE door closed, it is impossible to tell if it is day or night. The confines resemble bomb shelter meets spacecraft. A windowless cave with walls lined with dozens of small monitors, tape decks, an editing board, audio controls and all the buttons and switches to activate the mast and satellite transmissions. It happens to be daylight. I'm not sure whether to credit the added security, Shaman Richard's cleansing, which involved drenching us in the smoke and prayers, or the fact that we were too busy to pack up, but we stayed on another night at the guest house. Ben sits in a chair on wheels pushing and pulling himself along the long wall, using different editing decks to assemble clips of tracking dogs at the latest murder scene for our noon story.

"The chief says they finally coerced George into going to a legitimate treatment facility," I tell Ben. Silence other than the soft clicking of edit machine buttons. "He wouldn't share an iota of what's going on in the investigation."

"Probably because there's nothing to tell." Ben's crabby tone serves as a warning not to interrupt any further.

I prefer to suss out my leads with a partner. Instead, I quietly take inventory. I called Detective Sergeant Kowalski a couple of times this morning for an update, but was unable to track him down. I do know he interviewed each of the remaining Divas. I can take an educated guess that Tab and Lydia confessed their concerns about Halle. Halle likely tried to implicate Kasserman.

I don't have any evidence or even a strong hunch on whether either of them could be guilty of murder. I do know that everyone from Dale Lang to Bunky Bidlow say something happened in Florida. The question is what and would it really be awful enough to lead to such tragic consequences? I Google both Halle Frankel and Clive Kasserman searching for a Florida news article or police report. Nothing. I leave Sperry's sister Lucy a message asking if she could put me in touch with Raul. Maybe he would be willing to gossip. On a whim, I pull out the crumpled piece of paper that I found in the west wing lounge. I have no idea what I expect to glean from the escort service, but I give them a call. A young woman answers before I formulate a ploy.

"I know *exactly* why you're calling," says a voice that sounds like a bubbly 14-year-old. I truly almost fall off my chair.

"What?" I barely mumble, shocked that anyone in Florida let alone an escort service would recognize my number.

"I recognize the area code." The young woman seems much too giddy and immature to work at this type of establishment.

"So you've gotten other calls?" I ask, assuming other news agencies must have beaten me to this lead.

"Well not since the *incident*."

I do not utter a peep, leaving this overanxious schoolgirl to reveal a few more details.

"We knew Mr. Kasserman would be back. He's been such a great customer for such a long time."

"Yes," I say, feeling slimy as I play along. "Clive Kasserman."

"So is he coming down soon?"

"Yes, that's why I'm calling." I pause to make up a plausible story. I can't believe she'd jump to such conclusions over an area code. I'm not going to ignore the proverbial gift horse.

"Sorry that gal didn't work out last time. She was one of our best. Overqualified, really, in terms of class. She passed as the wife of a prince of one of those small Middle East countries. I don't know what went wrong with Mr. Kasserman. We have a couple of new gals. I can send you their portfolios."

Holy moly. What an unexpected stroke of luck. Maybe this so-called high-class gal was around and witnessed the questionable incident that transpired with Kasserman and the Divas in Florida.

"Let's not rule the last gal out. He said he liked her and they only had a small misunderstanding."

"She's not with us anymore."

"I'm new with Mr. Kasserman. She seemed his type. Could you do me a favor and send her portfolio for reference along with the new gals so I can look for someone similar?"

If this classy gal no longer works at the agency, she'll be far more likely to talk. I am determined to find her.

"I guess that would be okay," says the girl on the phone. "Our server is down. I won't be able to send them until a little later today."

"I can't run the photos by Mr. Kasserman until tomorrow morning anyway. Let me give you my email." I proceed to give her my generic Gmail address.

Ben twirls around with a giant question mark all over his face. "What was that about?" he asks as I disconnect the call. I shake imaginary green goo off my arms.

"That was gross. I've inadvertently pried into Clive Kasserman's secret sex life."

A loud knock at the door startles us.

I pop the door open and find Detective Sergeant Kowalski standing at the bottom of the steps. "Heard I'd find you in the truck. I hope you weren't recording."

"Nope. Just hanging out," I say.

"You left a message saying you may have something to help with the case," he says.

"We know you were watching people at the Lang funeral. We wondered if you wanted to review any of the footage we shot."

"Yea, what the heck," the detective says. "I'm here, let's take a look."

The footage starts with people walking down the aisles. The detective watches in silence as the tape continues with long pans of each side of the church.

"It was kind of odd that Clive Kasserman chose to stand at the back," I say, regretting overstepping my bounds immediately.

"Who's that blonde kid making his way to the front?" The detective ignores me.

"That's one of the grooms from Florida. Covey," I say. "Not sure of his last name."

"The other grooms are sitting together back here, correct?" The detective points to the grooms on the screen.

Ben pauses the tape.

"Can you zoom in on them? Mmm-hmm," the detective says, then reaches over and hits the play button to resume.

"We have family and close friends, as expected, sitting up front," Ben says as he hits fast forward to show the rest of the small church.

As we watch the replay I notice a void.

"I saw Halle Frankel before the service, did she ever come in?" I ask.

"She slid in late." The detective sounds blasé.

"If we could only rewind the past couple of days," I say. "This is all so surreal. Our trainer all but begged me to ride out with Christa yesterday. I should have been there to help her."

"Then you may have been lying there dead too," he says. "That brings me to the reason for my visit."

My stomach drops into the familiar *uh-oh* sink hole.

"You mentioned that you have been out walking on trails behind the horse facility recently?"

"Yes," I answer, hesitant that my alibi is going to be used against me again.

"I want to recreate the crime from the victim's perspective," the detective says. "Can you direct me to the path behind the facility?"

The word perspective gives me a brainstorm.

"I've got to file a report for the noon news," I say. "Can you meet me back here at twelve thirty?"

Kowalski agrees.

I'll be off the air a few minutes after twelve. That leaves almost half an hour to find Maggie and figure out how to pull the idea off.

28

"YOU HAVE A MUCH DIFFERENT VIEW UP ON TOP OF A horse than you do on the ground, don't you?" I ask Detective Sergeant Kowalski. His well-proportioned six-foot frame makes a nice picture in the saddle. "Now you are really seeing things from Christa's perspective."

We plod along on two of Maggie's dearest, and hopefully safest, retired horses, Shilo and Hank. I begged Maggie to help me figure out a way to allow the detective to truly see the trail from Christa's viewpoint, on horseback. Wanting to help the investigation, she pulled two trustworthy horses from a back pasture. My legs stick straight out over the Shilo's oversized belly making me look like a little kid in the saddle. The mare can definitely use the exercise. The detective sits on Old Timer Hank, a fine-boned, dark bay thoroughbred, who Maggie warned once had quite a propensity to buck. Evidently, arthritis now makes his trademark kick feel more like a hiccup. Hank likes to follow, so we risked putting Kowalski on his back.

"It looks like Christa Moldinaro may have happened across the perp unexpectedly," Kowalski says. "She may have startled him or even confronted him and he responded by killing her." We are following Maggie's directions to the tee, winding our way down the same trail I took a few days earlier when the women led me to Kasserman's estate. With woods on one side and a plowed cornfield to the right, it's nearly impossible to get lost.

"In your travels have you seen anywhere a perp may have set up a camp out in the woods?" Kowalski asks, as he searches each side of the trail. "This guy may be camping out in the area."

"Nothing obvious. Are you saying you don't think it's a she?"

"He is a figure of speech in my business," Kowalski responds. He smoothes his clean-cut hair after brushing a low hanging branch. Much to Maggie's chagrin, the detective refused to wear a helmet. "Working off statistics, our killer is likely a man."

The two old horses take their time, carefully plodding along.

"Have you found any tread marks out here?" I ask recalling Halle's comments about Kasserman's truck.

"Forensics is scouring the area."

Shilo snorts and raises her head as we grow closer to the crime area.

"These two aren't going to expect a team of people in the woods," I say. "We'll have to approach cautiously so they don't spook." I'm not a chicken, but I saw firsthand the other day what an unexpected commotion can do to even the calmest horses on a trail. I'm in charge of getting an inexperienced rider back safely.

"Are the dogs gone for the day?" I ask.

"Yes. Unfortunately, they proved inconsequential."

Rather than act worried, Shilo plunges herself into a clump of grass. Anytime we pass anything remotely green she reaches, trying to get a nibble. It takes all my strength to pull her head up.

"This mare acts like she's never had a meal." I give Shilo a good tug and a little squeeze with my legs to keep us meandering down the path. "The dogs didn't get a scent?"

"The K9 lead says he's not certain. They were out last night and again this morning. Both times the dogs chased around in circles."

Shilo spots a nice leafy spring fern and beelines off the trail yet again. This time Hank sees it too and rear ends us trying to get there first.

"This is not the most conducive way to carry on a conversation," I say. "These guys know every trick in the book. Keep your heels down and give him a little squeeze. It's a slow pace, but we'll make it to our destination. We have a nice open area ahead, that will keep them moving."

"It doesn't appear that the suspect purposely tried to trip the dogs up," the detective, undeterred by the distraction, continues his report. "Our best guess is he spent quite a bit of time coming and going from the woods, always traveling back and forth to this trail. The question is what has he been doing out here?"

We've done a couple of stories on meth or heroin labs out in the middle of nowhere. I know the women partake in prescription level narcotics, but street drugs hardly seem plausible. Yellow crime tape flaps in the wind, and a handful of workers in puffed up windbreakers continue to canvas the area making the horses predictably jittery as we approach the scene.

"We're going to have to lead the horses slowly through here so they don't whirl and run back to the barn," I say to the detective. I give Shilo a few reassuring strokes on the neck.

"We're directly over the key area," Kowalski says. "Look down. See the cluster of hoof prints? The altercation seems to have started out on opposite sides of this stretch of barbed wire. There is an opening where you can take another trail about ten feet up on the left. She seems to have stopped here, at least for a few moments. How could this guy have drawn her in close enough and have the leverage to pull her over the fence?"

Kowalski dazes off into a trance as if he can see the crime in action. There are more than a few hoof prints and scuffle marks in the ground. The barbed wire, which was in bad shape to start with, lies trampled. I listen to the detective, determined not to look over any further. I've seen enough death lately. I don't need to reinforce nightmare images. The detective, on the other hand, doesn't want to miss anything.

"She had to have hopped off her horse." The detective sizes up his mount, calculating the distance to the ground below him, at least four feet. "If she stayed on her horse she would have had the upper hand. She could have launched a kick to the face or galloped off."

"This may sound crazy," I say hesitantly. "When Christa left the stables, she was enthralled with being in the limelight. Could it be possible that Halle stood along the path with a camera pretending to get a little extra video of her friend, maybe even the alleged fake fall?"

Kowalski thrashes back and forth in saddle, evidently recreating the crime. He kicks his foot out of the stirrup, startling Shilo and me. I hold my breath, willing Shaman Richard's ritual to include protection from a horse related accident. Hank thankfully remains comatose. No kick, buck or hiccup.

"Did her clothes give any telltale marks of whether she fell?" I ask.

"There were marks. The scuffle that ultimately killed her would create similar dirt patterns." The detective continues to take in the view from his stance on the horse.

"Strangulation is an intimate kill, how did he manage to get so close to three different victims?" Clearly a rhetorical question. For once I manage to stay silent. I am strictly a catalyst for leading him to the scene. We'll work out what's on the record later. Shilo finds yet another nice clump of grass at the base of a tree. I float the reins on her neck and let her eat. It will keep her and me busy while the detective conducts business.

The detective wiggles his feet to steer Hank to walk a circle around the area.

"You already look like a pro," I say.

"I grew up going to horse camp. Thought about working with mounted at one point."

"You could have shared that with me a little sooner. I've hardly taken a breath since you sat in that saddle."

"You didn't ask."

"If I'm allowed to ask questions, I'd really like to know what happened in Florida." I glance at the yellow tape that hangs as lifeless as the body found beneath it. "Everyone I've interviewed has alluded to an incident. No one will say what."

"Right now we're focusing on the link to *this* area. All three bodies were found in very close vicinity," he answers.

All three bodies were found on the outskirts of Clive Kasserman's estate. He allegedly had issues with the women – and he's known for harboring grudges against equestrians in general. On the other hand, we're also next to Chanticleer, which is Halle's territory and a number of factors point in her direction.

I gather up the reins and walk Shilo up the path a little further to the other trail on the left that leads to the main drive of Kasserman's estate, and a large explosion erupts. My overloaded brain surely suffered an aneurism. Then another boom follows. This time I can tell it's coming from the woods.

"Duck!" The detective barks.

I distinctly feel a shot whiz past my ear. Someone is firing bullets, clearly aimed directly at Kowalski and me.

29

I MAY HAVE BEEN A LITTLE SLOW ON THE DRAW, BUT THE horses react to the warning shots immediately, prancing like crazy. Forgetting he can hold his own, I reach over and grab Kowalski's reins to steady Hank, who appears ready to spin and bolt toward home. The horses' nerves edge up further as a turbocharged golf cart with a gold Kasserman family crest displayed on the side races into close range. Sure enough, tall, dark, and handsome Kasserman is at the wheel and without any warning, lifts his gun to fire again.

Quick on the draw himself, the detective flips a black leather holder in the air, flashing his badge. Kasserman shoots it right out of his forefinger and thumb.

"State Police," Kowalski yells, as he rolls sideways off the horse military style and plops to the ground. He appears more concerned with fishing through soggy leaves to retrieve the badge, than getting hurt. Thankful I have both sets of reins, I jump off, as well, and run for cover behind the closest, biggest tree trunk I can find. There is no struggle to keep both horses in tow. They seem to want to seek shelter too.

"Next time announce your presence before showing up," Kasserman snarls. He yells something else about trespassing, then flees back down the same path from which he arrived.

"He shot at us! Go arrest him!" I yell, and slowly lead the horses out from behind our hiding spot. Somehow, I managed to hold both horses during the confrontation. With a quivering hand, I pass Hank's reins back to Kowalski.

"Na," the Detective answers as he brushes himself off. "It's not worth risking my life to chase him down and enlighten him about the fact that he broke the law."

It takes what seems like forever to find a fallen tree trunk big enough for us to use as a step ladder to mount back up on the horses.

"Not much of a mounting block," I say as I try gracefully to lift my foot three feet up into the stirrup and then clutch the front of the saddle to hoist the rest of my body up and over. Luckily, we both prove spry enough to lift ourselves back into the saddles.

"You learn after a while about picking and choosing your battles. We have a much bigger concern on our hands at the moment," Kowalski says while gathering up his reins. "And that's getting you and the horses back to safety."

"I'm fine," I fib.

"I want to take one more look from the victim's perspective," Kowalski says. He works his way to the barbed wire fence with an ease that would never reveal a shooting took place mere minutes ago. Kowalski assures the handful of CSI team members that we're okay.

"That Kasserman really is a maniac," I say, despite attempts to keep a lid on my thoughts.

"I'm starting to have some serious questions about what he is trying so hard to protect out here. I'm going to trust you to stay quiet about this until we can investigate further."

Kasserman surfaced early on my list of suspects, and has bounced on and off since. There is something distinctly haunting about this property. I doubt Shaman Richard could cleanse it.

"How well do you know Clive Kasserman?" Kowalski asks, twisting the ends of the braided brown leather reins.

"I don't."

"Interesting, we saw you speaking to him at the fundraiser."

"I met him that night." I don't believe it. That saying 'anything you say or do will be held against you' lights up in my mind like a neon sign. "That was it." I struggle to sound definitive.

The detective circles Hank around the area one more time.

"Damn it, Christa," the detective shakes his head staring at the site. "Talk to us. Tell us what you saw."

Attempting to give Kowalski some privacy, I walk Shilo along the fence line, looking for any of the signs he mentioned earlier, like tire tracks. Anything to clear my name. A piece of plastic glistens under brown soggy leaves. I hop off Shilo and immediately yell to the detective. "You might have gotten your wish!"

Thank goodness Shilo stands much closer to the ground than Cassidy. She follows me back to the tree trunk where I once again hoist myself into the saddle then circle back to hand the detective a Go-Pro camera. "Christa had a camera mounted to her helmet when she left the stables. It must have fallen off during the struggle."

"Let me see it," the detective reaches for the GoPro. He turns the small black camera around in his hand. "No playback screen." He and I both look on the ground in the area where I found it. "I'll have to take it back to the station and download the video to some other type of media."

"Or perhaps Ben could help," I offer.

"There you are!" a woman's voice interrupts us. I turn and see Tab and Lydia jog up the trail on foot.

"We were so worried!" Tab says.

The Divas jogged over a quarter mile from the stables to reach the site. Bunky Bidlow follows close on their heels, her short legs keep her a hundred feet behind.

"We heard the gunfire!" Bunky yells, not wanting to be left out.

"Maggie's calling 9-1-1," Lydia adds.

"I need you to keep this quiet," Kowalski mutters, as he hides the GoPro under his shirt.

"No worries."

"Must have been hunters," the detective says. "Sounded like it came from the property over that way." He points to a field way off in the distance.

"The gunfire sounded a lot closer than that," Bunky argues, raising her five-foot frame to confront the detective. "You know I work at the sheriff's office."

"Then as you must know, sounds travel and amplify in these open fields." Kowalski gives her a polite salute of the head. He looks my way expecting me to back the story.

"Do you think we'd be sitting her calmly if we got shot at?" I add. Thankfully, my voice doesn't betray me.

Sirens approach, once again the horses begin prancing. Fat Shilo manages to leap backward as Troy pushes his way through thick tree branches and pops out right in front of us. He must have intentionally gone around the crime scene.

"Report of gunfire?"

"False alarm," Kowalski says. "Hunters."

Before letting his guard down, Cute Cop focuses his attention my way. An unspoken *are you okay* passes between us.

"I don't have a signal. Can someone let Maggie know they're okay?" Tab asks.

"My squad car is parked along the road," Troy says. "Why don't you three hop in we'll get you back down there and you can tell her in person?" Troy all but pushes them into the thicket along the path he made, sending them on their way toward the road. As soon as the group vanishes out of earshot, Troy launches questions.

"What the hell happened? Did you fire at someone?"

"Kasserman shot at us," the detective says. "Claimed it was a trespassers' warning."

The minute I step foot in the guest house I grab the makeshift crime board. "Ben, wait 'til you hear this!" He meets me in the great room where I quickly fill him in on the incident.

"We've only heard Kasserman's name mentioned fleetingly," Ben answers with reason.

"We know some type of altercation happened." I watch Ben's face, I'm not moving the meter. "He was so mad he wouldn't fly them home," I add.

"Hardly evidence it was something so awful he would kill them. I know you're knee deep in this but stop and think about what you're insinuating."

"I absolutely need to find out what happened in Florida. We've got to find the gal the escort service mentioned. She may give us some insight." It dawns on me it's been hours since the call to the Prestige Escort Service. I fumble with my phone trying to open email as fast as I can. The profiles of the women arrived thirty minutes ago along with a short note:

> *Grace, It was nice to speak to you earlier. We're happy Mr. Kasserman will be back in town soon. Attached are the profiles you requested. Remember, Heaven is no longer available. You will love the newest members of our team. They are receiving rave reviews!*   *Yours, Dawna*

Grace, I didn't have time to be too creative with a fake name. Although *Heaven* isn't much more imaginative.

"What are our chances of tracking down a gal known only as *Heaven* a thousand miles away in Palm Beach?" I ask Ben. "Maybe her profile will give some background info that will help."

"I'm going out on a limb here, but I'm thinking Heaven is not her real name."

"Smart ass." Ben's negativity doesn't sway me. "If we can find her, I guarantee she's going to have a story. Maybe asphyxiation is Kasserman's perverted fetish and then it escalated into strangulation. Maybe he took it too far on their date and that's why she quit."

"Your imagination is out of control."

"He is a freak," I say demurely, trying to regain a pinch of dignity as I click on the file. It takes a few minutes to download the profile. "I will scour agencies with this photo if I have to. We have to find this girl." A minute later the file opens and when it does, I gasp.

I jump off the couch and race for the kitchen counter where I left my iPad. I have to blow the image up before uttering another word. Ben grabs the phone away from me. He, too, stares in disbelief.

I turn the iPad toward him with the photo enlarged full screen.

There's no doubt. The unmistakable big doe-brown eyes of Halle the Blonde Bombshell stare seductively at us in the photo. There's nothing bland about her in this shot.

30

THE NEXT MORNING, LIVE TRUCKS ONCE AGAIN ROLL UP along the stretch of dirt road where investigators work the Christa Moldinaro site. We all stand at our staked off stretch of ditch along the shoulder of the dirt road, pointing into the woods where viewers may or may not see tiny bits of yellow tape hanging motionless between trees. Pretty much the entire giant media pack, including me, broadcasts the exact same story: 'investigators continue to comb the site, call police if you know anything'.

Shortly after signing off the air Tab Chandler calls.

"What's happening this morning?" she asks immediately. How awkward. What's happening is that I know their dear friend worked as a call girl and I have no one to talk to about it. "Lydia and I have a great idea," Tab continues, unaware of my mental distractions.

"Yes, she called already this morning. A producer expects you on live at noon," I say. The black Escalade pulls into the Chanticleer gravel drive at 10:45. To my surprise, all three Divas arrive together. Tab hops out of the front seat, while the driver opens the back doors for Lydia and Halle. I hadn't expected the full flock. I returned multiple times to Heaven's profile last night. While I should be excited at the development, I feel more like a creeper, than an investigative reporter. I still don't know what Halle was 'busted' for or what led to such an explosive argument between Kasserman and the Divas. I can't divulge what I know to the detective. Even a hint of amateur investigating will surely land me in hot water.

"Here's our main mission," Tab says, taking the figurative reins. "We want to offer reward money to entice witnesses to come forward. Money talks louder than pleas."

We're huddled in the gravel parking lot in the main courtyard of Chanticleer. The Divas asked to officially announce a substantial reward for a tip that will help catch the killer. Ben chooses the stables with a pasture in the distance as the backdrop for the live report.

"We know someone out there has to know something," Lydia continues with the rationale. "If you look at past crimes, reward money typically pays off." While Lydia speaks, Tab wildly shifts her eyes toward Halle while maintaining an odd close-lipped smile on her face. The women function through plaster shells that could crumble at the slightest wrong touch.

"I talked to Cameron about it," Lydia keeps right on talking. "He says we have to push the public while the story is hot." She sounds like a politician on a platform. I'm thinking how great she'll be on camera, when my phone bings. A text message from Tab two-and-a-half feet away.

Don't want Halle to think she's a suspect. If we accuse, we could be next.

I give Tab a reassuring nod.

Bud Burkhart approaches as Ben stages the women in a horseshoe formation for the shot. Upon hearing their incentive, the Chanticleer owner offers to up the ante.

"We've got to nail this bastard," he says giving Tab a warm pat on the back. "Add another five grand to the kitty. I'll drop you a check later."

The noon anchor, Brett Levy, recaps the story, then tosses to us right off the top.

"Those closest to the victims are taking action to help catch the killer. They join our own Callie Kinsey live at the scene. Callie."

"Brett, the beauty of this picturesque landscape has long drawn the women out here to ride at Chanticleer Stables," I reference the gorgeous stretch of paddocks, "but police admit the rural surroundings might also be to blame for a serious lack of leads to date. With three murders now, all likely connected, a group of riders very close to the victims are banking that someone out in this sparsely populated area can lead police to a suspect. They join us now live to make a desperate plea and offer a substantial reward for anyone with information to come forward."

Lydia acts as primary spokeswoman, speaking of the overwhelming sadness and grief caused by the murders. She announces a one hundred-thousand-dollar reward for a tip leading to the arrest and conviction of the killer. Tab and Halle somberly nod in solidarity. We end with a reminder of the tipster hotline number, and the whole shebang wraps in a minute-thirty. Now, I need to pull off my real accomplishment, figuring out how to get a few minutes alone to ask Tab and Lydia what they know about Halle's extracurricular adventures.

"Can you pop into the guest house for a quick visit?" I ask, trying to use Tab's eye technique to relay a sense of urgency. Unfortunately, the heads of all three women are buried in text messages. Evidently a large number of people saw them on TV.

"Even Kasserman is texting offering to make a donation," Lydia says.

"We can review the text messages inside," I try again. I'm anxious to get back to the guest house for more than one reason. Maggie ran into town and I locked her dogs in the guest house so the Twins wouldn't disrupt the newscast. Who knows if they've been on good behavior. Finally, I text Tab and she agrees to follow me.

In a matter of minutes, our little posse gathers in the living room. Spanky and Spunky sniff and approve each of our guests.

"Now he's texting me," Halle says. "There's no way in hell I'm stopping by his house. It's a trap. We are damn straight taking his money though." She pounds keys on her phone. "I told him I'll meet him at Tip Up."

"Perfect," I seize the opportunity to get Halle out of the mix. "Tab, Halle can use the driver to head over, right?"

"Sure," Tabs says.

"We can finish sorting out if there are any other donors while she runs up there," I say.

The minute Halle heads out the door, Tab pounces. "Are you crazy?

We shouldn't be letting her out of our sight."

Rather than seize the coveted moment to ask Tab and Lydia about Halle, I have a better plan.

"Of course not," I come off sounding a pinch more smug than intended. "I want to hear for myself what's going on between those two. You still have The Ear on the property, right?"

"Explain that thing to me one more time," Ben's says. His large linebacker frame sits uncomfortably hunched over in the passenger seat of my little convertible. I fluff my hair in the small makeup mirror preparing to hide the earpiece.

"Haven't you seen it on late night infomercials?" I ask. "It's called The Ear. You wear it like a hearing aid, but you can hear conversations over a hundred feet away. Halle used it to listen in on my entire conversation with the station when this story first broke. The Divas bought it for fun in Florida and then became obsessed with using it to listen in on what people were saying about them."

"So you think one of these two could have committed the murders and you're going to spy on a private conversation. Did it occur to you that that will incite them and put you directly on the hit list?"

I hold up a skin-tone colored button that looks like a teeny megaphone. "Look how small it is. I am simply running into the restaurant for a takeout order. They will never see it."

"And you don't think this strung-out woman, and a man you called a maniac, will be suspicious when you walk in the very place they happen to be meeting?"

"It's lunchtime. We placed a legitimate order." While Tab and Lydia went to get The Ear for me, I placed an order for two large chef salads and two orders of chicken tenders.

Hoping to thwart any more misgivings from Ben, I turn the volume up on the radio dial. The remainder of the short drive, we listen to Alice Cooper's *School's Out for Summer*, while I say a small prayer that I'm right about not getting caught.

"Jump into the driver's seat so we can make a quick exit," I say as

I shut the door.

I press the little plastic piece into my ear canal, fluff my crazy, curly hair over it. "Try saying something after I get a good distance away. Let me make sure this thing works."

"Okay, I'm even going to talk in a whisper."

"You could probably hear a baby breathe with this thing." I flash Ben a thumbs up signal and climb the front steps to the Tip Up.

There's no way I arrived more than ten minutes behind Halle. She and Kasserman must not have started with any small talk or pleasantries. When I walk in, they look like they are already deep in a heated conversation.

"When Alan hears what you've been up to, he will dump you for good," Kasserman says pointing a finger at Halle, similar to the way she confronted him at the fundraiser. To my dismay the restaurant is almost empty. It's helpful for listening, however, the odds of getting caught increase to epic proportions. Halle and Kasserman sit across from each other at a dark wood four-top by the front window. I keep my back to their table and the volume up full blast on The Ear, as I slowly make my way into the restaurant.

"I came clean. I told him everything, and he says he'll go to the ends of the earth to protect me. I am not proud of what I've done. I might go to hell, but you can't use Alan as a threat. He understands that I did what I had to do to take care of myself."

"Callie!" Guy waves at me from the bar. Little does he know, he's interrupting my mission. Not wanting to draw attention, I smile and walk as slowly as possible toward him, so I can continue listening to this revealing exchange.

"How've you been?" With not one single person at the bar, Guy is intent on chatting, even from a distance.

"As good as possible with this nightmare," I answer. If I don't act natural, I'm bound to get caught.

"Yea. It's taken its toll around here. Business dropped off to nothing this week. Your order should be up any minute." Guy walks off toward the kitchen and I immediately hop sideways on a barstool, positioning myself with The Ear on the side of the suspects. I don't hear a thing. Fearing the super-bionic hearing device broke, I turn slightly toward the table hoping to pick up a little more with my own ears. Still silence. I ease around in time to see Kasserman pushing through the door in a huff. The whole meeting lasted mere minutes. I wish I had it on tape.

Halle sits staring forward into space. She wears a tailored, taupe suit with a high-neck floral blouse, chosen carefully to make her appear as the Bland Bombshell for the press conference. Even though she looks all business, my mind only sees the unmistakable, seductive eyes of the woman known as *Heaven* to the Prestige Escort Agency.

I plop into the passenger seat with the stack of carry out boxes on my lap and turn to Ben who is squeezed into the driver's seat with the car running.

"You should have heard her. Halle all but confessed."

"She actually said she committed the murders?"

"Well, she said she may go to hell, but her fiancé understood that she did what she needed to do."

Ben and I debate the merits of calling Kowalski with half-baked hearsay.

"That ear thing doesn't record, right?"

"No, and there's no way I'm going to the detective with anything I uncovered. He'll have me arrested for obstructing justice."

"They aren't wrong. You have been a little too involved in the case."

"Trust me, not by choice. The reality is, I still don't know what happened to Halle, or what type of relationship she had with Kasserman. It could be he and Halle were having an affair, and they found it kinky to pretend she was an escort," I say.

"This is no bedroom fantasy," Ben says. "Don't forget Halle's history with the agency. They said she entertained foreign dignitaries. She didn't hire in for a fling with Kasserman."

Ben turns on the final stretch toward home. The exact tree-lined stretch of road where all this started. I turn the radio back up again. I've missed my music. Van Halen wails *You Really Got Me*. I wish I could belt along with David Lee Roth. Instead, I sit silent, fighting the urge to look at the spot where I found Talia Lang. The little buds along the way are now becoming bursts of green leaves, the only sign of new life in the dismal area.

"Let's be logical." I break the silence. "If this was a lewd escort service and Halle was busted for prostitution, Kowalski surely knows her police record."

"Good. Then you don't need to play detective," Ben admonishes.

"No, but it will take time to build a case and, in the meantime, I need to let the women know that their suspicions seem founded. They need to seek protection. Let's hurry. I have to talk to them before Halle gets back."

31

I WALK INTO THE GUEST HOUSE WITH MY ARMS LOADED with takeout boxes and a chicken tender hanging out of my mouth. I wanted a little nourishment before tackling this delicate situation. Tab and Lydia remain in the living room, now with Chief Zurn.

"The chief is explaining the process for handling the reward money," Tab explains. "I hope you don't mind that we invited him in."

"Of course not," I say as I plop the boxes down and swallow the last bite of chicken. A low growl begins emitting from down the hall. The twins probably think I'm an intruder.

"It's just me guys," I say, opening the Styrofoam containers to make a buffet for our guests. I walk over to the cupboard to grab plates. The growls intensify to low deep snarls. I hope the mischievous mutts aren't planning to attack.

"What is going on?" I ask, coming around the corner to peer down the hall toward my bedroom and let them see me.

"They've been angels," Lydia says. She points to a round, blue throw rug. "They were sprawled right here the whole time you were gone."

"Well, they're up to something now. Come here you two."

The twins come roaring out of my bedroom, barking and snarling with such voracity, I fear for my ankles.

"Feisty little things," the chief says, shifting a little further down on the couch.

As they round the corner toward our guests, I'm mortified. It's not my ankles I need to worry about, it's my undies. I left my half-packed suitcase laying wide open on the bedroom floor. The twins plucked out my best pair of Hanky Pankys and are enjoying a thunderous game of tug-of-war. Those naughty dogs are turning thirty-dollar underwear into a Jack Russell chew toy.

"That about wraps it up for me," the chief says, sidestepping the dogs and taking a wide berth around the room toward the front door. I make a few attempts to swipe the panties away, but the effort escalates their antics to a game of keep away.

"We have to be going, too," says Tab as she stands. Lydia follows. The women hold each other's arms and tiptoe toward the door.

Once the company rolls out, the dogs settle. The underwear shredded to an unrecognizable state. I snag them off the floor and dump them straight in the garbage. The only good news at the moment is that Halle hasn't returned. The two Divas are stuck on the front porch waiting for the driver.

"I don't know if this will come as a relief, but I accidentally stumbled across what Halle was likely busted for," I say in the doorway, no choice but to jump right in. "I thought maybe if you knew I discovered her double life on my own, we could discuss it a little bit."

The women don't say a peep. They turn and walk back inside to the living room still clinging to each other.

"Let me grab my iPad, maybe it will be easier when you see what I obtained." I open the file, the system takes a few seconds to download the photos. "I take it you both know Halle was working at the Prestige Escort Agency?"

"Yes, we knew." Tab says.

"She's back," Lydia panics.

"She's heading toward the steps!" Tabs squeals. "Hide that thing!"

Lydia stands in front of the iPad, acting like a shield. I swipe the photo off the iPad screen, as the women power out of the house.

"Where is everyone?" Ben asks emerging from his safe zone of the news truck back into the house.

"You don't want to know."

"Your talk didn't go so well?"

"There was no talk." I twist my curls into a bun on top of my head, then let the hair fall free again. "I confirmed that they knew Halle worked at the escort agency, but that's as far as I got. Tragedy has subdued these women, at the core they can still be mean-girls. I can only imagine the Diva-sized drama when the women found out Halle worked at as escort – or worse if she was arrested for prostitution." I look for the crime board. "This revelation catapults Halle back to the primary suspect. She does have a lot to hide."

Ben beats me to it, swooping the crime board from its hiding spot behind the couch. "I can't believe I'm saying this," he says, "but add that motive to the list."

News of a rich housewife, turned call-girl, turned murderer, will make an amazing exposé for a national crime show. Right now, I have to focus on day-to-day coverage, and that includes finding out what the Go-Pro revealed.

"I can't believe I caught you on the first try," I say when Kowalski answers his cell.

"That's because I was about to call you."

"Does that mean you have something to report from the GoPro footage?"

"We do," he says, followed by his trademark pause. "And there are a few things I need to question you about." I thought we were past all this. I have no choice but to agree to meet with the detective later that afternoon.

"I'm going to get some air," I tell Ben when I hang up. I have to shake off the anger – and frankly a little fear. It's unfathomable how every piece of evidence that should clear my name, instead puts me back on the hot seat. I no sooner hit the bottom of the porch steps when Bud Burkhart pounces.

"I thought those women would never leave. What the hell were you thinking setting that camera up here today?" he thunders. As if I weren't already fragile enough. "Coverage down the street is one thing," he continues. "But we don't need bad publicity for Chanticleer. You realize you put an APB out there on our exact location? It's irresponsible!"

I summon every ounce of composure in my five-foot six-inch frame. "You chipped in money toward the donation right before we went on the air."

"You're not that naïve, kid. What am I going to say, 'stupid idea ladies' and have them move their horses out with all the others? I expected you to dissuade them from going public. That's your job."

"My job is report the news. It is my responsibility to create public awareness. If there's a threat to the community, we use our reach to prompt witnesses to come forward and help solve this case."

"Well, my boarders are coming forward alright. To tell me they're leaving. Now that you've exposed the facility, we have a mass exodus underway. I want you out as well. You and that photographer of yours can start packing."

I turn and head right back into the guest house. "Our landlord is a little upset," I say to Ben.

"I heard him. What's his deal?"

"He's mad we did the live shot from the property today. He kicked us out."

"Hopefully not right this minute." Ben hands my phone to me. "Sperry's sister called. The hair stylist, Raul, is at the funeral home right now and agreed to do an interview."

32

I ALWAYS ENTER ANYWHERE THAT CONTAINS DEAD PEOPLE with trepidation. The front door of the funeral parlor activates a polite chime, alerting the undertakers as Ben and I enter the foyer. Imitation red velvet texture on everything from furniture to wallpaper creates a cushy, yet creepy environment.

"We're from Channel 5," I tell the greeter in a hushed tone. Lucy arranged for us to meet at the funeral home. Raul is here to style the hair of his former client for the last time.

"Mrs. McCauley and the gentlemen are in the back. I'll check to see if they are ready for visitors." The woman, at least six-foot tall, wears an old-fashioned floral dress with a belted waist. She looks like she's had her gray hair poofed in the exact same style each week for decades. She makes her way through the door marked *Private*, in sensible, low-heel pumps.

I watch the flicker of a votive candle, trying to keep myself calm while we wait. Ben inspects the pictures and awards on a wall. I take a deep breath to release tension forged in my body and am overpowered by the sugary sweet aroma of the fresh flower arrangements synonymous with funeral homes. Small bouquets smell heavenly. In mass, too much floral reminds me of death and, well, funeral homes. Dozens of large sprays pile up in the parlor, most fuchsia and white, peppered with exotic flowers, roses and lilies. A memorandum for staff to weed out cheap carnations could probably be found in the will.

"A—A—K!!!!" A horrific outburst shatters the silence and knocks me right off my heels. I grab Ben's arm to steady myself. He, in turn, clutches the red plush top of an antique Queen Anne wing back chair.

"What was that?"

The wake-the-dead scream is followed by a series of hysterical shrieks.

"That has to be to Raul."

Ben bolts through the door marked *Private* into the back room. I follow. A man with hair as shiny black as Elvis, and a bright pink custom-made dress shirt falls to one knee, wiping sweat from his forehead. Sperry's sister, Lucy McCauley, runs off to a side exit.

The man looks up, revealing a matching sleek, black goatee and meticulously groomed magic-marker black eyebrows. A magician without the cape.

"Did you see..."

He shakes uncontrollably, unable to form whole sentences.

"I can't even..."

"Raul?" I ask.

"Yes, yes," he answers. "I've been violated! This place -- violated! Just violated!"

In the middle of the commotion lies the casket holding Sperry Davis. Her body remains completely still, impervious to the clatter. Ordinarily, I would be freaked out at seeing a body, but she looks remarkably better than the last time I saw her.

"I can't believe," Raul chokes. He uses a wooden chair to lift himself up, still unable to form a sentence. He gasps for air.

"He, he had the audacity to enter this sanctuary." Raul lets his knees buckle and falls to the ground once more, this time perhaps more for effect. Raul, who appears capable of ultra flamboyant snap-snap entrances, must figure sinking to the ground shows off his flair in a way that's a little more appropriate for the somber surroundings.

From his knees, Raul gazes up at the casket, waist-high on a table.

"I wasn't ready to reveal my princess yet!"

"What happened? Who was here?" I finally ask.

Breathing in deeply through his nose, Raul makes an attempt to compose himself and lift his crumpled body off the ground. He reaches an arm outward to his beloved Sperry, as if she can give him the energy to endure. Pure theatrics.

"I don't blame him for clinging to her. She was vibrant, beautiful," he says, glancing at Ben and me, finally acknowledging our presence, "divine." He bursts into tears again. This time I'm unsure whether it is over the loss of his "goddess" or because he catches sight of the mess he made of her hair during the hysterics. Even without having been privy to the will, the cost of Sperry's final public appearance would be obvious. The glow on her wrinkle-free face and Paris couture Chanel suit take her a step beyond stunning. Ironically, that exact apricot suit made headlines during one of the hottest fashion shows earlier this spring, something about the tweed being made of rare and ridiculously expensive cashmere. Lined with a deeper apricot trim, the ensemble pops, even on a corpse. A testament to one of the finest fashion houses in the world. The airbrushed makeup adds to the truly exquisite picture.

"You almost expect her to sit up and welcome her guests," Ben whispers to me.

Sperry's hair, by sharp contrast, falls victim to the turmoil. Several strands bolt straight out toward the head of the coffin, as if hit by a strong electric shock. A round brush and hair-pick lay tossed in the casket where Raul had evidently been creating magic before being scared senseless.

Lucy hustles back in, immediately attending to Raul before greeting us.

"I know this was a long day for you," Lucy says. She takes Raul by the arm and turns him to sit in the wooden chair that he's been using as a crutch. "You said you had a few sedatives for the flight, do you feel woozy?" Lucy's voice sounds soothing, while she accuses the distressed stylist of hallucinating. "We're all under so much stress," she reaches out to comfort him with a half hug. "I scoured the parking lot. I didn't see a soul out there."

"He ran when he saw me. We spent intimate time together in my styling chair. I transformed him from a grotesque Q-tip bleached white to a golden Adonis. I hit him with a 20-volume developer and the most awesome 30-D Flaxen Blonde. He looked fab, but of course, I couldn't stop there. I threw in chestnut low lights to ripen the look. It was gorgeous. Perfection. I'd know that head anywhere, even with that hideous two-inch grow out."

I'm confused. The main blonde in these parts is Halle. Clive Kasserman has a thick head of dark brown hair, with perhaps a little gray tapering his temples.

"Who did you see?" I question him again.

"Oh, Callie Kinsey, let me introduce you," Lucy says, with sweeping arms that exude the persona of an old movie actress. She presents Ben and me to Raul and the funeral director, Mr. Gower, who also waits nervously for news of what transpired.

"I went to the restroom," Raul says, as he lowers his voice and turns his head to avoid offending his client. "We all have to do what we have to do, especially after a long flight. I returned to find him lingering over the casket." Raul recreates his earlier *a-a-k*, with a little less conviction than the initial shrieks.

"I startled him and he ran off before I could," shakes, shivers and quivers emanate head to toe, "before I could," he pauses, "speak."

"I was with Mr. Gower discussing service details in a private room at the time and missed the entire altercation," Lucy interrupts. "I raced for the side door. By the time I reached the parking lot, there was no one in sight."

"I have so many questions," Raul continues on, as if there were never an interruption, "he knows them all so well. He and Sperry were 24/7 all last year, until he started getting a little too possessive. In Palm Beach if you can't have fun with a fling, you get flung, and that's exactly what happened. She ditched him. The little Casanova endeared himself with the other women. I mean, he must have, because he made the trek to Michigan."

"Covey?" I ask. I know how he came to Michigan. He was helping Talia fool her husband into thinking she was having an affair.

"Are you really sure you saw him dear?" Lucy puts a hand on Raul's shoulder. "It seems odd that he would visit a funeral home, especially through the back door."

"Yes," Raul says definitively, taking a step to brush Lucy's hand away. "Covey stood right here." Raul positions his body facing the casket, and hunches over, imitating Covey's exact stance. "He adored my dear Sperry."

"I think we should call the police," Ben suggests. "You're right, people don't usually enter a place like this from the back."

"That's how he operates," I say. "Covey has an allusive nature. I've been trying to find him to do an interview for days. He comes and goes on a whim." I make my way to the side door and peer out. Nothing. If he was here, he vanished again.

As I make my way back over to the group to start over with introductions and pleasantries, Detective Sergeant Kowalski sends a text saying he heard we are at the funeral home. I show the phone screen to Ben. He wants us to stay put until he arrives. I can't believe I'm under surveillance. I need to get Raul's interview in the can before they get here.

"I highly recommend we add security to the premises for the showing as a safeguard," the funeral director offers.

"Absolutely!" Raul jumps on the cause.

"Why not?" Lucy caves, clearly exasperated. "This is going to be in the record books for most exorbitant funeral in history."

Raul agrees to begin our interview. The still rattled stylist insists on recounting of the entire run-in with the former groom, including more details of Covey's hair color and protective nature.

"That's excellent," I say to appease Raul. "We're on a deadline. We'd like to hear about your recollections of Sperry."

"Honey, do you want the story or not? I'm telling you what's important." Raul tugs the right cuff of his shirt, then the left, to straighten his designer look. He sits up a little straighter, then continues. "Ah, Sperry, Sperry, my Sperry," he says, his voice reaching over to the casket longingly. "Verve. She had a zest for life reserved for few humans."

As Raul recollects some of Sperry's antics, he lightens up and the stories quickly shift to the glam life in Palm Beach and the victims in general. The stylist forgets about the camera and surroundings and dishes like he would while working on the head of a client.

"For the most part the women were simply fun loving," Raul continues. He puts on a pair of purple leopard reading glasses to glance over at his dead client, then turns back and peers over them at me. Ben gives me a reassuring nod to let me know he's keeping the shot nice and tight, nothing morbid.

"Sperry attracted men like a magnet. Talia, on the other hand, was different. She was a tease. No action. She really did love her husband you know."

Raul shudders. "I can't believe Talia and Dale are both gone. And my Sperry." He looks down at his client with reverence. "It's all in the past now. What's that horrid, overused saying? 'What happens in Palm Beach stays in Palm Beach'? Well, in this case it should have." Tears roll down his cheeks. "Girl, this woman had it all," he says. "Men lavishing her with gifts galore. And I'm not talking trinkets. In one season, Sperry received a Mercedes SL 500, designer purses, top-shelf champagne by the case, you name it. She was a catch and suitors knew it."

I've never heard of someone being the recipient of such huge amounts of cash and prizes without being on a game show. I know I should wrap the interview, but the stories about private jets, parties on yachts, endless champagne and polo ponies are mesmerizing. If I do produce a national tell-all, a look into the glitzy lifestyle will come in handy.

Kowalski walks in the room unannounced. I freeze. I still don't know what he wants. Seeing he tracked me down, my paranoia imagines I'm about to be arrested. The shoot goes kaput before I can ask Raul about Halle.

"Detective, just in time," Ben greets Kowalski. "Thanks for the interruption. My back is aching."

"I'm sorry," I apologize to Ben.

"These women were top shelf," Raul says, upping the flair for the newcomer. "And you, my pet." He fluffs my hair. "You need to call me."

Kowalski barely gives me time to say goodbyes. I leave Ben and the others in the backroom, while the detective escorts me outside where Chief Zurn waits in the parking lot. Both men look grave.

33

"WE HAVE TO TALK PRIVATELY," THE CHIEF STARTS. PER usual, the burly leader motions toward the squad car. I follow with dread in every step. I can't comprehend what they will accuse me of now. I search longingly for Troy. He seems to be the only one who firmly believes in my innocence. He's nowhere to be seen. Maybe it's best he not see me being loaded into the back of a squad car. For the first time since this story broke, I finally want to go home.

"We want to talk to you about the footage we found on the GoPro," Kowalski begins once we're all seated in the car.

"There can't be anything incriminating me on it."

"Actually, you were instrumental in discovering some key evidence," the chief says.

"I need to take you into confidence once again," Kowalski jumps in. "Unfortunately, the camera was not mounted or used properly and shows very little of the altercation." He lifts himself to turn all the way facing me from his perch in the passenger seat. "I need you to promise to keep what we're about to reveal to you completely confidential."

"Always. Hopefully you'll tip us off when you're ready to make an arrest."

"We'll see what we can work out on that one. It may not happen any time soon. The recording doesn't show the perpetrator. State police labs are working to zoom in on the few images we have, and to enhance the little bit of audio exchange. The video picked one element up clearly, and that's what we want to talk to you about. Off the record."

"Absolutely."

"Prior to Christa falling, there's clearly a syringe being stabbed into her leg."

"Are you suggesting heroin?" I ask with doubt strewn through my tone. We have had a huge number of well-bred suburbanites die in heroin houses in the inner city in the last year. A husband fed it to his wife in cereal in a deadly plot recently. Other than that case, rarely has it been used as a weapon.

"All three women appear to have been drugged with some type of sedative. It's not a common pharmaceutical."

"Given the horse connection, the chief suspects you may have some insight."

"A horse tranquilizer?" I ask, again in complete disbelief.

"The medical examiner will follow up with the textbook side of things, what we need from you is the reality of what's readily available out here. What type of equine drugs are kept at the stables? What could someone get their hands on fairly readily?"

"I'm still pretty new to the sport."

"We need a general idea of what to look for and, more importantly, to figure out who has access to those types of drugs," the chief interjects.

"The liquid appears to be yellow," the investigator adds.

"The only thing readily available that comes to mind is Ace," I say.

"Ace?" the detective and chief question in unison.

"Acepromazine. I assume it's a type of sedative. Maggie uses it for minor things like clipping, or farrier visits with nervous horses."

"Do you give it by injection?"

"Usually."

"What size syringe is used? Are the needles larger for horses?"

"They look like regular human-sized shots to me."

"Who besides Maggie would have access to ace?"

"She keeps it in a cabinet in the office. I don't think it's considered any big-time type of narcotic. It does not knock a horse out. You can ride a horse on a light dose."

"That might be true, but we're talking about injecting it into a human."

"For once, I'm not the suspect," I tell Ben as we head back to Chanticleer.

"What did they want?"

Maintaining confidentiality with my partner sitting two feet away in the front seat of vehicle is practically impossible. "They swore me to confidence. What I tell you stays in this van. Evidently the killer used some sort of sedative. That would explain how someone as petite as Halle managed to take her victims down."

"How could she get her hands on horse tranquilizers?" Ben asks.

"That's the crazy thing. Vets do the heavy sedating, but light stuff is pretty readily available. I never thought of the substance as a narcotic before. It's in the office on a shelf. Maggie and George don't even lock it up."

The route back to Chanticleer takes us down a dirt road on the opposite side of Kasserman's property from where the crimes took place. All the country roads out here run straight east-west and north-south around square parcels of picturesque land. I'm wondering where the horse trail I took with the ladies pops out on this side. As I scan the landscape for signs of a path, I can't believe my eyes.

"Stop!" I bark.

"What?" Ben screeches to a stop. He's so used to being in heavy traffic, he immediately checks the outside mirror to make sure we don't get rear-ended.

"I swear I just saw a blonde head jog into the woods."

"Did Raul give you whatever he was on?"

"We're only two miles from the funeral home. Do you think Covey is heading back to wherever he's staying?"

"I don't see anyone."

"Give me a minute." I hop out and jog a ways up the path through a mowed down cornfield calling after him. A few birds tweet, a pheasant jumps out of a hiding place. No sign of the elusive groom. I slump back in the news truck.

"It was a blue heron. I am certifiably going nuts."

"Your phone dinged twice."

I look at the screen. Troy. I wait until we're back at the guest house to call him back.

It's a quick call. Troy says he wants to find time on our calendars for a date. Swooning over the invite, I whoosh through the bedroom door and throw myself on the cushy queen-sized bed like a schoolgirl swept up in a crush. I hug a pillow, roll over with a giant smile on my face and then gasp. A figure stands over me.

"A-A-K!!" I scream, an exact imitation of Raul earlier, as I face a stranger standing menacingly next to the bed. I sit up and peddle my feet to smash myself up in a fetal position against the headboard. It's a woman with a shoulder-length brown bob, wearing oversized sunglasses.

"Who? What?" Like Raul, I can't form a sentence. Instead, I try another screech. My vocal cords are still bruised, but even a strong scream won't help. Ben is outside in the news truck. He will never hear me.

"Don't scream," the woman says. She lurches forward and holds a brightly-colored silk scarf over my mouth to muffle my cries. The intruder's brown hair tilts slightly askew, obviously a wig. I'm certain I recognize the voluptuous body. And now, I'm even more certain of how a petite woman could pull off multiple murders. Halle not only used sedatives, but the element of surprise by being in disguise.

"Calm down," she instructs as she pulls off the glasses, making no attempt to conceal her identity. It is late afternoon. The short spring days already steal light from the room, but I clearly meet the sultry eyes that I stared at repeatedly on the escort service profile picture.

"Calm down?" I launch a good shove with my foot toward her abdomen. She's standing and easily sidesteps the move. I jump off the bed intent at grabbing the scarf away from her.

"Stop!" Halle throws her hands in the air. "I came to ask for help."

"What?" I back up a couple of inches. I keep my eyes on her hands.

"I'm sorry I scared you," she says. With shaky hands and crumpled posture, she does appear nervous.

"I… I… I don't know what to say," I stammer back.

"Please," Halle motions for me to sit back on the bed. "I'm not going to hurt you. This is going all wrong."

I'm dealing with an unstable, frantic woman wearing a tilted wig. I don't know if I should follow her instructions or try to bolt.

"What are you doing here?" I ask, putting my hands in the air to show I mean no harm. "Ben is right outside. You're going to get caught."

Halle looks in horror at the tightly held silk scarf in her grasp. "I would never hurt you!" She stashes the scarf into the pocket of her black quilted jacket. "I was wearing it when I got here. I didn't want you to scream. I really need your help."

Perhaps this is the ultimate femme fatale technique. Halle gains leverage over her victims by disarming them with charm. And she's good. If I didn't know her background, I would almost believe her.

"What do you want?"

"I was interrogated by the police all afternoon. They let it slip that you know about my background. I want you to understand why I was forced to work for that agency. I have a good reputation, and I want to keep it that way."

She's going to kill me to ensure my silence. My only choice is to let her talk until I come up with an escape plan. Hopefully, Ben will get anxious and come looking for me soon.

"Alan only took me back last month. For the last two years I've been really struggling. In our last divorce he left me the house, complete with a four-thousand-dollar mortgage payment, and, of course, car payments and credit card bills. I needed to find a way to keep up. I was stupid. When you've become accustomed to a certain lifestyle and running with these women, you feel backed up against a wall. I'm not an educated woman. There weren't a lot of options to come up with the kind of cash I needed to stay afloat."

Halle pulls the wig off and sinks to the bed. Her blonde hair cascades down around her shoulders. "I guess what I'm trying to say is, I can't change the past, but the whole world doesn't need to know about my desperate mistakes."

"Why go to such lengths in order to keep that secret?" I back up a little. I'm hoping to get the bedside table lamp within reach. "You're creating a much worse situation for yourself." Halle looks directly at my hand reaching for the lamp. Her eyes bulge.

"Oh, my God! You think I had something to do with the murders? Are you kidding me? Call the police. Ask them. I'm innocent! I'm in disguise because there's a maniac on a rampage." Halle stands and grabs me by both arms in near hysteria. "And *I'm* next on the list!"

34

HALLE HAS BEEN A SUSPECT TOO LONG FOR ME TO LET MY guard down. Thank goodness I know about the sedative technique.

"If you are innocent, keep your hands out where I can see them," I direct as we make our way to the bedroom door. I remain one step behind her, as if she's at gun point, to the kitchen counter and call Kowalski.

"You need to move away from the stables," he scolds. "You could be in danger, but not from the Frankel woman. Keep this to yourself, but the video indicates we're looking for a male suspect." I hang up, apologize to Halle and watch as she launches a Xanex the size of a small torpedo into her mouth. She makes her way to the billowy couch, where she sleeps like a baby as I head out for the evening newscasts. I've now wrongly accused two people – three if you count Dale Lang – and had the wits scared out of me twice. With nerves frayed to the point of jumping at the chirp of a cricket, I fully plan to pack up when we wrap the eleven o'clock news. When I find Halle sitting up watching television, I sidle up. Finally, time for questions.

"So, you think Clive Kasserman is behind the murders?" I ask bluntly.

"That maniac. You know he's an ex-navy seal?" I did not. That explains how he and Troy are familiar with each other. "He vowed revenge on us women in Florida. He thought we were playing him and making him look foolish." Halle pulls the throw blanket over her lap. "He's systematically killing each of us."

"Where's your bodyguard?"

"Alan fired the security detail," Halle sniffles. "I think he was threatened by their buff bodies."

"Isn't he worried about your safety?"

"I told him I'm in meetings at the police department where I'd be safe. He's on a buying trip in Malaysia, so I raced over here when I was released. I was so worried you'd go on the air with an incriminating story about me."

"Go back to Kasserman. I still don't get what made him this mad."

"He's an insecure, sniveling weasel," Halle says. She sinks back into the country blue floral couch. "Two years ago he briefly dated Sperry. He couldn't begin to keep up with her. He acted wildly jealous and obsessed. She kept trying to break it off, but she didn't want to set him off, so she wasn't as definite as she should have been. Fast forward to this year. When we first arrived in Palm Beach, Sperry caught Kasserman stalking her while she was on a date. She finally told him to back off for good. To make her jealous, Kasserman wooed Tally. As a favor to Sperry, Tally agreed to play along with Kasserman's flirting to keep him occupied. It worked for a while, but ultimately Kasserman erupted when he discovered Tally had no intention of delivering in the love department." Halle lifts the comforter up over her shoulders. "You heard he has anger issues, right? Court ordered anger management classes and everything."

"It doesn't surprise me."

"Anyway, completely unbeknownst to me, he decided to make both women jealous by calling the escort service. And they sent me! I was strictly on the list to entertain foreign dignitaries. Big money and no chance of getting caught. I don't know what Kasserman paid the agency, but he talked them into sending the best, and somehow that was me." There's not an ounce of pride in Halle's tone, only remorse. "Of course, he used an alias, and I was using an alias – it took a face-to-face meeting before we realized we were both busted."

"Didn't you recognize his address when they sent you to his home?"

"We met at the private back bar at the Polo Lounge. I should have known not to go to a place where I know so many people. The back room has reserved seating areas. I thought it would work out. When he saw me walk up, that man turned shades of red I didn't know possible. He fully believed we were messing with him." Halle sighs. "I was so mortified that people might find out about my secret job, I ran with that story, acting like we had set him up. He called the agency demanding to find out who leaked his private business, which made them blow the whistle on me working for them."

"Wow."

"It doesn't end there. Kasserman vowed revenge. He was determined to ruin all of us. First, he called Dale and told him that he and Talia had a wild affair, and that Tally slept with an entire polo team. Next, he called Alan to rat me out. Then the lunatic packed up and flew home in the middle of the night, leaving us all in a bit of a lurch. We hoped that was at least the end of his tirade. But then Talia…" Halle crumples.

"Did you and the others stay at his place in Florida?"

"No. Never. Tally and Tab Chandler both have gorgeous places down there. I don't even know why we agreed to fly down on his plane. Sperry arranged it."

"Why did you meet with him alone yesterday to pick up the check?"

"I started all this. I owed it to the girls. I didn't want to put them at risk."

"The police know the entire story?"

"Yes, but they need solid evidence. He always brags about his militia background. Those types don't leave clues."

"Why would he leave the bodies in plain sight on his own property? At the very least you think he would have hidden them in the pond or way out back?"

"I know exactly why. He was trying to frame me. It worked. You thought it was me." So do all your friends, I think to myself. "Every piece of evidence was created to set me up. Now that his plan isn't working, I'm positive I'm next." The Bland Bombshell lifts her feet up on the couch and pulls herself into a ball. "It's my fault he snapped. I haven't been able to function since we got home."

"It's okay. You are safe here for now." I tell her. Really, I'm thinking we better get out of here. Now.

"Please, promise you won't reveal to the world that I worked at that disgusting job."

"It's not relevant to the story right now. I can't make a promise that it won't come out at some point in police reports." I'm fraught with guilt. A rich divorcee working as an escort definitely plays a factor in the national exposé on rich housewives gone wrong.

"When you were with the investigators today did they give any indication that they were closing in on Kasserman?" I ask.

"No. I overheard that they found Talia's car. Hidden on Kasserman's property."

35

"IT'S INEVITABLE, WE'RE GOING TO NEED THE FOOTAGE. We're out here now, we might as well get it." Ben and I stand outside the news truck in the Chanticleer parking lot. The sun has been up for a couple of hours. Frost still coats the vehicle and surrounding grass. We have full intention of heading out, I just have one final pursuit before we go.

"Ggrrrrrr," Ben literally growls at me as if he's an angry animal. He shifts from one foot to the other, lightly punching the driver's door. "I should have peeled out when you went to say goodbye to that horse."

While I was checking on Cassidy, my agent, Sara Beardsley, finally returned a call. She thinks my idea for a story on the elite equestrians will not only fly, she thinks it will bring a pretty big payday. The problem now is I need some critical footage and hopefully even an interview. The notion leads to a complete standoff with Ben as my BMW sits packed, the guest house returned to its pristine order, and the two of us ready to head out.

"I need to make one attempt to talk to Kasserman," I say. "At the very least, we need footage of his mansion for the stories. We pull up the drive, while I ask for an interview, you casually shoot footage of the rod iron gates and mansion."

"To recap, you expect me to send you up to a firing squad while I stay back and capture your demise on camera?"

"You're being a little too negative. I want you to catch me doing my journalistic duties of giving Clive Kasserman the opportunity to do an interview. And, while we're at it, get a few candid shots of his estate."

"Not happening."

"I'm not going to let on that he's a suspect. I'm strictly going to ask about the bodies being found on the outskirts of his property."

"Nope." Ben doesn't budge.

I sigh. "I get it. You're a new dad. I don't want to put you in harm's way. I'll shoot a little footage on my phone."

"You are impossible," Ben says. "Come on."

We head up the road together in the news truck. It takes no effort to find the main entrance to the estate. To Ben's dismay, the wrought-iron gates emblazoned with giant *Ks* hang open. We pull in slowly, expecting the home to come into view. Instead find ourselves on a never-ending, winding drive lined with pine trees.

"There it is," I say pointing to the right. "Pull over before he sees us."

"I'm not sending you up that last stretch of drive by yourself."

"If he sees the truck, he might chase us off before you get a shot of me asking for an interview. The gates were open. He must be expecting some type of service. I'll wear the wireless mic. You'll be able to hear everything going on. Look, there's a clearing for you to get a good shot of the porch through those trees."

Ben reluctantly helps wire me up.

"Take this too," he says, handing me the handheld mic with a bright block logo of Channel 5 news at the top. "This will at least identify who you are."

"And it will serve as a weapon, if I need it." I take a swipe at Ben.

"Now remember, the transponder can only pick you up for about 100 yards and in line of sight. Don't take any offers to go inside the house. Stay on the porch. I'm sure he has heavy duty surveillance. I don't know what his system will do to the transmission." Ben puts his head set on. "Go ahead and talk."

"One, two, one, two. Hello, Channel Five News," I recite our usual test.

"Talk to me the entire way. Tell me exactly what you're seeing. Don't lose contact."

Armed with a business card, notebook and station mic, I make my way to the front door. The gray McMansion I once thought was an apartment building sits off to the right side. Straight ahead, an eight-car garage with an overhang that leads to some sort of a car park courtyard between the garage and main house. To the left are smaller residences. One looks like a caretaker's home and the other a guest house. The entire center of the complex is lined with a circular pattern of gray brick paver stones. A helicopter could land there.

"This last stretch of driveway is the length of a football field," I whisper to Ben. "It's going to take a minute or two to reach the porch."

"He's not here," someone yells, as I approach the bottom step.

I turn and see none other than Covey poking his head out of the guest house. He looks more than a little surprised to see that it's me.

"Hi, Miss Callie. He left early this morning. The landscape crew is here. They must have left the front gate open, huh?"

"Ben" I whisper, "K not home. Covey is here. I need to get an interview with him too. Call you in a minute."

Covey in cahoots with Kasserman, wait until the Divas find out their boy toy defected. Another outrageous development. That explains how Kasserman had access to acepromazine.

"Any idea where Mr. Kasserman went?" I turn and stride across the center of the courtyard.

"Not my turn to watch him."

I make my way toward Covey, who remains in the doorway of his little home. His blond hair tousled, his t-shirt looks like it was thrown on as I arrived. I wonder if I am interrupting something other than sleep.

"So this is where you've been staying?" I ask.

"Not quite what I'm accustomed to, but suitable for the moment." I can't help but recall Sperry talking about Covey's delusions of grandeur. It's difficult to picture the groom being any type of lackey for Kasserman. Yet, here he stands, peering out into the courtyard. My mind spins with questions. I want to get them on camera before Covey pulls another disappearing act.

"Ben is here." I try to sound carefree. "We would love to get an interview with you."

"Not a good time," Covey says.

"You knew the Divas best. It will only take a minute." I try to play to his ego. "I'd really like to hear your take on of all the stuff going on around here." We've now had three full blown crimes and I still can't bring myself to use the word murder when I speak to people who knew the victims. *Stuff* suffices.

"It's not my place to talk," Covey says.

"You don't have to talk about the case. I'm trying to capture how elite this world is. We can talk about the amount of wealth in the horse world." I keep the mic propped upward for Ben to hear what I'm up to.

Covey contemplates the offer. "I'm trying to pack up. I'm done with this scene."

"Are you heading back to Florida?"

"Guess so. I lost my wheels. Trying to put a few logistics together."

"Ben is waiting for me in the news truck. I'll call him. We'll make it quick. I promise."

"The news truck?" Covey leans out the door looking quite concerned. "Don't let him pull up here. We can use the golf cart and drive to him. You said you want footage of the elite. Have him start with those ridiculous front gates. Let me get my coat," he says. As Covey steps away from the doorway, a trashed guest house comes into view. A dozen square white Styrofoam containers sit piled in the sink, a duffle bag with blue jeans and t-shirts in the center of the floor and stacks of open newspapers on the dining table. He is far from the ideal houseguest.

"He keeps the cart at the far end of the garage," Covey directs, ushering me toward the motor court.

An entrance at the front of the massive garage deposits us into a car museum. Everything from a new Ferrari to a vintage Rolls Royce are parked on angles across the giant expanse.

"The guy never drives any of these," Covey says kicking the tire of a yellow Lamborghini. Whatever friendship or agreement Kasserman had with the groom has clearly soured. I wonder if Covey discovered his host was responsible for the murders. I'll wait until the camera is rolling to ask. The luxury car barn and its contents are a world away from the shavings, hay and smells of the horse barns that populate the surrounding area.

"It's not hard to understand how someone obsessed with this type of horsepower and cleanliness has no tolerance for horses on his property," I say to Covey.

"All his big security to protect the property and he doesn't even know –" Covey stops himself but it's too late. I know the rest of the sentence. I was completely confused over how a guy that hates equestrians enough to chase them with a shotgun, knew how to enter the stables, find the appropriate lead lines and hunt down acepromazine to frame Halle. The pieces fall into place with a thud. The most obvious person who had access to the horse related murder objects stands right in front of me. I pray the surge of misgivings don't show on my face.

"What's wrong Miss Callie? You look like you've seen a ghost." What I'm seeing are the faces of the three victims and suddenly with great clarity, Covey's packed bag on the floor. Clearly he plans to escape.

"We've been on the run all morning, I haven't eaten. I'm probably a little low on blood sugar." My mind fires on all cylinders and I now realize how he quote *lost* his wheels. The car was Talia's. Halle said police found it on Kasserman's property.

"Feeling weak?" Covey turns and slowly walks toward my face.

"Maybe it's the fumes," I sidestep toward the door. "I feel lightheaded." When I hit the drive, I'll yell like crazy. If Ben can't hear me, hopefully the lawn crew will. I don't have the chance to reach for the door handle. In one smooth movement, Covey strikes from behind. He grabs the back of my shirt and takes my left arm and twists it behind my back.

"I think you'll stay right here with me." He tweaks my arm enough to let me know the excruciating pain the slightest movement will cause.

"Ben is with me," I speak to the mic as much as I speak to Covey.

"Oh and we're carrying a microphone are we? Why is there not a woman on earth that can be trusted? Hey, big guy. Your girl's with me." Covey leans over my shoulder putting his mouth right in front of the mic. "She's safe as long as you don't go causing trouble. Stay where you are. Don't call the police or I will hurt her." He flips the baton shaped mic on end and turns the battery switch to *off*. Hopefully Ben can listen to the lavaliere mic attached inside my shirt – *if* it's capable of picking up conversations this far away.

Back inside the one room guest house, I get a better look at the table where I clearly see a box of syringes and a bottle of acepromazine. There's no denying what I'm dealing with now.

"So, you dragged me back to your place. What's the plan?"

"You're going to help me get out of town."

"So the car you lost was Talia's? You've had it here since she went missing?"

"Stupid police. I was just about to head out. I guess we're both going on a little trip now," he says, tightening his fingers on my arm as he stoops down for the duffle bag. "Don't let out one squeak." He shuffles me toward the table and grabs a syringe filled with yellow fluid. Any hope I had of feigning ignorance vanishes.

"I don't get it. You're working for Kasserman?" I ask.

"That weenie?" Covey retorts with disgust. I look out in the courtyard trying to gauge the distance back to the truck. It looks like way more than one hundred yards. Sweat beads form along my hairline. "Mr. Tough Guy," he continues. "So into protecting his property, he doesn't even know I've been staying right under his nose in his guest house. It's hilarious."

No sign of the truck or Ben. I'm sure I'm out of range. I didn't bring my cell phone. Although in this vice grip, I couldn't use it.

"How did you get away with having a car here?"

"I kept it hidden by the construction entrance. Now that it's confiscated, I was trying to figure out a new way out of town when you showed up."

"We can give you a ride to the airport."

"You're a smart woman. I know you won't try to play me as stupid. I will take you up on your offer, but we'll do it my way." He gives one more twist to my arm. I wince. "Have you ever been a hostage before?"

36

"WHO HIDES THEIR KEYS?" MY CAPTOR SAYS.

Once again, Covey and I stand in the massive garage. In a childish tantrum he hauls off and kicks the side of a gorgeous light blue Bentley. Less than ten minutes have passed since I told Ben to hang down the driveway. Covey swept me into the house, threw his clothes together and marched us out to the car park in swift fashion. With duffle bag slung over his shoulder, clenching my arm with one hand and the loaded syringe in the other, he looks for an escape vehicle. We've checked the F-150 Super Duty, an antique four-door silver Rolls, and now the Bentley. At the far end of the garage sits the super charged golf cart. Covey pushes us toward it.

"You can't get far in that," I squeak, before a squeeze on my arm renders me silent.

"We'll take it to your car, which I'm assuming is back at Chanticleer." He bears down on my arm again. I can only shake my head yes. My body trembles so severely I can barely put one foot in front of the other.

"Someone will surely see you driving a golf cart down the road."

"I've learned every trail around this place. I can make it the entire way there without being detected," he brags. Covey pushes me to a back wall of the garage, which turns out to have dual-facing doors. He presses a button to open the one leading to the back side of the property.

"Get in," he shouts. The blonde groom shoves me on the black bench seat through the driver's side of the golf cart. "Slide over. Do not attempt to run. This shot will knock you out in one second flat." He holds the point of the needle on the skin of my bicep making a tiny indent. "If you make even the slightest motion, you'll find yourself like the others." With that, he plows his foot on the pedal. We jolt through the back door of the garage, speeding toward the trails with the same ferocity of Kasserman chasing riders with a shotgun.

"How did you get mixed up in this? I'm sure we can help you out," I did a piece on a self-defense class once. The instructor said to treat an assailant as a friend while you figure out an escape. Plus, I am truly curious.

"Those tramps—" Covey sounds like George, our barn manager when he's drunk. "They thrived on keeping a corral of men, basking in constant attention. My mom was just as bad. She was always out partying round the clock with a rotating bunch of men."

"I'm confused. Halle thinks she caused all of this drama."

"Halle is the only innocent one." Covey glances over at me like we are legitimately on a road trip. "She might be embarrassed that she worked as a call girl, but at least she was honest about taking a guy's money."

"How did Christa get involved? She wasn't even in Florida."

"That little wench. Thought she could control everything and everyone. I meant it when I said I would defend you. I protected both of us."

The golf cart races along the dirt path. I sit precariously on the edge of the seat so I can feign getting bounced out to the ground. Unfortunately, the vehicle handles the bumps with surprising ease. We turn left onto a very narrow passageway. I recognize it. It's the path the Divas tried to take on my first ride out to this area. This is the most direct route to Chanticleer, the same path Kasserman piled several logs across to prevent riders from entering his property. I distinctly remember the horses getting crabby with each other as we turned them around on the cramped path. We are about to hit the dead end. I need to distract Covey so he doesn't see the obstacle coming.

"Tell me about Sperry. You two seemed to get along so well."

"Here's the thing about Sperry," he begins. *Bingo*! Covey turns to me with interest. Sperry told me Covey relished in elaborating stories.

Now he has a meaty bone to chew on. "I loved her. When that girl was fun, she was fun." With pedal to the metal and the super charged golf cart racing at top speed, he turns to give me a raise the eyebrows, you-know-what-I-mean look. I meet his gaze, holding his eyes long enough to distract him from the impediment quickly approaching. Bam! The cart crashes into the logs. I keep my eyes locked on the syringe. As Covey reels from the impact, I grab his hand and smash the needle into his leg, pushing the hub to inject the sedative all in one motion.

"You bitch!" he yells. I swing at him with the handheld mic. It's enough to knock him back and off balance enough where he can't reach me. I lean back and heave my foot at his midsection. He thumps off the cart to the ground. I slide over, throw the vehicle in reverse and hit the pedal. The golf cart goes as fast backward as forward. I race in reverse, trying to keep the cart straight. There's no room to turn around, and there's no time to slow down. I don't even look to see if Covey chases after me. I steadfastly watch over my shoulder, flying back toward the estate. My hands and hair drip sweat by the time I reach a clearing. I turn the cart around, put it in forward, flooring it once again to head up the main trail and bang! Low hanging branches blocked my view. I crash – smack into the chief's old beater truck.

"Covey, the groom, he's out there. I don't know if he's knocked out," I pant, pointing down the trail as I stumble out of the cart. "Get him." The chief, Ben, Troy and Kowalski come and go from focus. "I don't know where he is," I keep repeating.

"Stay with her," the chief instructs Ben. The chief opens his driver's door. Troy and Kowalski, guns at the ready, jump back into the truck bed, the same way they arrived.

"It won't fit. The horses barely fit," I eke out. I'm dizzy. I've never gone into shock. I can hear my voice coming from somewhere. I'm pretty sure not from my body.

"Over here!" Ben yells. He throws the camera on the seat of the golf cart and motions the chief, Kowalski and Troy to join him. It takes only seconds to load up the cart. All four men race down the trail from the direction I just came. I lean up against a tree to hold myself steady.

It doesn't take long for the super charged golf cart with the K emblem to amble back. Ben remains in the driver's seat with the chief up front. Kowalski sits on one side of the rear facing seat beside Covey. His blonde head hangs to the side, drool oozes from his mouth. Troy stands on the back platform holding a top rail on the opposite side of Covey, using a knee to keep the murder suspect from rolling off.

"We've got an ambulance and back up on the way," the chief tells us.

"What knocked him out?" Kowalski asks me.

"The same thing he used on the others, acepromazine. He used the needle like most people would wield a knife to threaten me. We crashed into some logs and I stuck him with it, then pushed him out of the cart and peeled out. How did you know where to find me?"

"You have one astute partner there," Kowalski says and nods toward Ben.

Ben rolls footage as EMTs load Covey into the ambulance. I'm placed in a waiting squad car yet again. Kowalski conducts preliminary questioning on site, then agrees to meet us at the police station to finish the paperwork. Once we're back in the news truck, I'm recovered enough to hear Ben's side of the nightmare.

"Could you hear me? How much did you get on tape?"

"Honestly, once you told me Kasserman wasn't home, I started to move the van off the property. I didn't want to be a sitting idle if he pulled in. As I was pulling a U-turn I heard 'safe, trouble and police' through crackles. That was enough for me to call in the troops. Thank God I did. He didn't waste any time whisking you out of there."

"Did you call the station?"

"I didn't have time."

Ben and I call the station together on speakerphone and help prepare a short story for the noon news saying police have made an arrest in the multiple murder case, and that we expect a press conference later in the day. We have the entire arrest on camera. No other station in town can compete at this point.

When we arrive at the police station, I am faced with a mound of paperwork and a new round of interrogations with a much larger group of law enforcement officials. The process takes over an hour. The chief and detective both promise interviews, so I take a little time to relax and freshen up before returning to evening news mode.

From the police station parking lot, I sneak in a call to Zari Gold, Christa's publicist. I feel a little ridiculous, but I know she's in town for her former client's funeral and I could use her assistance to make the most of this opportunity.

Back at the station, Rick chooses to handle the coverage personally. He divides the story out into two parts: Covey's arrest, followed by a separate piece on how I became involved in catching him. I write the copy for both while Ben edits his best footage, and then we return to the police station for the key interviews.

"Where is everyone?" I ask the desk sergeant in the lobby.

"Meeting."

After being abuzz with masses of personnel earlier, the building sounds like a library.

"I saw cars still in the parking lot."

"They're all in the back room. Some type of briefing."

"That's odd," I say turning to Ben. "Are we being left out of the press conference?" I ask startled.

"Internal meeting," the desk sergeant says.

What's going on? We're on deadline. Time for interview? I text Kowalski.

No response.

Where is everyone? I text Troy.

Nothing.

"You're sure they're still in the building?" I question the desk sergeant while pacing. When the door finally opens there's an entourage of authorities, most I don't recognize. Kowalski finally appears in the mix. He nonchalantly tilts his head, indicating to meet him off to the side.

"You gave that kid quite a dose of the tranq. He's going to make it, but it looks like he might be incarcerated in a hospital bed for a good few days," the detective says.

"Do you have time for a quick interview?"

"Our big boss, the executive director, took over. She's calling a press conference for five o'clock at the hospital. We've got a substantial development on our hands. As a thank you for your assistance, I'll give you a heads up so you can do a little research."

"Pull any images you can of Gloria Gaitland," I tell Rick. "This kid Covey is her son. Gerald Covington Gaitland, III. A spoiled rich kid. Let me correct that, a deeply troubled super rich kid."

"You're sure?" Rick's hesitation is completely founded. No one could believe the connection, which is why the authorities huddled behind closed doors so long.

"They thought it was a case of stolen identity at first," I say. "Sure enough, Covey is from the prominent family. And wait 'til you hear this: Looks like his murder spree may stretch back to college days in Florida. Officials here are currently working with Feds, the state of Florida and Dade County law enforcement."

Ben and I follow the detective and company to the hospital where we plan to go live from the press conference. As I brief Rick by phone on the wild new twist to the story, I feverishly use the iPad to Google as many facts as possible about Covey's famous family.

37

"SHOCKING NEWS FROM NORTH ANTRUM COUNTY THIS morning, where State Police arrest the son of the country's wealthiest cosmetics tycoon in connection with recent serial killings. Our own Callie Kinsey helped take the suspect down. She joins us now live from Lapeer Regional Medical Hospital with this remarkable story."

"Let's start with the facts," I begin. I'm wearing a fitted, burnt-orange wool peplum Escada suit, by far the fanciest outfit I've ever imagined. I can't help but knock the story out of the park. "Gerald Covington Gaitland, III, son of celebrity businesswoman Gloria Gaitland, will be arraigned this afternoon from his hospital bed in connection with all three murders. Police are preparing a press conference behind me, where they are expected to announce that the only son of the queen of cosmetics may also be responsible for another killing spree in South Florida. We have been covering the story since it began 10 days ago. Typically, we stick to covering the news, not becoming a part of it. This morning I went in search of a routine interview and instead was taken hostage by the man police believe is behind the slew of murders."

Zari Gold stands beside Ben at the camera. With impeccable timing, the publicist returned my calls and scooted over in time to help me navigate the pending media implosion. She insists it starts with image, so when she raced in with choice pieces of wardrobe, this time I accepted.

The station rolls our pre-taped package.

"The bodies of all three women were found on the grounds of another wealthy heir, Clive Kasserman. I paid a visit to his estate to ask for an interview this morning where I was intercepted by the young man now being arraigned for the murders." We begin with the limited footage of me approaching Kasserman's steps, followed by a dramatic U-turn as I hear Covey call out. The story goes on to recount my tale of ultimately escaping and leading police to the suspect. Ben has footage of me being escorted, wrapped in a blanket, to the squad car, and of Covey being transported by golf cart and transferred to the ambulance. We include interviews with Kowalski and the chief.

"Callie, from where we sit you look unharmed. What a horrific ordeal. How are you holding up?" Anita Bainbridge asks from the anchor desk.

"I experienced moments of pure terror this morning, but for all of our sakes, I'm thankful the ordeal helped capture the killer."

"You are a brave woman," Co-anchor, Tim Rexroth, says, jumping in from the studio. "I understand the suspect worked for a short time at the stables. Had you met him?"

"We spoke a number of times while I was out here covering the story. Covey, as the suspect is known in this community, worked as a groom on the prestigious Palm Beach horse circuit and traveled to Michigan earlier this spring under the pretenses of caring for the victims' horses. To find out he's responsible for his clients' deaths sends shock through all of us." I promise the anchors we will stay on site to cover the pending press conference and sign off the air.

"That's an Emmy in the bag," Zari says. "No one can top that."

"The press conference has been postponed," Ben says. Rick sent a text while you were on the air. "Something about trying to confirm a little more information with officials in Florida." The photographer looks at his phone. "They're planning to address the media at a little after six at this point."

"I don't know how much you know about local news," I inform Zari. "Local authorities are great at coordinating their announcements with the top of the five or six o'clock newscasts."

"Oh they are, are they?" Troy appears from the sidelines. I didn't know he had been watching. "Nice job."

"And, how about the outfit?" I gush.

"You always look great." I'm so thrilled to have Cute Cop finally catch me on top of my game and not the crumbly mess I've been lately. Ben and Zari, sensing the magnetic shockwaves bouncing between us, conveniently meander off.

"While you're tethered, little lady, I need to have a talk with you."

Fearing faulty connections with all the high-tech hospital interference, Ben secured a wired microphone and earpiece rather than the usual wireless. Troy is right. I am literally tied to the scene.

"So, here's the scoop," he starts. "Before our upcoming date, I want to come clean about why I am working at this job when I don't particularly have to."

"He's quite handsome." Stu the director pipes in my ear. We are clear from broadcast airwaves, but the mic I'm wearing is still live in the control room.

"Just let me--" I reach for the microphone clipped on the orange lapel. Troy grabs hold of my arm, determined to get his story out.

"Full transparency, I own a very successful company. Well, two or three actually." The admission catches me way off guard and, for a second, I forget that he can be heard loud and clear in the control room.

"What?"

"I told you the truth. I was released from the FBI with honors and invested in a simple computer data tracking company. What I left out, is that it struck gold. I chose to hide the success when I first moved back," he forges on. "I don't want to sound sexist, but I had this image of women looking for a free ride and I wasn't ready for all that."

"Awwww," I hear in the headset. I don't know whose voice that is. I'm mortified. I can only imagine the amount of people jammed in the control room during coverage of a huge breaking story.

I inch myself back in front of the camera, and give a chastising look to the lens while Troy, evidently relieved to get the secret off his chest, picks up the pace. Knowing he'll be humiliated over revealing his private story publicly back in the newsroom, I try again to stop him, but he won't let me interrupt.

"I thought working for our small-town agency again would provide a cover while I get used to what the company has become."

Woo hoos erupt in my earpiece.

"Callie's got a boyfriend," I hear a female voice say.

"Please." I put my hand up to stop him. Everyone down to the interns are likely gathering around to watch. I give another stern look to the camera, pleading with them to ease off.

"Let me finish," Troy says.

I glance at the small monitor used to watch the broadcast feed. We're in a commercial. I'm sure even the studio anchors watch us now.

"Wait, wait." I try to stop Troy again.

"We finally have a moment alone." He talks right over my protests. "Here's my problem now. I'm hesitant about our upcoming date because you might be turned off by the fact that I haven't been honest about who I am. Whew." *Whew is right.* I hope he's finished. "What I'm trying to say is, my whole plan jumped up and bit me." I look at Cute Cop. He's so innocent and handsome and awesome. I don't know how to respond.

"Go on, kiss the guy!" the voice of Elena, one of our veteran producers chimes in through the earpiece.

"Tell him you'll marry him!" It's Wally, evidently working as ENG tech today.

"But don't quit your job!" I don't believe it, even Rick is weighing in on this private moment.

"Stop it!" I yell to the studio. Troy takes a step back.

"No, not you." I hold his arm. "Them." I point to the camera, referencing thin air. He's going to think I'm bonkers. This situation renders a girl who gets paid to talk, completely unable to form words.

"This could only happen to me," I say.

"We're not on the same page?" Troy's face sinks. He looks like the poster boy for complete and utter rejection.

"No, not you!" Heat fills my cheeks. I struggle to unplug the microphone. "Don't say another word until I'm out of these wires." Someone likes me for me and I like him back. I can't wait to tell him. It's not going to be booming through a speaker back at the station.

"Come on, help me out!" I cry. Ben jumps out of the truck and runs to my aid.

"Where were you?" I chastise my usually trusty partner.

"Watching from inside the truck. I agree with Wally." I turn eight more shades of red, making my complexion clash drastically with the new suit.

"What's going on?" Troy asks. Released from the tethers, I pull him out of view of the camera, waving to those back at the station as we disappear.

"I'm tempted to tell you nothing, but if we're coming clean," the idea of telling him is easier than executing it. "Well, er,"

"You have a boyfriend?"

"No."

"You're married?" His look of gloom makes me come clean.

"No, I'm all yours if you'll still have me. The problem is, um, your private talk was beamed to half the people that work at the station, including my boss."

"What?" Troy spins on one foot in a circle.

"You'll be happy to know they were all rooting for you!"

"Some relief," he says and starts to walk away.

"Does this mean you're not going to ask me out?"

"That's where I'm going," he says in an Eeyore tone, as he straightens his hair and shirt walking back to the camera, gesturing for me to join him. "Come on. We can't leave them hanging, can we?"

38

"THE BULK OF THE MONEY COMES FROM THE FIRST-HAND account of the heir-turned murderer you've been asked to pen."

I'm on the phone with my agent extraordinaire. My mom stands beside me mouthing *what, what* in the kitchen of her condo, where I was forced to spend the night due to a mass of media trucks staked out at my place.

"You get one-point-two just for signing," Sara Beardsley relays details of the top offer for the Gaitland story. A staggering seven figures. "You will also collect royalties once the book is released. And I haven't even told you about the details for the Nation Watch segment. They want a full hour special!"

"Are you sure?"

"Face it. You're in the bigs," she says. I sink to a chair. "There are a lot of nuances to the contract. I can fly in tomorrow and show you the fine print on paper."

"After the toll of this story, I could really use a getaway," I counter. "I would love to visit New York. I'd like to bring my mom." My mom starts jumping up and down and clapping like she won a prize on the Price is Right, and she doesn't even know the full extent of the news yet. "Should we book the tickets or does someone there handle that?" Sara, who stands to make fifteen percent of this deal, patches me immediately through to her assistant to handle the arrangements.

"I get to go to New York?" My mom squeals, bouncing in place, her curly hair springing up and down with her.

"And that's not all," I say, in my best game show announcer imitation. "You'll be watching your daughter sign a seven-figure deal for the rights to the story!"

With that, my mom drops to the floor.

"I know it's not tuna niçoise or salmon on a bed of spring greens," I say surveying a spread of pizza pies. "Our pal Justin has been delivering pizzas fairly regularly out to the scene, and it seemed appropriate to order from him one last time for our makeshift wrap party."

"Hey, when it's the only thing available," Tab Chandler says, hoisting a slice in salute.

"I'm always for a guilty pleasure," Halle adds with a naughty wink.

We are gathered in the West Wing tack room at Chanticleer. The Divas eagerly offered to host a briefing party. They even pulled china dishes and crystal champagne glasses out of the cupboards. I arranged for Detective Sergeant Kowalski and the chief to come to the stables to give a full overview of Covey and his arrest. Tab, Lydia and Halle hover at the food table acting as hostesses, pouring champagne for a packed room filled mostly with boarders. Maggie, Ben and his wife, Brianna, huddle on the couch, where they are forced to listen to Bud Burkhart brag about his efforts in solving the crime.

"I made a call to the lab," he tells the chief. "They've been instructed to release any evidence needed to authorities."

Zari and Raul bond instantly. The new besties lean arm in arm on the counter, toasting each other every so often with the champagne flutes. After her fainting spell, I figured it best to bring my mom along, too. She mills around collecting compliments about her hero daughter.

Although I arranged the pseudo-celebration, I feel horrid. Not for jeopardizing the Divas' size zero waistlines by feeding them pizza, but for selling them out. Part of my contract includes a tell-all, and I'm concerned it won't paint the Divas in the best light.

"So Chief, we've been talking it over," Tab says. "We should issue Callie the reward money."

"It's your money to be dispersed at your discretion," the chief answers.

"Callie?" Tab checks to see if I heard her. All eyes in the room turn toward me, as a glop of cheese dangles between the slice of pizza and my mouth. I quick swipe my chin with a napkin.

"Actually, I'm waiting to share a little news." I look at Zari. She nods. My mom beams with pride. "I've been asked to produce a television special and write a book about the events, so I'm already being taken care of quite well."

"We collected the money. We should put it toward some good," Tab says. "What about putting the money toward a memorial class in honor of the girls at the Classic this summer?" The Classic refers to the area's largest and most prestigious horse show. "Or creating a young equestrian scholarship fund?"

"I'm sure Sperry would be honored to have a memorial in her name," I say.

"We're up to about a quarter million," Lydia crows. "We can probably do both."

"Let's make a foundation and appropriate funds from there," Halle suggests. I never knew the Halle prior to this story, but it's good to see her minus the jitters.

"Before we begin a formal debrief, it seems appropriate for all of us to give a round of applause to Ms. Kinsey," Chief Zurn says, walking to the front of the room. "Without her brave actions yesterday we might not have the suspect in custody." The group claps, making me want to hide.

"Mr. Gaitland, as we're coming to realize, is very a troubled young man," Detective Kowalski takes the helm. "A team will continue to evaluate him. So far we have ascertained that he harbors a strong hatred toward his mother, a classic foundation for deviant behavior. Like many serial killers, it appears he took the displaced anger out on his victims."

"That boy took spoiled tantrums to a whole new level," Raul chimes in from the back of the room. "I have several clients who know Gloria Gaitland personally. They say she craves men swooning over her. I feel a little sorry for Covey. She ignored him something terrible during his formative years. His nannies say she'd drop him like a hot potato at the prospect of a date." I can see the detective lean forward attempting to regain control. I know what it's like to try to stop Raul when he's on a roll. The stylist pauses to take a sip of champagne, and still manages to continue before Kowalski can jump back in. "As soon as he was old enough she conveniently sent the boy off to boarding school, where everyone knows he quickly took to drugs and alcohol."

"I'm sure all of that will come to light during psychological evaluations," Kowalski inserts as he literally places himself in front of Raul to recapture the floor. "Sadly, this does not appear to be his first rampage. As you know, we are currently working in conjunction with authorities in Florida. We suspect Mr. Gaitland may also be wanted in connection with a series of co-ed murders at a college he briefly attended. The message we want to give all of you this evening is that we are very sorry for your loss. We promise that you are now safe, and as you heal, you can confidently return to your normal routines."

"Here, here," says Bud Burkhart, raising his glass of champagne.

"This is where the action is," Bunky Bidlow says as she pokes her head into the tack room. "Sorry for being late everyone. I just got off work."

"Come on in," Tab quickly offers. Bunky hustles over to the table where she plops a few slices on a plate, then hangs close to Tab, Lydia and Halle, beaming to be in the affluent mix.

"I know the question on everyone's mind," Raul says, as he stands twirling his champagne glass. The bubbles have apparently gone to his head. I can't imagine what he'll announce.

"She's ravishing!" he gushes, giving every last detail of Sperry's appearance for the next day's viewing, as if he were a reporter on the red carpet of the Oscars.

"Oh, but that Covey, I shudder to think he ever sat in my chair," he adds, as a very real tremble rips through his designer dressed body. "Before I get back to Florida, I'm having it replaced." Without missing a beat, the stylist then turns to me.

"Girlfriend, this story is going to make you a super star, and I will not leave town until we give you a makeover!" Raul studies my face. "You must look fantastic when you tell the nation about the poor little rich kid going ballistic." As Raul carries on, it dawns on me. I don't have to expose the women from Chanticleer as wild. The stories will focus on Covey and the Gaitlands. I can work the national angle of glitz and glamour gone wrong without creating enemies.

"Oh Raul, you are wonderful." It's my turn to gush. "No wonder the women adore you. Not only do you make us look great, you make us feel great too." I don't mention it out loud, but Raul will be getting plenty of camera time. What I thought was the boring ramble about the blonde Adonis during the interview, provides excellent snippets for the ongoing coverage. Whenever we need an eccentric sound bite to liven up a story, we lean on the Raul video.

The briefing lasts less than an hour. I think we are all anxious to get home for a good night's sleep.

"We've become quite a duo since this coverage began," the chief tells my mom warmly as we walk out to the car.

"We had a couple of challenges, but you were always fair," I say.

"I considered you trustworthy 'til proven not." The chief reaches into his pocket and pulls out his cell phone. "I had a little firepower on my side in case you tried to get out of line." He clearly calls up a photo.

"Please tell me that is not a photo from the first time we met," I wince.

"I took a couple because I thought you were either a ballsy prostitute or a young drugged-out teen. Thought I might need evidence in court. Nothing perverted," the chief assures my mom. "Did you tell your mom you were hanging out on a stretch of country road in your skivvies?"

"It's her fault," I say and put my arm around my mom. "You'll be so proud of me, mom. I pulled over to change clothes on the side of the road."

"See darling, it kept you from getting a ticket."

"Actually it caused a lot more trouble. Unfortunately, the chief caught me striking quite the pose." I shift attention to the chief. "I am still embarrassed."

"They'll be deleted. You've got my word," the chief says as he turns toward his truck.

"Are you already forgetting the little people?" Troy jumps off the porch swing at the guest house where he's been waiting for me and jogs over to the parking lot.

"Troy!" I introduce Cute Cop to my mom, who, after a nice greeting, quickly and obviously makes herself scarce by retreating to the passenger seat.

"Now that the case is closed – " His smile beams in the moonlight the same way it did the night we first met. I smile back at him. I can't believe how he makes me feel like a silly teenager.

"Boy, do I have a lot to tell you," I say.

"We have all the time in the world now. How about we start with dinner Friday night?"

"Oh, no," I whine. "I have to fly to New York to sign the contract," I explain.

"Contract?" he raises his eyebrows. "You do have a lot to tell me about. Then promise you'll make time when you get back?" he asks.

"Of course," I reply. "Let's seal the deal with a hug."

As Troy pulls me in for a bear hug, I catch a glimpse of my mom over his shoulder. She positively beams with excitement. Forget that a bad guy is behind bars or that my career is on the fast track. This is my mom's proudest moment. Her daughter may actually have a date.

Read on for a Sneak Peek of the next book in the Callie Kinsey series:

A SECRET, A PSYCHIC, AND A SCAM

BY MARY CURRAN

1

"HAVE A SEAT," THE SHERIFF SAYS, SOUNDING RATHER somber. "We have an interesting situation on our hands." I have no inkling what he's talking about, so I sit in silence. "You do know why you're here?" he asks.

"You called and asked to meet." How odd. We're sitting in his office. I know the sheriff could not have forgotten that he called me two hours ago. Then I remember. He didn't call once. He rang repeatedly until I finally picked up.

My name is Callie Kinsey. Visiting the sheriff's department used to be routine when I worked for local television news. Now I work for the network and I can't recall the last time I stopped in. After covering the story of a serial killer, who turned out to be the troubled son of a world-famous cosmetics queen, my agent scored us a deal on par with winning the lotto to write a book and produce a two-hour special. Those, in turn, put me in the national spotlight. These days I spend most of my time commuting to New York, where I guest host a nationally syndicated true crime show.

"There were six missed calls from your office. It must be something important," I say.

"Ms. Bidlow came in to see me this morning," he says. "I understand she was at your home last night."

My *home*. That's another wild change. I bought Chanticleer, one of the most elite equestrian facilities in Michigan, on a whim after coming into the unexpected cash. Maggie, my horse trainer and good friend, stayed on at the French rustic main farmhouse and at the helm of the riding program. I sold my condo, donated the cheap furnishings to a charity thrift shop and moved into the super posh, fully furnished guest house.

Bunky Bidlow boards at our prestigious Chanticleer Stables. She also works dispatch at the sheriff's office. A mix of extremely low maintenance, yet irritatingly high energy, Bunky falls into the misfit category, especially at Chanticleer. In the height of spring fever, I invited her to join Maggie and me for drinks yesterday afternoon after a riding lesson. She must have gotten popped for drunk driving on the way home. To the best of my recollection, she barely had three sips of that wine.

"Yes, but—" I'm not sure what to say. I don't want to incriminate her by admitting we had been drinking.

"She brought this in this morning," the sheriff says. He lifts a photocopy of a pencil sketch off his desk. Trying to better herself, Bunky's been taking online forensic artist classes. In the morning light, the drawing looks even better than it did yesterday.

I cherish the serenity of looking out over rolling hills and horses grazing in paddocks, but lately, horrific dreams of being trapped in a shallow grave plague me. Symbolic, I'm sure, of being buried in debt. The facility constantly drains my savings. Blame the wine – or me for drinking it – I shared the tale of sleepless nights with the ladies yesterday. All of us believed Bunky sketching an image of the dream would help me confront my fears.

"She did a marvelous job," I admit, still surprised that Bunky possesses even an ounce of talent. The woman in the sketch looks nothing like me, however, the rendering carries the exact essence of the nightmare, from the dirt surroundings to conjuring the muffled screams. I scold myself for letting Bunky in on my secret. Since I first met her four years ago, I've kept her at arm's length. Not out of rudeness, simply self-preservation. This is the perfect example. Despite pleas to keep the drawing confidential, she paraded it straight into her boss's office.

"This was just a silly exercise to help me get past –" I hesitate. I've embarrassed myself enough by letting Maggie and Bunky know I'm having nightmares; I don't need local law enforcement gossiping about my mental or financial state.

"Ms. Kinsey, let me caution you, please don't implicate yourself."

"I don't understand. We were goofing around doing sketches. How can I be implicated?"

"I showed the drawing to several deputies this morning. They all had the same reaction that I did."

I literally am sitting on the edge of my seat waiting to hear their consensus.

"At first we thought Ms. Bidlow traced a photo from one of our files, but she insists she took dictation from you."

"She did," I admit.

"Then you must know, this is an exact likeness of Jewell Rhodes. The young woman that went missing five years ago."

"I don't know a Jewell Rhodes," I say, taking a good look at the rendering. "I don't even remember a missing person's case with anyone that resembles that drawing."

"And that's what concerns me most. You're right. The case never received media attention. The usual sad story. Young girl fell to using drugs and men to crawl through life. Some presume the girl's dead. Others figure she drifted on to the next location. She has a down-and-out mom who never pushed to find her daughter. With not much to go on, the initial report landed up in a cold case file in less than three months." The sheriff adjusts a manila folder containing the meager pieces of Jewell Rhodes' paperwork. He tosses it to the side of his desk and sits forward. "So you can imagine our surprise when you ask one of our employees to draw the victim. That raises curiosity." The sheriff leans his full weight onto his elbows, pushing his frame toward me. "What exactly do you know about this young woman," he pauses, "and her whereabouts?"

Visit www.MaryCurranBooks.com to sign up for updates on each new book release!

A Note from the Author

Thank you so much for reading DIVAS 'TIL DEATH!

If you enjoyed the read, I would greatly appreciate it if you would take a moment to give the book a rating or short review.

It's uncomfortable to ask, yet it's become standard practice to check reviews before reading a book or going to a restaurant. Ultimately, we all help each other by taking a few minutes to share our thoughts on any experience. Thank you in advance for taking the time to give honest feedback.

Also, if you'd like to know in advance when the next Callie Kinsey Mystery is released, follow me at Mary Curran Books on Facebook or visit www.MaryCurranBooks.com and sign up for email alerts.

I promise not to bombard you with content – I'll only send emails when I have news.

Thank you,
Mary

Acknowledgements

First, I need to apologize to my early readers. Writing is a craft and I saddled you with some pretty horrific writing early on. I apologize.

To my current Beta Readers -- Carrie, Tiffany, Maggie and Shelley -- thank you for your encouragement and enthusiasm. To my critique partners and Sisters in Crime, Bobbi, Theresa and Jan – thank you for all your thoughtful reads and input. You've really helped me add a new layer of polish to the page.

A huge shout out to the team that helped make the dream of becoming an author, a reality. Phenomenal artist, Kristi Rauckis, called and offered to 'take a crack' at the cover art, then nailed the image in less than 24 hours! If you haven't seen her work, make a point of checking it out. My Florida horse trainer, Macy Newman-Coleman, also a gifted graphic designer, ran with the image to create the cover. And now Ellen Maze Sallas, yet another horse person, joined the mix to take the cover to the next level. You all exceeded my imagination.

I also want to thank Erin Mitchell. She's listed in my phone contacts as Erin Mitchell Book Guru and lives up to the name daily. Thank you for your tireless efforts peddling the book to publishers and now your expertise in getting *Divas 'Til Death* out into the world. I know I've been a bit of a pest during the process, but I couldn't be on this journey with a more savvy and accomplished partner. I am forever grateful to have been introduced to you by Pam Stack.

Speaking of Pam – thank you Pam, for creating and hosting Authors on the Air, and thank you to Dan Simpson for creating and hosting Writer's Routine. Both are top on my list of inspiring podcasts, filled with great insights into the world of writing.

Of course, I have to thank my husband, who is endlessly supportive of my writing, riding, passion for animals and occasional monkey business.

Finally, I thank those of you taking a look at the book. I hope you enjoy it and I would love to hear from you.

Made in the USA
Monee, IL
21 July 2025